Praise for Maryse Condé

"She describes the ravages of colonialism and the post-colonial chaos in a language which is both precise and overwhelming. In her stories the dead live close to the living in a world where gender, race, and class are constantly turned over in new constellations."
ANN PÅLSSON, Jury, New Academy Prize in Literature

"Condé is a born storyteller."
Publishers Weekly

"Maryse Condé is a treasure of world literature, writing from the center of the African diaspora with brilliance and a profound understanding of all humanity."
RUSSELL BANKS

"Maryse Condé is the grande dame of Caribbean literature."
NCRV Gids

•

Praise for The Wondrous and Tragic Life of Ivan and Ivana

"Condé has a gift for storytelling and an unswerving focus on her characters, combined with a mordant sense of humor."
The New York Times Book Review

"What an astounding novel. Never have I read anything so wild and loving, so tender and ruthless. Condé is one of our greatest writers, a literary sorcerer, but here she has outdone even herself, summoned a storm from out of the world's troubled heart. Ivan and Ivana, in their love, in their Attic fates, mirror our species' terrible brokenness and its improbable grace."
JUNOT DÍAZ

"The breadth, depth, and power of Maryse Condé's majestic work is exceptionally remarkable. *The Wondrous and Tragic Life of Ivan and Ivana* is a superb addition to this incomparable oeuvre, and is one of Condé's most timely, virtuoso, and breathtaking novels."
EDWIDGE DANTICAT

"Condé's latest novel is a beautiful and dramatic story with its origins in the Charlie Hebdo attacks. Masterly."
Afrique Magazine

"Brilliantly imagined, Maryse Condé's new novel presents a dual bildungsroman of twins born into poverty in the African diaspora and follows their global travels to its shocking ending. Once again, Condé transmutes contemporary political traumas into a mesmerizing family fable."
HENRY LOUIS GATES, JR.

"Maryse Condé offers us with *The Wondrous and Tragic Life of Ivan and Ivana* yet another ambitious, continent-crossing whirlwind of a literary journey. The marvelous siblings at the heart of her tale are inspiring and unsettling in equal measure, richly drawn incarnations of the contemporary postcolonial individual in perpetual geographic and cultural movement. It is a remarkable story from start to finish."
KAIAMA L. GLOVER

"Maryse Condé's prodigious fictional universes are founded on a radical and generative disregard for boundaries based on geography, religion, history, race, and gender. In *The Wondrous and Tragic Life of Ivan and Ivana*, the most intimate human relationships acquire meaning only on the scale of the world-historical, and as we follow the twins in their fated journey from the Caribbean to Africa and

Europe, we learn about love, happiness, calamity, and, at last, the survival of hope."
ANGELA Y. DAVIS

"With this story of a young man from Guadeloupe who finds himself persuaded by the pull of jihad, Condé has written one of her most impressive novels to date, one that seamlessly resonates with the problems of our time."
Le Monde

"Maryse Condé addresses very contemporary issues in her latest novel: racism, jihadi terrorism, political corruption and violence, economic inequality in Guadeloupe and metropolitan France, globalization and immigration."
World Literature Today

"This new novel, written in an almost exuberant style, contains many typical Condé elements, in particular the mix of a small family story with global events and the nuances of existing images."
De Volkskrant

•

Praise for Segu

"Condé's story is rich and colorful and glorious. It sprawls over continents and centuries to find its way into the reader's heart."
MAYA ANGELOU

"The most significant novel about black Africa published in many a year ... A wondrous novel about a period of African history few other writers have addressed. Much of the

novel's radiance comes from the lush description of a traditional life that is both exotic and violent."
The New York Times Book Review

"Exotic, richly textured and detailed, this narrative, alternating between the lives of various characters, illuminates magnificently a little known historical period. Virtually every page glitters with nuggets of cultural fascination."
Los Angeles Times

"With the dazzling storytelling skills of an African griot, Maryse Condé has written a rich, fast-paced saga of a great kingdom during the tumultuous period of the slave trade and the coming of Islam. *Segu* is history as vivid and immediate as today. It has restored a part of my past that has long been missing."
PAULE MARSHALL, author of *Daughters*

"*Segu* is an overwhelming accomplishment. It injects into the density of history characters who are as alive as you and I. Passionate, lusty, greedy, they are in conflict with themselves as well as with God and Mammon. Maryse Condé has done us all a tremendous service by rendering a history so compelling and exciting. *Segu* is a literary masterpiece I could not put down."
LOUISE MERIWETHER

"A stunning reaffirmation of Africa and its peoples as set down by others whose works have gone unnoticed. Condé not only backs them up, but provides new insights as well. *Segu* has its own dynamic. It's a starburst."
JOHN A. WILLIAMS

Praise for Crossing the Mangrove

"Condé writes elegantly in a style that beautifully survives translation from the French. She gives readers a flavor of the French and Creole stew that is the Guadeloupan tongue. In so doing, Condé conveys the many subtle distinctions of color, class, and language that made up this society."
Chicago Tribune

•

Praise for Tales from the Heart

"Honest, exquisitely measured—inspiring in its reminder of the human spirit's capacity to endure."
The New York Times Book Review

"An astute study of family and place."
Washington Post Book World

"Upon reaching the final page and the start of Condé's journey to adulthood, readers will regret that this brief, colorful, and lively remembrance has ended."
Publishers Weekly

"A useful look at the psychological consequences of intolerance."
Kirkus Reviews

Praise for Windward Heights

"Condé is a masterly storyteller who also proves deft at reinterpreting other people's stories, as she shows here with this energetic reimagining of *Wuthering Heights* set in Cuba and Guadeloupe at the turn of the century."
The New York Times Book Review

"Through Condé's transformation of the tragedy in *Wuthering Heights*, she creates a narrative that seduces, evokes, and makes us think about the kinds of emotions that have moved human beings throughout our existence."
Chicago Tribune

"Condé gives Brontë a cultural context—a fine and unique accomplishment."
Washington Post

"Exotic and eloquent. Condé takes Emily Brontë's cold-climate classic on obsessive love and makes it hot and lush."
USA Today

"A confident and incisive Caribbeanization of a European master-text by a master novelist of African descent."
Village Voice

"The author weaves in the history of the region along with themes of passionate love, color prejudice, oppression, and social unrest to create an engaging and well-written book that is difficult to put down."
Multicultural Review

"Condé has given readers an astonishing new way in which to contemplate our ancestral past."
Black Issues Book Review

The Wondrous and Tragic Life of Ivan and Ivana

MARYSE CONDÉ

The Wondrous and Tragic Life of Ivan and Ivana

Translated from the French
by Richard Philcox

WORLD EDITIONS
New York, London, Amsterdam

Published in the USA in 2020 by World Editions LLC, New York
Published in the UK in 2020 by World Editions Ltd., London

World Editions
New York/London/Amsterdam

Printed by Lake Book, USA

Library of Congress Cataloging in Publication Data is available

ISBN 978-1-64286-069-6

First published as *Le fabuleux et triste destin d'Ivan et Ivana* in France in 2017
by JC Lattès

Twitter: @WorldEdBooks
Facebook: @WorldEditionsInternationalPublishing
Instagram: @WorldEdBooks
www.worldeditions.org

Book Club Discussion Guides are available on our website

For Richard and Régine, without whom this book would never have been written.

For Maryse "savannah of clear horizons, savannah that quivers from the fervent caress of the wind from the East" (so sung Léopold Sedar Senghor).

For Fadèle, whose world perhaps will be entirely different.

Gradually your life knocked you out.

Alan Souchon, Le Bagad de Lann-Bihoué

IN UTERO
OR
BOUNDED IN A NUTSHELL

(Hamlet by William Shakespeare)

As if acting on a signal, an invincible force besieged the twins. Where did it come from? What was its purpose? They got the impression of being brutally dragged down and forced to leave the warm and tranquil abode where they had lived for many weeks. A terrible smell clung to their nostrils as they gradually, helplessly, made their descent, a smell that resembled a noxious stench. The twin who had a button between his legs preceded the smaller less developed other whose sex was hollowed out by a large scar. He butted his way down the narrow passage whose walls slowly widened.

Up till now their routine had been dominated by the single fact of being huddled one against the other. Their only inclination was to cling to each other and breathe in the sour but agreeable smell in which they were wrapped. The abode where they had spent many long weeks was somber: dark, but nevertheless porous to every sound. Among the many sounds they heard they had ended up recognizing one in particular and realizing it came from the woman who bore them. Soft, lilting, and consistent, it washed over them its wave of harmony. Sometimes it alternated with other sounds, sharper, less intimate and pleasant. Then all at once there would be a genuine hullaballoo, a concert of indistinct, metallic tones.

While the fetuses continued their helpless descent they suddenly found themselves between two rigid walls that seemed to go on forever. Then they landed in a circular, oddly mobile space. Once they had made their way through, they abruptly fell onto a flat surface and were blinded by the light. Here they were gripped by the shoulders, a feeling that afflicted them as much as the light that hurt them. They instinctively rubbed their eyes with their fists by way of protection. Meanwhile a strange wind filled their lungs, making them suffocate and unconsciously open their mouths to let out uncontrollable cries. Without further ado they were soaked in a lukewarm liquid which neither smelled nor tasted like the one they were accustomed to. At the same time they became aware of their bodies as they were wrapped and laid onto a cushion of ample flesh whose penetrating smell filled their nostrils with perfume. Such was the feeling of well-being that it made them forget the horrible downward journey they had just made. They guessed they were lying against the breast of the woman who had borne them, recognizable only by her voice. With voluptuous pleasure they discovered her smell, they discovered her touch. They began to suck greedily on the bloated nipples full of a sweet-tasting liquid which were placed in their mouths. It was then, at that very moment, their life began.

Simone whispered into the ears of her new-born twins:

"Welcome, my two little ones, boy and girl so alike that one can easily be mistaken for the other. Welcome, I tell you. The life you are about to embark on, and from which you will not get out alive, is not a bowl of arrowroot. Some even call it wicked, others an untamed shrew, and some a lame horse with three hoofs. But who cares! I'll grab a pillow of clouds that I'll put under your heads and I'll fill them with dreams. The sun that lights up the desolation of our lives will not burn brighter than my love for you. Welcome, my little ones!"

EX UTERO

The twins' first months on earth proved difficult. They were unable to cope with living distinct lives: sleeping in separate cradles, being washed one after the other, and taking turns to suck their baby bottle. At first all it needed was for one of them to start gurgling, crying, or screaming and the other would immediately follow suit. It took time for them to rid themselves of this annoying synchronization. Gradually the world around them took shape and color. They were at first filled with wonder by the ray of sun that entered through the shack's wide open window and landed on the mat where they lay. On its way through it took on mischievous shapes which made them laugh, and this laugh tinkled like small bells. They rapidly remembered their names, pricking up their ears and waving their little feet at the mention of these syllables so easy to retain. What they didn't know was that the priest at Dos d'Âne, a fat, dull-witted man, had almost refused to christen them.

"How could you give them such names," he shouted angrily at Simone. "Ivan, Ivana! Not only do they not have a father, but you want to turn them into true heathens!"

Simone's family was used to both multiple and singular births. In the nineteenth century, her ancestor, Zuléma, the first of a litter of quintuplets, had been invited to the Universal Exposition in Saint-Germain-en-Laye in order to prove what could become of a descendant of a slave when he breathed in the effluvium of civilization. Dressed in a tie and three-piece suit, he was a surveyor by trade. He had learned opera arias all on his own by listening to a program on Radio Guadeloupe called *Classical? Classical indeed!* It was he who instilled the love of music that had trickled down to all his descendants.

The twins quickly discovered the sea and the sand. How wonderful it was to feel the warmth of the sand that cascaded through their chubby fingers, their nails pink like seashells. Every day Simone would put them in a wheelbarrow which served as a pram and push them to one of the creeks near Dos d'Âne where the sea breeze caressed their faces mingling with the sounds of an ample maternal voice.

How many years passed blissfully, four or five? They discovered very early on the beautiful face of their mother, who was always leaning over them, and her black velvety skin and sparkling eyes which changed color depending on the mood of the day. She hummed songs to them, much to their delight. When she went off to work with sweat on her brow, she placed them in a sort of basket which she covered with a cloth and set down under the trees. And the women who worked with her came to peek at them in raptures. They soon realized their mother's name was Simone: two harmonious syllables easy to remember and repeat. Gradually the decor of their lives took shape. They had neither brothers nor sisters and had only to share their mother's love with an old grandmother, and that was okay. They never tired of letting that wonderful sand trickle through their fingers: golden sand, endowed with a smell that filled their nostrils, sand that made an imprint of their bodies and could be tossed playfully into the air.

After a few months they began to stand up and walk bowlegged until their legs straightened and turned into two pretty pillars. They soon began to speak and endeavored to put the world around them into words. When silence was required they learned not to make a sound. Consequently Simone could take them to her choir of an evening. They sat on their little benches as good as gold, sucking their thumbs, beating their hands in rhythm to the music. Famous from one end of Guadeloupe to another, the choir specialized in the island's old melodies, one of which, "Mougué," dated back to the time of slavery when the slaves were in irons.

Mougué yé kok-la chanté kokiyoko.

The song "Adieu foulard, adieu madras" dated back to the time when the crowds sang on the quay while the steamships of the Compagnie Générale Transatlantique left for the port of Le Havre, their berths loaded with civil servants on administrative leave.

Adieu foulard, adieu madras, adieu gren d'or, adieu collier-chou.

As for "Ban mwen an ti bo," it was composed during the schmaltzy *doudouiste* period when Creole was considered to be nothing more than bird twittering and not a language of protestation.

Ban mwen ti bo, dé ti bo, twa ti bi lanmou.

After her singing Simone would dance barefoot and throw back her shoulders, her silhouette standing out from the other women who were incapable of rivaling so much grace and beauty. She was often accompanied by her mother, who was just as black, but with hair powdery-white like salt. Her mother was called Maeva. With no milk in her breasts she would feed the babies with spoonfuls of savory cereal. Maeva and Simone would take each other by the hand, bow, and do entrechats. For the two children this was the first such performance they were to see.

Simone never failed to tell them why they were called Ivan and Ivana and why she had stood up to the priest. Ivan was named after the Czar of All the Russias, a capricious and atrabilious man who had lived in the sixteenth century. Ivana was a feminine version of his name. When she was younger Simone was too poor to afford a seat at the cinema on the Champ d'Arbaud in Basse-Terre. She only watched films when Ciné Bravo, a cultural association, set up a white cloth on the main square in Dos d'Âne. That was how she sat in awe through a series of films comprehending little of the cavalcade of images and matching music that filled her eyes. The children sat on numbered metal chairs in the first row. The older generations crawled out of the woodwork of their shacks like cockroaches on a rainy day. Everyone went on chattering loudly until a gong called for silence. Then the magic began. One of these films, *Ivan the Terrible*, had made a deep impression on her. She couldn't remember the name of the director or those of the actors. All she could recall was the lavish jumble of images.

While Ivan was born first, Ivana took refuge behind her brother as if he were destined to be forever and wherever in command. He was the first to learn to dance, filling all those around him with admiration for his instinctive sense of rhythm.

One particular date comes to mind. When the twins were five years old Simone gave them a thorough wash, put on their best clothes, two unbleached linen body-suits embroidered with cross-stitch, and took them to have their photo taken at the studio Catani. This was one of the obligations that no inhabitant of the actual island of Guadeloupe (as Basse-Terre was called at that time) could shirk. Louis Catani was the son of Sergio Catani, an Italian who arrived from Turin in the 1930s because he had no intention of marrying a Fiat like his brothers. Car engines and bodywork did not interest him. He was more interested in portraying men's grim, pimply faces, or those with a fresh face and smooth skin, languishing looks or piercing eyes. Comfortably well-off from his wife's dowry, a rich white Creole heiress, Sergio Catani opened a photo shop he called *Reflections in an Eye*, which was the talk of Basse-Terre. On weekends he set up his camera in the countryside and captured everything that caught his eye. He published three books, now forgotten, but which at the time were highly successful: *Gens de la Ville*, *Gens de la Campagne*, and *Gens de la Mer*.

The portrait of Ivan and Ivana appears on page fifteen of Volume One, entitled "The Little Lovers." It features two children holding hands and smiling at the camera. For some reason the boy is darker than the girl, but just as adorable.

Ivan and Ivana lived in the company of women—their mother, their grandmother, aunts, cousins, aunts-in-law, and cousins-in-law—who each took turns washing them, dressing them, and filling their stomachs with food.

Of the two, Ivana was more inclined to dream. She would examine flowers and leaves, smelling their scents, and seeking the company of domestic animals. She was especially fascinated by birdsong and the color of butterflies which her chubby, clumsy hands tried to capture as they flew by. Her mother devoured her with kisses and as proof of her love invented light-hearted songs especially for her.

Ivan considered his sister his own personal property and grudgingly accepted the love she showed for their mother. As soon as he was old enough, he was the one who washed her, chose her clothes, and tied her mop of picky hair into braided buns glistening with black castor oil. At night, more than once, Simone found them sleeping in each other's arms, which was not to her liking. Nevertheless she didn't dare intervene. The power of their love intimidated her.

The first years therefore went by in perfect happiness.

The place where Ivan and Ivana were born was called Dos d'Âne, a village no uglier or lovelier than the others scattered along the Leeward Coast. Their only claim to finery was the immensity of the sea, the pink and blue sky over their heads, and the emerald green of the sugarcane.

The school stood in the center of Dos d'Âne. It had been rebuilt from top to bottom by the Conseil Général after Hugo, one of the most terrible hurricanes Guadeloupe had ever experienced. It was built at the top of a hill on whose slopes the shacks were terraced. Ivan and Ivana very soon realized they had no father in Guadeloupe. Their father, Lansana Diarra, was part of a Mandingo traditional ensemble that had come to perform in Pointe-à-Pitre. No sooner had he made Simone pregnant than he returned home to Mali. He had promised to send her a ticket to come and join him but never did. Simone had seldom left her island. Occasionally the choir was invited to Martinique and Guyana. Lansana Diarra, however, regularly sent postcards and letters to his children. And that was the reason why Ivan and Ivana grew up with the dream of a wondrous country where their parents would be reunited: *Papa plus Maman*.

Lansana Diarra was originally from Segu in Mali and belonged to the royal family who had previously ruled the kingdom. Now ruined by the consequences of colonization, they had withdrawn to Kidal and got by trafficking kola nuts. Instead of attending school Lansana and his brother Mady sat on the back of an ill-natured, raucous camel and transported huge sacks of nuts. Sometimes they journeyed as far as the great city of Taoudenni, known for its salt mines. Shadows emerged from every wall and every thorny copse. When they were not traveling with their father, Lansana and Mady sat beside their mother in the noisy, filthy market. One day Lansana came across a house he hadn't previously noticed and was struck by the music which suddenly filled his ears. Two musical instruments were answering each other, one shrill and slightly piercing, the inimitable *ngoni*, the other, which he had never heard before, ample, majestic, and deep-sounding. The music stopped and a human voice rose up, that of a griot, of an indescribable harmony. Lansana stopped in his tracks. The following morning as if guided by a magnet he returned to the same place. Then again the day after and the days after that. This little game lasted for about a week when all of a sudden the door opened. A tall, scrawny man emerged with an emaciated face under a long head of gray hair as tangled as a fetish doll's.

"What do you want?" he shouted at Lansana.

Lansana's only thought was to run but the man grabbed him by the wrist and said in a gentler tone, as if he regretted his bluntness:

"Why are you running away? You are not doing anything wrong. Music is a sweet sugary loaf which we can all share."

He dragged Lansana inside the house, where another man, a white man with a mop of curly hair, was clutching an enormous instrument in the shape of a violin. These two men were the famous griot Balla Faseke and the no less famous cellist Victor Lacroix. That was how Lansana became the pupil of two of the best musicians of his time.

At the early age of seventeen he too had acquired a reputation beyond compare. When he was twenty he was invited all over the world from Tokyo, Jakarta, and Beijing, to Paris, where he gave a concert in front of an audience in raptures.

From her very early years Ivana proved gifted at school. The teacher would read out to the class her French homework and give her top marks. She was also an obedient, well-behaved little girl, never without a kind word and the budding flower of a smile at the corner of her mouth. Everyone adored her, especially the aunts in the choir. They claimed Ivana would go far and had a voice of gold that would captivate admirers in Basse-Terre and beyond.

Nobody, however, could put up with Ivan, who was disobedient and always prepared to hurl abuse, a real little hooligan. With his shirt gaping open on a chest glistening with sweat, he dared to constantly defy and disrespect men and women much older than himself. He fully deserved the nickname of "hoodlum." But as the years went by the affection that united the two children never dwindled.

Ivan's sharp, raucous voice took on a softer tone when he spoke to his sister. As soon as Ivana appeared Ivan would holster his bravados and become as meek as a lamb. Ivan vaguely remembered the pleasure he got from his sister's body. When? He could no longer recall. Perhaps in another life? As a result Ivana frightened him somewhat because of this desire that never ceased to haunt him: her brown skin, the small cups of her breasts, and the tight curly hairs of her pubis.

The second date that comes to mind is when they were ten years old and Simone took them to Basse-Terre. Basse-Terre is a small, nondescript town; only the monuments built by Ali Tur make an impression. This Tunisian architect was commissioned by the government to repair the damage wreaked by the hurricane of 1928. The Conseil Général and the Préfecture especially are worth a visit. Simone regularly traveled to Basse-Terre to buy manuscript paper on which she noted her compositions. She seldom took her children with her. Where would she find the money to pay for three round-trip bus tickets? How could she even afford to buy a codfish sandwich from one of the cheap restaurants on the edge of the market?

But this time she got it into her head to let them enjoy the ride. They climbed into the bus *Hope in God* that drove for a good hour. The road from Dos d'Âne to Basse-Terre is "magnificent," as the tourist brochures say without exaggeration. It is lined by flame trees that turn scarlet in season. It overlooks the sea and you travel between the blue of the sky and the phosphorescent blue of the ocean that unrolls to your left.

When they arrived at the noisy, multicolored market, typical of the tropics, they decided to buy those brown-skinned fruit they call sapodilla, which have given their name to a black woman's velvety skin. Nobody knows exactly how the quarrel broke out with the market woman, but the fact remains that under her ill-fitting yellow and green madras head tie, her cheeks glistening with sweat, she insulted Simone who was clutching her children. She berated them in no uncertain terms in a thick, aggressive Creole:

"Just look at these good-for-nothings, miserably black, who are complaining my fruit is not sweet enough. People like you shouldn't be allowed on this earth."

From that day on Ivan and Ivana realized they belonged to the most underprivileged category of the population, the ones anyone could insult as they liked. At Dos d'Âne they weren't aware of social differences. Except for the school and the town hall, there was no building of significance, no fine houses, no flower-bedecked garden. Everyone lived in the same miserable shacks seeking to earn a living as best they could and hoping to find a little happiness.

In an instant they realized their skin was black, their hair kinky, and that their mother worked herself to the bone in the sugarcane fields for a pittance. Ivana was heartbroken and she promised that one day she would avenge her mother and give her the gentler way of life that she deserved. Yes, one day her life would be coated with barley sugar. Ivan, however, was filled with rage against life and against his fate which had turned him into an underprivileged subordinate.

Simone guessed only too clearly what was going on in her children's hearts. For her the quarrel with the market woman was banal and of no consequence. She was more affected perhaps by Lansana, who had promised her a country where color didn't count and where there were neither rich nor poor. Lansana was a smooth talker, that's all there was to be said.

When Simone, Ivan, and Ivana left the market they

made their way to a shop called Au Lac de Côme, near the Conseil Général, where they sold accordions, saxophones, string instruments, and all kinds of drums: drums you could sit on and drums you could just tap.

The shop's star attractions were a guitar that had belonged to Jimi Hendrix, and John Lennon's sitar. The owner was an old mulatto who had had his moment of glory accompanying Gérard La Viny when he sang at La Cigale in Paris.

"Please don't touch anything," he strongly urged the children.

Coming so soon after the quarrel at the market this remark ended up exasperating Ivan, and, small things sometimes having lasting consequences, here began the perfect breeding ground for revolt.

From that day on Ivan's marks at school got worse and he truly became the hoodlum he had been playfully nicknamed up till then. Despite his young age, he began to steal and pilfer. Simone didn't know which way to turn. Gradually the idea germinated in Simone's mind that she would have to get Lansana to realize that the son he had neglected might soon become a public menace.

It did not take long before it happened. The start of the school year in October saw the arrival in Dos d'Âne of Monsieur Jérémie, a high yellow *chaben*, with short graying hair and a square face half hidden by an ayatollah's beard. He was no ordinary teacher. You would never guess from his cheap cotton shirt or his coarse commonplace canvas jeans bought at a discount that he had traveled the world. Where exactly, nobody knew. It was rumored he had been sent to Dos d'Âne for disciplinary reasons. Some claimed he had made as many women pregnant as he had hairs on his head, others said he had

had love affairs with men, while yet others maintained he had got rich from drug trafficking. Nobody could get to the truth with certitude.

Monsieur Jérémie was put in charge of the class studying for the primary school diploma, up till then the pride of Dos d'Âne, whose pupils passed with flying colors every year. Alas, as soon as he arrived, the pupils who had worked so diligently were left to their own devices: gone were the tests, the essays, and almost all the compositions. Monsieur Jérémie passed the time churning out endless tirades during which he claimed to be able to fix the world: for example, he said we needed to combat Western ideas; he described the superiority of certain religions and certain doctrines. He very quickly made friends with Ivan who was repeating his school year. Very soon Ivan spent all his free time round at the primary school teacher's home.

Out of bravado, he would repeat the teacher's words without thinking.

"France is a country of white people," he repeated, echoing his master's voice. "It's a fact! People as high up as General de Gaulle said so. We Blacks have nothing in common with them."

Simone tolerated his blasphemy with the indulgence she reserved for her children. Ivan was foul-mouthed, everyone knew that, but no one paid much attention to what he said since deep down he was not a bad kid.

When one evening she received the visit of Monsieur Ducadosse, the deputy mayor, Simone was dumbfounded. Monsieur Ducadosse was a little man with skin the color of night, and oddly red hair. His excessive smoking had blackened his gums and teeth.

"Make sure you look after your son," he said solemnly. "Monsieur Jérémie is planting strange ideas in his head.

He is turning him into a critic, an enemy I would even say, of France who transformed us from African savages to civilized men."

Simone had trouble understanding his words. She had spent her life working amidst the sting of the sugarcane and had never questioned her condition or that of her country. She endured a sleepless night, and in the morning decided to act. But she didn't yet know how.

In actual fact, Monsieur Jérémie was neither homosexual nor *makoumé*, as it was rumored. He didn't like women either. He was obsessed only with politics. A denunciatory letter had informed the Ministry of Education that his five-year disappearance had been spent in Afghanistan or Libya. That sounded fishy. What was he doing in these countries of ill repute? As usual the Ministry of Education had taken its time before opening an inquiry. When it finally made a decision the trail had gone cold and they couldn't prove anything against Monsieur Jérémie. As a result there was no way he could be struck off the list and all they could do was send him back to his native Guadeloupe and appoint him to the school at Dos d'Âne, that godforsaken hole. Monsieur Jérémie, first name Nicéphale—a name you wouldn't be seen dead with, a phrase invented by a sixteenth-century innkeeper who refused to lodge a traveler because of his name—became besotted with Ivan for reasons that had nothing to do with his athletic build, his muscular frame, or his prominent member, which always seemed to be in a state of erection. Firstly, he had calculated that Ivan would have been the same age as his unborn son, killed along with his mother in a NATO bombing raid. He sensed that in the breeding ground of this uneducated and unrefined mind, his ideas would germinate into a burning bush. He especially liked the way the boy listened to him: slightly bored and slumped in an armchair, his hands locked over his stomach. Monsieur Jérémie, therefore, didn't hesitate to speak his mind:

"You have no idea what winter is like in the desert. The wind roars and rages in every nook and cranny, howling '*Faro dans les Bois*.' Crystals cling to the branches of the scant trees rigid as roadside crosses. They change color with the rays of the bluish sun and especially when the moon rises over the immensity of the desert, triggering a world of enchantment. Although my *gandoura* was too light and my cardboard boots too flimsy, I was not afraid of the cold. I loved that country more than my own because it was Alya's. It was Alya who chose me, me the foreigner, black what's more, and who didn't speak a word of her language. Because of my color, her family, especially her brothers, did not want us to marry. They repeated their demands, which I endeavored to satisfy. In the end they demanded I become a Muslim. I accepted, not knowing that the circumcision would be so painful and cause so much blood. All that for such a tiny piece of flesh. But now that my member was patched up I could penetrate Alya as many times as I liked and make her moan beneath me. Our happiness lasted seven months. Seven little months. Then they killed her. They killed my beloved. One evening while I was in a bar drinking green tea with friends of mine, a crackling of gunfire made us rush outside. Facing us the entire neighborhood was in flames. Orange flames were already licking the sky. 'They're all dead!' shouted those running to escape, covered in blood. That's when my life came to a grinding halt."

The morning after Monsieur Ducadosse's rather troubling visit Simone went to find her friend Father

Michalou. He was called Father because he had a mop of totally white hair. In actual fact he wasn't that old, fifty at the most. He had lived for a long time in France. Then he got tired of assembling cars, unable to pay for one himself, and tired of traveling on the regional express metros, which were always crowded, always late, and always breaking down. So he had returned home and taken up the trade his grandfather and father had practiced before him. There had been a time when he wanted to move in with Simone and live as husband and wife, but she had refused, claiming that her twins would never accept a stepfather. In actual fact she still had a stubborn dream in her head that one day Lansana would come back and they would make up for the lost years. Michalou didn't mind since her bed was available whenever he liked.

When she arrived he was mending his nets. He listened to her, shrugged his shoulders, then declared:

"In our country there are some who say we would be better off if we went our own way, politically speaking. It's not true, just look at the Haitians and the Dominicans, for example. Monsieur Jérémie is perhaps an activist for independence. Who knows? It might be wise to keep your son well away from him."

"But how?" lamented Simone. "What do you expect me to do with the boy? Where do you want me to send him?"

"How old is he? You could put him to work somewhere. Even a small wage would help you."

Simone was not content with his opinion. She also went to ask for advice from her mother. Although Maeva, now in her sixties, seemed vacuous, she was once considered one of the most formidable women of her generation for she possessed the incomparable gift of second sight. It had swept down on her one day without warning. At the age of sixteen, while she was taking her siesta, she had seen her father, Ti-Roro, a stone mason, tumble off the roof he was building and land straight on the splintered rubble below, which was sharp as a saw. After that she had seen Hurricane Hugo wreak its desolation. Then she had seen the Blanchet factory's sugarcane glow in the night and children suffocate from an attack of tape worms and men and women drain themselves dry with a green-colored diarrhea. From Basse-Terre to Pointe-à-Pitre people were frightened of her predictions. Then Father Guinguant had arrived from his native Brittany and drawn her into his confessional. "What did she think she was doing?" he asked her. Didn't she know that God acts in secret and mysterious ways? She risked eternal damnation if she went on like this. From that moment on Maeva never said another word and blended in with the crowd of churchgoers dressed in black who took communion daily. But this did not mean her gift was dead. She could see her grandchildren wrapped in a thick red veil, oozing blood. What did that mean? What would be their fate? Maeva listened carefully to her daughter then shrugged her shoulders.

"Take Ivan out of school? Why not?"

Since the two women had come to an agreement, Maeva turned the key in her door and mother and daughter made their way to choir practice. Rehearsals took place every day and sometimes lasted for hours. When the singers dispersed of an evening the moon had often risen and its soft light bedecked the extreme ugliness of Dos d'Âne with an unexpected charm. The toad-like shacks turned into chrysalises ready to become butterflies and take flight. Other times it was pitch dark. Stumbling over the rough stones as they felt their way home the women got the impression of pushing open the doors of hell and following their own hearse.

The choir's repertoire was a mixed bag. They avoided facile and hackneyed melodies such as "Ban mwen un tibo" or "Maladie d'amour" and delved straight into serious research on the island's fundamental traditions. They were not opposed to modern composers such as Henri Salvador or Francky Vincent. That was how one evening Maeva introduced a song by a singer whom nobody had ever heard of: Barbara. The women listened to it with their undivided attention:

One day
Or maybe one night
Near a lake, I had fallen asleep
When suddenly, seemingly tearing the sky apart
And coming from nowhere
Appeared a black eagle.

At the end of the song they all had the same expression.

"That's not appropriate at all," one of them had the courage to declare.

"Nobody will like that," affirmed another.

Maeva went into a fit of rage:

"Why ever not? Barbara is one of the greatest singers of all times."

She was wasting her time for she never managed to get the others to change their minds.

Years later at the inauguration of the Mémorial ACTe, the monument dedicated to the history of slavery, the choir met with huge success singing a well-known song by Laurent Voulzy; at the time it had caused an uproar and infuriated those who defended the Creole language. How come this sudden liking for French songs? Moreover the choir had the ridiculous name of Les Belles du

Soir. This was ample proof the singers were alienated. The President of the Regional Council, however, had donated several thousand euros, which had enabled them to travel to Martinique.

Simone, therefore, set about looking for a job for her son. On an island where 35% of the population is unemployed this was no easy task. However hard she climbed up and down stairs, rang doorbells, sent his cv, made constant phone calls, and waited for hours and hours in empty waiting rooms she was always met with the same answer: no job available.

She was on the point of giving up when La Caravelle Hotel, which was opening on the Leeward Coast, accepted to interview Ivan. La Caravelle belonged to the Coralie chain, which had hotels all over the world. Its flagship undoubtedly was the hotel in the Seychelles. However, since tourism in Guadeloupe was of the modest, family kind, no major investment had been made. La Caravelle was a nondescript building set behind a garden. Standing on the lawn were two traveler's trees with their rigid arms outstretched.

Ivan was given a job as a security guard. Violence had now settled on the land. There were villages, areas, and neighborhoods where nobody dared venture after a certain hour. Parents told their children, who couldn't believe their ears, that there was a time when nobody locked their doors and windows and when keys and safes were unheard of. Ivan was given a pair of blue, rough canvas trousers, a T-shirt, and a same-colored cap. Above all, he was given a gun, a Mauser. He had never imagined owning a weapon, even in his wildest dreams. Monsieur Esteban, a retired police officer, an expert under oath, came to teach the team how to shoot.

"Never aim at the legs of the hooligans you'll meet," he

recommended. "Once they're back on their feet they'll return to the scene of their crime. Aim for the head, aim for the heart, so they'll die and never come back to trouble you."

From that day on, Ivan had two passions: One for his sister whom he loved and desired more every day, to the extent he would wake up at night convinced the irreparable had been done. And the other for his weapon, his Mauser. He liked to feel the weight of this piece of cold, rigid metal, strike a pose, and pretend to aim at a target. He dreamed of lodging a bullet in a living prey. That's how he killed a series of white hens that Simone was keeping to make ends meet and sell in the market. He felt he was God, a king, all-powerful.

Alas, his happiness, as is often the case, was short-lived. First of all he learned that his Mauser was antiquated and wasn't worth anything. It came from a miscellaneous batch, bought for next to nothing from a French man who took to his heels as fast as he could to leave Guadeloupe. One night he had fired at a burglar come to raid his house and had mortally shot him in the head. He had escaped a prison sentence but his house had been smeared with blood and graffiti with the words "murderer" written on his doors and windows. Consequently he realized he would be better off putting the Atlantic between him and Guadeloupe.

This discovery deeply affected Ivan. His arm therefore was worthless, a toy, nothing but a cheap toy. The worst was yet to come.

He hadn't worked for more than a week at La Caravelle when the director of human resources, a fat, sweaty French man, summoned him to his office. He stared at Ivan with eyes as blue as the sky and asked, "Is your name Ivan Némélé? How old are you?"

Ivan remained dumbfounded. He was used to fooling people about his age since he was strong and well-built. But this time he sensed danger.

"We have information on you," the French man continued. "Which says you are not yet sixteen. We cannot, therefore, entrust a weapon to a minor without running the risk of serious prosecution. Give me your gun! Give it to me!"

Since Ivan remained petrified, the man grabbed the belt around Ivan's waist. But they didn't fire him; they simply changed his job. He was given a fluorescent-colored uniform and put in charge of the pool for children. Ivan took this as a terrible humiliation, trapping him like a force of evil.

It was from this moment on that his radicalization began, a word that is bandied about today, rightly or wrongly. It does not originate from his time in prison as the experts would like us to think. Up till then Ivan had listened to Monsieur Jérémie's tirades as a lot of hot air. Now he understood that the world was far different from what he had imagined; that the earth was not round but full of fissures and faults in which a defenseless individual without a foothold, such as himself, could lose his life.

Now that he was no longer a security guard at La Caravelle he had time on his hands to visit the primary school teacher. The latter was fond of these visits and would chatter on, returning again and again to the wound that had cast a bloody shadow over his life.

"After Alya's death, bomb attacks, ambushes, and reprisals no longer meant anything to me. You understand, I'm not a real Muslim. I never believed I would see my beloved again seated in Paradise with everything I had lost. I knew I would never see her again. My happiness was gone. So I returned to France and laid siege to the Ministry of Education, who ended up giving me a job in a mediocre college in a godforsaken suburb. Surprise, surprise, the students began to worship me. They loved the meanderings of my life. They wanted to visit the countries where I had been. My lessons were spent telling them of my adventures and advising the most brazen among them where best to travel the world. Alas, the director of the college got suspicious and denounced me. You know the rest."

Yes, Ivan knew the rest. People content with happiness don't make history, goes the popular saying.

As for Ivana, she was happy. She was lovely. She was top of her class in French, Math, and even Sport since she had just been appointed captain of the school's female volleyball team. She had also been gifted with a pretty, high-pitched voice and had been chosen as soloist in the school choir. One day while she was singing in the church at Dournaux, a small coastal town situated twenty or so kilometers from Dos d'Âne, a retired music teacher had noticed her and taught her the "Ave Marias" by Gounod and Schubert, which earned her an invitation to Guyana to sing in the church at Apatou in front of an audience of maroons. We know, too, that in order to be happy on this earth we need to shut our eyes to a good many things—something Ivana was good at doing. That's how she refused to confront the environment of extreme poverty she was growing up in and was convinced that one day all that would change. That's how she refused to admit that Simone was languishing and working herself to the bone in the sugarcane fields at harvest time or behind her stall at the market. She was convinced that a time would come when she would be able to change the course of her mother's destiny. There was only one point on which she was totally lucid: the nature of her feelings for her brother. She vainly attempted to put it down to their being twins, but deep down she knew it wasn't normal. There were times when she was profoundly troubled such as when she saw him dressed in his old black undershirt sweeping the courtyard and around the house, or when their hands touched on a bowl of coffee or a braided loaf of bread. Of course they had never uttered an inappropriate word or made a single uncalled-for gesture. But she knew that this burning bush they carried deep down inside would one day flare up and consume them. Ever since Ivan began to leave early in the morning for La Caravelle she had seen less of her brother and was given a rest.

One day when she was returning from the gully, a demijohn of water balanced on her head, a red moped drove straight towards her, almost making her fall over.

"You shouldn't be carrying such a load. You're far too lovely," a voice cried out. "Let me carry it for you."

Ivana was surprised to see Faustin Flérette, the son of Manolo, the baker. Manolo was a mulatto who had a place of his own in Dos d'Âne. He was looked upon as being rich. He was on first-name terms with the mayor and hosted dinners for the regional and general councillors from Basse-Terre. He had grown up in Marseille, where his father had taken refuge during the war in order to save his Jewish girlfriend. He had not learned much and was expelled from the René Char College during seventh grade, having merely learned how to make focaccia and panisses. Nowadays on Sundays the cars of the well-off jammed the only street in town to buy up all his special pastries. Faustin, his oldest son, had passed his baccalaureate exam with flying colors. Nevertheless, owing to an administrative error, his file had disappeared and he didn't get the scholarship he deserved. While waiting for this error to be rectified he worked at the college as a tutor and taught algebra and geometry to the children who were having difficulty in these subjects.

"You're saying you don't want me to carry this load," Ivana joked. "And you're the one who's going to put it on your head?"

"No, of course not," he protested with a laugh. "I'll put it on the back of my bike."

From that day on a budding relation formed between the two teenagers that was not easy to define. From Faustin's point of view there was no doubt a young man's desire for an alluring young girl despite her inferior social class. He hoped to get her into his bed, without daring to allude to such crude thoughts. As for Ivana, she was flattered; but for her it was mainly a way to get away from Ivan, and an attempt to transfer to someone else what she felt for her brother.

So Faustin now came to pick Ivana up every morning. She would strap on an admittedly ungainly helmet, sit on the back of his moped, and be driven to the college at Dournaux. Faustin would bring her back to Dos d'Âne every evening. There is nothing more delightful than to drive along the Leeward Coast. When the powerful rays of a cruel sun have not yet emerged, erasing every shadow and flattening every contour, the landscape is bathed in a magical, milky light. Of an evening it is the realm of pitch darkness. All you can hear is the vast, howling voice of the sea whose waves swell and roll in from as far back as the horizon.

One evening Faustin and Ivana came face-to-face with Ivan who, for once, had come home for dinner. While Simone was cooking conch for her beloved son, Ivan was watching a football match on the extra-flat TV screen. Seeing the couple arrive he got up, eyes and mouth rounded in stupefaction. Ignoring the hand Faustin held out, he shouted at his sister.

"Where did he come from?"

Ivana launched into a confused explanation while Faustin cautiously headed for the door without further ado. Simone set down on the table plates with slices of avocado, creole rice, and a conch fricassee that looked extremely appetizing. Throughout dinner, however, not a word passed between the mother and her two children. Ivana was afraid. She had a terrible foreboding. And she was not mistaken. Around one in the morning, hiding his mother's kitchen knife in his clothes, Ivan laid in wait for Faustin who was getting drunk with his friends at the local Rhum Encore bar. When he emerged, Ivan hurled himself upon him and chased him as far as the beach. Here the silhouette of the two teenagers disappeared into the darkness. What happened? We shall never know. But the fact remains that the following morning, two fishermen returning from Antigua discovered Faustin's dislocated body lying in a pool of blood. There was no end to those who had witnessed the fatal brawl between the two boys, and Ivan was arrested around ten in the morning at La Caravelle. Some tourists took offense and immediately packed up and left. It gave the place a bad reputation. A helicopter flew Faustin Flérette as an emergency to the hospital in Pointe-à-Pitre where three doctors went to work on him.

It was Ivan's first conviction and the first time he "entered jail," as they say in Guadeloupe. For having wounded Faustin he was sentenced to two years' imprisonment. He owed this relative leniency to his court-appointed lawyer, Mr. Vinteuil. Mr. Vinteuil had already made a name for himself as a defense lawyer. Some thought him excellent. Others found him tendentious, bearing the mark of a total incomprehension as to the realities of Guadeloupe. He depicted Ivan as a furious *maléré*, enraged at seeing his sister used like a plaything, as flesh for the pleasure of the son of a semi-well-to-do family. In actual fact, nothing had gone on between Faustin and Ivana except for a few kisses and some necking. But how could you prove that?

Manolo, Faustin's father, was still angry. A two-year prison sentence for having made a mess of his son— Ivan had got off pretty lightly. He decided to take his revenge. Oh yes! This family and its putrid miasmas needed to be wiped off the face of the earth. He urged his friend the mayor to strike Simone off the list of those in need who received a monthly allocation of several euros, but, above all, to expel her from the rent-controlled apartment she had occupied for twenty years, since well before the twins were born.

One morning Simone and Ivana were dragged out of their beds by the police and thrown onto the sidewalk with all their meager possessions. But the police hadn't reckoned on Maeva. Not only did she welcome her daughter and granddaughter into her cramped little shack, but she also begged Kukurmina, the master of the invisible—who hides in the infinitely small and influences the infinitely big—to come to her aid. The powerful could no longer continue to crush and humiliate the weak and go unpunished. Apparently Kukurmina heard her, for three days later while getting up in the middle of the night to take a piss Manolo's feet struck an unknown obstacle and he fell flat out, smashing his skull against the edge of the bath. The entire island went into a state of shock. What a to-do was Manolo's funeral!

His parents and relatives emerged from all over the place: Paris, Marseille, Strasbourg, Lyon, Lille. For it's a well-known fact that there are two types of Guadeloupeans: those who are without a job on the island, and those who just get by in metropolitan France. There are a lucky few who are an exception to the rule and take refuge abroad, but such privileged individuals are few and far between. Manolo's family transformed this period of mourning into a stroll around the island. Some rented cars and went for a dip in the icy waters of the red and black rivers at Matouba. Others took selfies and had themselves driven to the pre-Columbian site at Trois-Rivières and the Lucette Michaux-Chevry roundabout at Montebello. Another group flew off to the islands of Les Saintes and Marie-Galante for the day.

"It's not true the Caribbean sea is bluer than the Atlantic," claimed one of Manolo's sisters who lived in Saint-Malo and was married to a Breton, the perfect example of the age-old attraction the Bretons had for Antillean women.

Adding to the festive nature of the event were the succulent dishes served up in abundance. First came the blood sausage: "one kind two fingers wide, twined in coils, another thick and stocky, the mild one tasting of wild thyme, the hot one spiced to an incandescence" (the description is by Aimé Césaire). Then came the stuffed crabs, curried goat *colombo*, tuna casserole, octopus, and conch fricassee. During the church ceremony the mayor refused to let the priest read the homily and went straight up to the pulpit himself.

"There is an African proverb that says when an old man dies a library goes up in flames. Manolo knew things which nobody knows today and he takes this knowledge with him."

Should we correct the mayor? This is not an African proverb but a famous quote by Amadou Hampâté Ba, one of West Africa's greatest intellectuals. It would be a waste of time. The mayor is already posturing for photos and publishing them on Facebook.

At the end of the ceremony it began to pour with a sharp, drenching rain, proof that the deceased regretted this life.

Now Maeva and Simone, who never really got on together, were forced to live under the same roof. In fact as soon as Simone reached fifteen she left home, tired of the constant sanctimonious atmosphere alternating with visionary fits. She moved in with Fortuneo, a gangling Haitian who sometimes hired himself out to the factories for harvesting the sugarcane and sometimes manicured people's gardens. Fortuneo never stopped talking but Simone was never tired of listening to his constant chatter.

"When I was born," he would say, "I was so black, blue in fact, that the midwife couldn't tell the difference between my front and my behind. She dropped me and I still have an enormous bump on my head. Could it be a stamp of madness? When I was in my maman's womb I wasn't alone. I had a brother, a twin you might say. But he died or, to be exact, he merged into me. He must have been a musician. Sometimes he fills my head with his melodies. I am deaf to the people around me and look at them like an idiotic *ababa*. Other times his voice goes round on the vinyl of my brain, as hard as a sapphire stylus."

It was Fortuneo, an instrumentalist with an extremely harmonious voice, who introduced Simone to the world of music. Thanks to him she delved into her memory and recalled those lullabies, those chants she heard in her childhood to which she had never paid much attention. They spent hours of an evening singing in their patch of garden, leaning against the hedge of hibiscus while the moon sailed back and forth high in the sky like a round, moonstruck lantern.

Unfortunately after five years living together Fortuneo went to join his brother in the States. His brother assured him it was a country where there was plenty of work to be had. Consequently there followed a bleak period for Simone, who went from bed to bed, from man to man, from macho to macho. Then the wind of love and music produced a miracle.

One evening no different from any other, she attended a choir rehearsal. Around ten in the evening a group of men arrived dressed in unusual attire. They were wearing cotton robes over baggy trousers. Simone learned later that these were African costumes, namely *boubous*. The men were holding strange musical instruments. One of them, obviously the leader of the group, addressed the choir, who were both intimidated and repelled by the strangeness of these new arrivals.

"This instrument," he explained, "is called a *kora*. Its voice accompanied the heroic deeds of our kings and followed them into battle. This one is a *balafon*. Each of its metal strips emits a different sound, and learning how to harmonize the notes is essential. This stubborn little one is called a *ngoni* and it dodges in and out all over the place."

The speaker who cast a fiery gaze over the audience while he spoke was cousin to the famous Mori Kanté, who had delighted Guadeloupe the previous year and filled the stadium of Les Abymes with thousands of spectators. His name was Lansana Diarra. Between Simone and him it was love at first sight and it changed their vision of the world in an instant. Stars lit up their eyes and it was as if they had known each other for years. Forever, in fact.

After the rehearsal they went out into the night. The stars, which had made their eyes sparkle, climbed back up into the sky and left behind a gentle glow, the glow of mutual comprehension and commitment. Lansana and Simone held each other's hands.

"Are you a woman or a spirit?" Lansana asked. "Although my life has been filled with the sounds of love, I have never met anyone like you. Tell me about yourself."

Simone laughed good-heartedly.

"There is nothing to tell. I think my life begins today. There was nothing before you came."

Lansana departed after spending two weeks in Guadeloupe, during which the two never left each other. At the airport they kissed passionately and Lansana had murmured, "I'll have you come to Kidal where I live. You'll see how this town is like no other. It defies the desert from which it derives its force."

Not long after, Simone realized she was pregnant and sent Lansana letter after letter but to no avail. She couldn't get over it. This man who had brought her the hot breath of the Sahel—was he in fact no better than the others? As the months added up, she gathered he was no better. Once Ivan and Ivana were born she became a single mother. Like so many others around her. Why are some lands more fertile in single mothers than others? Are the women lovelier and more attractive? Are the men more hot-blooded? On the contrary. They are lands in dire straits. The sexual act is the only godsend; it gives the men the impression of having achieved an exploit and the women the illusion of being loved.

After an exhausting day at the market where she had

tried to sell her hens, Simone returned home to her mother's. In the cramped but meticulously arranged dining room the table had already been laid. A delicious smell of rice and smoked herring, *diri et arengsaur*, floated in the air. This irritated Simone no end. She knew what it meant. Her mother, who had always blamed her for being disorganized, was giving her a lesson in good manners. Maeva emerged from the kitchen wiping her hands on the apron which she always wore.

"I've had that dream again," she said anxiously.

"What dream?" Simone asked in exasperation.

"The same one where I see Ivan and Ivana in a blood-covered fog. What can it mean?"

"Nothing bad, I can assure you," Simone said, shrugging her shoulders. "They love each other too much to hurt one another."

She did not know that being in love is as dangerous as being out of love and that a famous English writer once said, "Yet each man kills the thing he loves."

Crouched on top of a hill and edged on two sides by ruthless cliffs, the prison at Dournaux dates back to the eighteenth century when the rebels who dreamed of ousting the king were dispatched as far away as possible to meditate on their crime. Numerous events have marked its history. The most spectacular was The Great Escape dating back to 1752. Armed with solid Manila ropes, the rebels slipped down the cliffs to a small creek where their accomplices were waiting for them. These accomplices then rowed them out to sea to a three-master named *La Goëlette*. What happened after that? We shall never know. Did a quarrel break out? The fact remains that the rebels fought each other to the death and the ghost vessel drifted past Dominica and dumped a crop of stinking corpses on the coast of Martinique.

Wings had been added over time to the main building since the prison was overpopulated, as were all prisons the world over. It's quite easy to see why. There are more and more people wherever you look who have no respect for the law, make a mockery and turn their backs on it.

It was here they took Ivan. He was thrown into Building A, which housed petty offenders. Here there were a good number of prisoners guilty of having abused their partners. Covered in bruises and blood, the battered women had had the strength and the audacity to go to the police and press charges. Their cases had been accepted and much to their surprise their abusers had been arrested. What! You can no longer beat up your wife nowadays? From time immemorial our ancestors were used to practicing this little game. Is the world about to change?

Ivan was mortified at being imprisoned together with a group of petty delinquents. He would have preferred being locked up in Building B or C or in the high-security ward where you sometimes caught sight of the prisoners doing the rounds in their courtyard surrounded by barbed wire under the supervision of a horde of prison screws who were the subject of many stories in the press. One of the prisoners was nicknamed The Locust since he was as thin and destructive as a cricket, and capable of reducing a crowd of individuals to pulp. Another one was called The Mongoose because he was deceitful and cruel. And yet another The Black Mamba, who outdid all the others in cruelty.

Patience, a voice whispered to Ivan from deep down, *your day will come, when you will write your name in the sky with letters of fire and everyone will remember you.*

Ivan became friends with Miguel, the son of Dr. Angel Pastoua. Five years older than Ivan, Miguel took him under his wing. He had been imprisoned because he had blinded his wife Paulina in one eye, suspecting her of being the mistress of a Lebanese cloth merchant, rue de Nozières. Miguel was the son of a "draft evader," so called by the Antilleans because they refused to do their military service and had joined the ranks of the FLN in Algeria. Once Miguel's father was amnestied he had returned home and become a reputed cardiologist. That is all it took for Miguel, constantly confronted with this image of a valiant father, to turn into a delinquent from an early age. Like Monsieur Jérémie, he would chatter on to Ivan: "Albert Camus said: 'Between justice and my mother, I choose my mother.' You know who Albert Camus was, don't you?"

Ivan didn't answer since he had never heard the name. Oblivious to his ignorance, Miguel continued, "Albert Camus was so right. My father bored me stiff with his stories about the FLN, how he had gone into combat, how he had met Frantz Fanon and so on and so forth. It was so boring. For me Algeria boiled down to Blida where my mother was born. I lived with her until I was seven; then my father had the terrible idea of having me come to live with him."

Miguel decreed a number of peremptory rules: never set foot inside a church, above all never confess or take communion. The Catholic Church had defended slavery. Priests such as the Père Labat had owned slaves. On the contrary, focus on Islam, a religion despised by Westerners, but filled with grandeur and dignity. Leave Guadeloupe, where nothing ever happens, as quickly as possible and join other regions of the world where the struggle against the powerful is raging.

These two years in prison were beneficial, dare we say, for Ivan. In the mornings they made tennis balls and rackets. They assembled parts for record players and various musical instruments. Afternoons, volunteer teachers came over from the surrounding colleges. They taught French, Math, History, and Geography. Ivan was already familiar with Victor Hugo, of course, but soon got to know Rimbaud, Verlaine, Lamartine, and above all a certain Paul Éluard:

> On regaining health
> On ignoring risk
> On hoping without looking back
> I write your name.
> And with the power of one word
> I begin my life again
> I was born to know you
> To call you
> Freedom.

Ivan realized that he didn't understand what these lines actually meant. But he knew deep down that it didn't really matter. Poetry is not meant to be understood. It is designed to invigorate the mind and vitalize the heart. It is meant to quicken the blood in one's veins. After his time in prison Ivan passed his college diploma with flying colors. The jury made a surprising mention:

"If Ivan Némélé would only make an effort, we would have nothing but compliments to give him."

When Ivan got out of prison, he and Ivana met up again and were paralyzed by shyness. For two long years they had only seen each other once a week amidst the chaos and disorder of a crowded visiting room, communicating through a meshed window and sometimes forced to shout in order to be heard. Snatches of conversations in foreign languages mixed in with theirs.

Now they were back together again they didn't dare look into each other's eyes or touch each other, and even less to kiss. They both agreed to set off for a place they particularly liked: the Pointe Paradis, a creek where privateers of every nationality laid in wait for the Spanish galleons loaded with the bullion they were coveting. This is where the famous Jean Valmy had been ambushed by the king's soldiers. Shipped back to France as a traitor he was hung on the Place de Grève.

Ivan laid his head on the soft cushion of his sister's stomach and murmured, "I think of you all day long. I wonder what you are doing, what you are thinking. When I imagine your thoughts they end up becoming mine. All things considered, I am you."

Ivana stopped herself from asking him what he was going to do with his brand-new diploma when he asked her the last question she was expecting.

"Have you heard of a certain Paul Éluard?"

She shrugged her shoulders in amazement.

"Yes, of course."

"What do you know about him?" he insisted. "Was he deprived of freedom? Was he sent to prison? And for how long?"

"That, I don't know."

Thereupon she began to rattle on about the platitudes she had learned regarding Paul Éluard: Surrealist poet. Disciple of André Breton until he was evicted from the movement, a great friend of René Char's.

It was obvious her brother was no longer listening to her. He had constructed his own version of Paul Éluard, a writer made to suit him. Simone de Beauvoir wrote that a writer should never meet her readers. In my opinion, the reverse is true. Readers always think of a writer as being good-looking, handling their words with elegance, and being full of good humor and sparkling wit. They risk being disappointed with reality.

Idleness is the mother of all vices. Ivan had been out of a job for almost a year. At La Caravelle he was persona non grata, an ex-prisoner. However often he made regular visits to the association in charge of helping him reintegrate into society, they came up with nothing. At one point he found work with a circus, the Pipi Rosa circus from Venezuela, which traveled throughout the islands of the Caribbean. But the sight of these unfortunate animals locked in their cages, especially a couple of lions, looking dazed in their shabby mane of fur, depressed him. After two weeks he resigned. It was then that Father Michalou offered to help him and invited him to come aboard his fishing boat to confront the open sea. As early as four in the morning, while the two men set sail, a thick fog that had accumulated during the night came and settled on their shoulders. Rapidly the sky would brighten and they would throw out or haul in their nets several times. But fishing today is not what it used to be, and they returned to land, their boat half empty, and Ivan got fed up.

Finally, an extraordinary event changed his life. Monsieur Jérémie opened a private school and asked Ivan to be one of its tutors. Consequently all three women, Maeva, Simone, and Ivana, were showered with all kinds of questions. They were lost in conjectures. How come Monsieur Jérémie who, everyone knew, was out of favor with the Ministry of Education, who had no connections and not a cent to his name, could open a private school? In actual fact the Institute of Blinding Light was a branch of a flourishing open university founded in France by a popular philosopher whose initials BC (not to be confused with the meaning "Before Christ") will be the only indication so as not to run the risk of legal proceedings. While he was in France Monsieur Jérémie had gone to Noirmoutier to visit BC's university. The two men had become friends and grown even closer owing to the similarity of their partners' deaths. Usually austere and taciturn, BC mellowed when talking about his late wife.

"Our two lives fused into one. We looked in the same direction. We smiled at the same moment. We were one and the same person."

His wife had been run over by a reckless driver and was killed on the spot together with the baby she was carrying. BC and Monsieur Jérémie both came up with the idea of creating a university in Guadeloupe but they were unaware it would take them almost eight years to achieve their aim. The Institute of Blinding Light comprised three sections: Humanities, Social Sciences, and History. There were no lectures but conferences, colloquiums, and seminars instead moderated by leading experts from France and especially from England and the United States. Monsieur Jérémie's modest title was Assistant Director of Social Sciences but everyone knew he was in charge of everything.

He was the one who rented Dr. Firmin's former clinic which had been left abandoned for years. He was the one who had it repainted and proudly signed in majestic letters *The Institute of Blinding Light: Center for Fundamental Research.* He was the one who gave an interview to an anti-establishment private radio which caused a sensation. He was the one behind the choice of speakers and their topics; for example, Slavery, A Crime Against Humanity; Capitalism and Slavery; What's the Purpose of Literature; Raising Awareness of the Oppressed; The Ravages of Globalization; On Liberating Mankind. On the surface Ivan played a minor role. He was in charge of making sure the DVDs and Blu-Rays were available for the speakers when they were required. He also supervised the cleanliness of the place and oversaw an army of cleaning women equipped with brooms and constantly lamenting the cost of living. This period was the best time of his life. The world deconstructed and reconstructed under his eyes. The lies, myths, and shams were unmasked. He understood that years of unjust and arbitrary imperialist power had caused the suffering in the world today. He returned home of an evening radiant and talkative. He would take his sister by the hand and have her dance the Charleston and boisterous boogie-woogies, somewhat out of fashion but an excuse for making comical contortions and entrechats. For the first time in his life he had a little money of his own and consequently showered his sister with presents of Creole jewelry such as a *collier gren d'o* necklace and *zanno créole* earrings. The most striking of them all was a ring in which he had engraved the words *ti amo.*

How lovely Ivana was, in all her finery! She was reaching the age when the teenager turns into a young woman. The round contours of her cheeks, her stomach, and her thighs had melted and she was sprouting up straight for the sky like a Kongo cane. Simone contemplated her with an emotion unwittingly bordering on jealousy.

Was I as lovely as her at her age?

Of course not! Maeva had put her to work in the sugarcane fields. It's a fact the work was not as hellish as in the old days; now machines were used to cut the cane. The cane bundlers dressed in those padded clothes so dear to Joseph Zobel have now disappeared. But the remaining work is still terrible. No matter how thick Simone's cotton stockings were, her legs were covered in scratches and her hands callused. Her skin was blackened and chapped.

As soon as it opened, the Institute of Blinding Light was met with great excitement. Three hundred students registered during the month of October alone, mainly because the fees were minimal and admission was accepted at high school diploma level. The institute was also the target of angry criticism. How could the powers that be tolerate such a monument of hatred towards metropolitan France? the affluent asked. How could they allow some of the teachers to claim that the Crusades were the first colonial enterprise, that the great Napoleon Bonaparte was nothing but a vile slave driver, and that a much-admired president of the republic was in league with the collaborators during the war?

The final straw was when BC came in person to give a lecture entitled "The Psychic Wounds of Domination." Given his reputation he was invited to speak on television during prime time. He was a handsome fifty-year-old. The sound of his voice, the way he carried his head, and especially his way of looking at you indicated he believed he was one of the most intelligent men on this earth. He calmly explained that the dependency in which the Antilles had been maintained for centuries, a dependency which had changed names but still remained fundamentally the same, had caused an irreversible trauma in the minds of its inhabitants. On second thoughts his opinion merely repeated the words of Césaire in *And the Dogs Were Silent*—when the slave covered with the blood of his master he has just killed shouts, "This is the only baptism I remember today." It also mirrored the thoughts of Frantz Fanon.

Given the age in which we live, however, such remarks

were dangerously loaded. Hardly had a week gone by after BC climbed back on his plane than a company of riot police, booted and helmeted, raided the Institute of Blinding Light. They dispersed the students who happened to be there, invaded Monsieur Jérémie's office, where a gigantic photo of Martin Luther King had pride of place, and informed him the institute was closed by order of the Minister for the Interior. Before leaving they placed seals just about everywhere.

The students were appalled, and organized a march inviting every political party from the right to the left to join them in demonstrating against such a major attack on freedom of expression. Their plea went unheard. A trickle of men and women assembled on the Place de la Victoire. There was a growing atmosphere of fear. There were reports that riot police had landed from Martinique and Guyana. It was then that Monsieur Jérémie committed suicide. He walked into a cane field not far from his home and put a bullet in his head. Some field workers found his body already devoured by chicken hawks.

Monsieur Jérémie's funeral was totally different to that of Manolo's a few years earlier. This time you could count the number of mourners on one hand: his old mother who never stopped sobbing and asking what she had done to deserve such a son as well as his half-brother who had never got along with him and drove an unregistered taxi in Fontainebleau. Monsieur Jérémie had never had a mistress nor had he kept a woman on the side. As a result, there were no bastards, no illegitimate children born of adultery. BC was unable to attend the funeral as he had been invited to Tunisia by the Muslim Brotherhood. But he attached great importance to the events at the Institute of Blinding Light and named a lecture room at his university after Nicéphale Jérémie.

Monsieur Jérémie's death completely shattered Ivan. He could not have cried more if Monsieur Jérémie had been his father. As always in such cases he blamed himself for such trifling things as looking bored every time Monsieur Jérémie rambled on about his love for Alya or looking skeptical when he started in on his favorite theory:

"Africa will dominate the world after China. And when I say Africa I don't mean Black Africa or White Africa, as the Western World calls it. I mean the entire continent: people united by the same religion."

Consequently Ivan set off every day to the local bar and spent entire nights there. He was picked up dead drunk at every crossroad night after night. Simone and Ivana were scared to death and wondered whether he was not suicidal.

One afternoon he received a visit from Miguel with whom he had remained close. Miguel was on to a good thing and wanted to let Ivan in on his plan. Alix Avenne, a well-known wine merchant, had a debt towards Miguel's father who had operated on his heart a few years earlier. He had just opened a fish-canning factory and was looking to hire reliable young people for deliveries to hotels, restaurants, and individual clients. They would collect the sums due and pay back the SuperGel Company each month.

"Frozen fish!" lamented Maeva. "*Ka sa yé sa!* Whatever next! When I was young we used to throw the fish still alive and wriggling straight into the court-bouillon."

Ivana did not agree. She had never liked Miguel, who had committed the abominable crime of having blinded his partner. This angel face could hide nothing but foul thoughts. Obviously Ivan did exactly as he pleased. Won over, he piled his meager possessions into a rucksack and followed Miguel who had offered to lodge him.

The first few months everything went brilliantly. Every Saturday Ivan arrived in Dos d'Âne at the wheel of a van displaying the words: *Our fish is fresh, only our customers are spoiled.* He was dressed in a dapper uniform and carried loads of frozen fish: slices of red tuna, sea bream, red snapper, and the same sort of colorful tropical catfish that his mother used to cook in her stews.

During the All Saints Holiday, Ivana went to join him. Like all those who lived on the Leeward Coast, the little town of Pointe-à-Pitre seemed distant and foreign. Ivana had only been there once or twice to sing the "Ave Maria" by Gounod in the Cathedral of Saint Peter and Saint Paul. Its crowded streets, with Lebanese stores bellowing out the latest *zouk* songs, were a frightening place. But Paulina, despite being blinded in one eye, had come back to live with Miguel and had even given him a son. She took charge of making sure Ivana changed her opinion, and arm in arm would drag her on endless walks.

"For those who don't know Pointe-à-Pitre, it's true the town might appear unattractive," she said. "But it's quite different when you live here. I was born in the Canal Vatable district in a house belonging to the diocese because mother hired out her services to the presbytery. She scrubbed the floors, polished the silverware, and made the priests' beds. It was rumored that me and my two brothers were the children of one of the priests, a South African from Durban, because of our blue eyes and our yellow mop of hair. Nobody could prove it and my mother took her secret with her to the grave. When I was a child, everyone who lived in the poorest neighborhoods was terrified of fires. Whole blocks of houses would go up in flames. People lost their possessions and sometimes even their children.

"One late afternoon my mother and I went to the cathedral to attend the coronation of the Virgin Mary. You know, the one that takes place every August 15th. When we arrived home our house was glowing like a torch with my two brothers inside. Ever since that day I've loathed the unhealthiness and precariousness of poverty. That's why I stay with Miguel. However much he acts like a low-down nigger and claims that nothing counts in his eyes, he's a bourgeois and son of a bourgeois. His mother was an Algerian peasant his father refused to marry. He preferred a lovely mulatto girl like Marie-Jeanne Capdevielle, whom he placed as a center piece at home."

Ivana was at a loss for an answer. As for poverty, she didn't know whether or not she hated it; it was her daily lot. She attended the school's film club. She read everything she could lay hands on: Balzac, Maupassant, and Flaubert were part of the school curriculum as well as Jules Verne, Marguerite Duras, Yasmina Khadra, and René Char, whose poetry she saw as a beautiful but indecipherable dream:

Behind your maneless running I am bleeding, weeping; I gird myself with terror, I forget, I am laughing under the trees. Pitiless and unending pursuit where all is set in motion against the double prey: you invisible and I perennial.

As soon as she passed her baccalaureate she would choose to become either a nurse in order to take care of the weak and the destitute or a police officer in order to protect them. She couldn't make up her mind.

After four months everything changed. Miguel vanished

with his wife and son. First it was thought they had gone to Guyana, to Saint-Laurent-du-Maroni where Paulina came from. That turned out to be untrue. They couldn't be found in Blida at Miguel's mother's place either. In the end the police had been notified and discovered they had flown to Paris and then on to Turkey. From that point on all trace of them had been lost. Alix Avenne then realized they had left behind a totally unsuspected mess. The orders had been overbilled. Some remained unpaid. There was a huge deficit in the accounts. They arrested Ivan. He was obviously an accomplice since he lived with Miguel and they were two of a kind. For the second time then, Ivan went back to jail and Simone sobbed bitterly.

It was then that her vague desire to write to Lansana Diarra took root and grew. Ivan was growing up as best he could without a father to hold his hand on the road of life. Did Lansana remember the dreams they had dreamed together while she was pregnant? But then she wondered how to get in touch with him. Nowadays nobody writes with paper and envelope. You've got to know your correspondent's email address and use a computer. After some musing and a good many tears she made up her mind to send a letter to Monsieur Lansana Diarra, musician with the instrumental ensemble Bamako, Republic of Mali. At the post office the sympathetic lady behind the counter advised her to write her address on the back of the envelope.

"That way, if it doesn't get delivered, it will be returned," she advised. "At least you'll know."

Simone sobbed even louder and Ivana's whole being revolted at the sight of Ivan's photo on the front page of the local newspaper. The photographer had contracted his forehead and eyes and blown up his jawbone and ears giving him the features of a perfect hooligan. It was also the tone of the article that went with it, the work of a journalist obviously in the pay of Angel Pastoua. He made Ivan out to be the brains behind the affair. It was this good-for-nothing from Dos d'Âne who had corrupted the son of a notable. The trial seemed to be a done deal. But they hadn't taken Mr. Vinteuil into account. Not only had he not returned to his native Clermont-Ferrand but he had recently married a black woman: not a white Creole or a mulatto, not a light-skinned coolie or a mixed-blood Indian, not a high yellow girl or a light-skinned, brown, or red girl. But black. Mr. Vinteuil had helped Ivan once before and now asked to be his officially appointed lawyer. He was not going to let the weak pay for the powerful and be ruined because of them once again.

An ultramodern prison had recently been opened at Bel Air. In order to avoid any attempt at escape it was lit up every evening like an ocean liner. As a result nobody could get any sleep for miles around and a petition had been circulated. The prison housed a number of offices equipped with computers and Dictaphones. Mr. Vinteuil met his client here on a daily basis and interrogated him about his life.

Ivan discovered the joy of talking about himself, of plunging deep down inside and coming up with long-hidden, secret thoughts.

"Why did Monsieur Jérémie become your role model?" Mr. Vinteuil asked.

Ivan hesitated, turning the question over and over in his head until finally he said, "Before I met him, nobody took any interest in me except for my sister, my mother, and my grandmother."

"What did he talk to you about? What books did he give you to read, for example?"

"A bunch of books: Frantz Fanon, Jean Suret-Canale, and especially a lot of African-American authors translated into French. I must confess I didn't read them much since they bored me a little."

"What did interest you then?"

"Monsieur Jérémie's life. His actual life. He had lived in Afghanistan and Iraq. He was in Libya the year Gaddafi was killed."

Hearing these words, Mr. Vinteuil gave a start.

"How would he describe Gaddafi? A dictator or a hero?"

"In his eyes he was a hero. He worshiped him."

"Did he encourage you to leave for either Syria or Libya?"

Ivan rolled his eyes.

"Leave? How could I leave? He knew I didn't have a cent to my name, not even enough to buy a bus ticket to Basse-Terre or Pointe-à-Pitre. He insisted my duty was to improve the world around me."

"Improve? By doing what?"

"He said everyone should do his part. I never really understood what that meant."

All this ended in an acquittal pure and simple, together with a sentence of community service.

During Mr. Vinteuil's defense speech some people, especially the women, wept. Others applauded. At the end, the court rose and gave him a standing ovation.

Ivan returned to Dos d'Âne victorious. His mother had rented a van with flag flying and sounded the horn continuously. All along the road people emerged on their doorsteps wondering what was going on. Numbed by their own problems in life, they had never heard of Ivan and had no idea that for once justice had been rendered.

On the main square in Dos d'Âne the schoolchildren sang the Marseillaise while waving little tricolor flags. The mayor, who as we have already seen was partial to homilies, couldn't let such a perfect occasion slip by. He boasted of a just and tolerant France who could not allow one of her sons to be wrongly accused. Many spectators were shocked that Ivan did not want to speak and join in the concert of voices praising the Mother Country. The truth was that he couldn't put one word in front of another. It was as if he had been put through a washing machine, wrung, and hung out to dry. He felt no gratitude towards Mr. Vinteuil since he had no understanding of what was going on around him. He recalled Miguel's enigmatic words:

"I'm going first," he had declared mysteriously, the day before he disappeared. "I'll let you know how it's going and whether you should come and join me with Ivana."

As soon as they could, Ivan and Ivana set off for their favorite place, the Pointe Paradis. Ivan showered his sister with passionate kisses while Ivana whispered in his ear:

"Please don't go back to jail again. Think of me. It hurts me so much when you're not here. All year long while you were in prison I thought I was going to die. I had trouble even studying at school."

Ivan sat up on the sand and looked at the sea as it frothed at their feet. Without realizing it he repeated Miguel's words: "One day we'll leave. We'll go somewhere else."

"Where do you want us to go?" Ivana said, astonished.

"I don't know. But we'll go to a place more just and more humane."

Six months later Ivan's community service took him to CariFood, a company founded by two nutritionists, fathers of extended families. CariFood had been declared state-approved and was generously financed by the Ministry for Overseas Territories. It was also largely subsidized by the Regional Council. This was not surprising since CariFood maintained an argument likely to find favor with the nationalists. The two nutritionist directors had demonstrated that the jars of baby food in the Caribbean did not contain a single Caribbean nutrient: neither yam nor sweet potato, neither cassava nor dasheen, neither breadfruit nor plantain nor green banana. Consequently, this baby food could develop a dangerous alimentary alienation and was at risk of altering the infant's palate by accustoming him to regrettable foreign tastes.

Ivan got the cold shoulder from the dozen or so men and women who worked in the spacious facility that had once belonged to the Darboussier factory. Can you imagine, working with an ex-convict whose photo had been spread over every newspaper? He was allocated a tiny studio in a block of flats not far from the Morne de Massabielle. Since Ivan had never lived alone and couldn't cook, he used to go twice a day to the café-restaurant A Verse Toujours. He was recognized immediately, the word "ex-convict" began to be rumored, and he found himself relegated to sitting all alone. This had a deep impact on him but didn't prevent him from frequenting the café, as he liked the surroundings. It's true the Massabielle neighborhood was unlike any other. A fourteen-story tower block was its only sign of modernity. All around it were wooden houses that recalled olden times, built between courtyard and garden, as well as upstairs-downstairs houses where potted palms flourished behind wrought-iron balustrades on their narrow balconies. There was also a private school of good repute and, consequently, every morning clusters of schoolchildren in white and blue uniforms played hopscotch while waiting for classes to begin.

By dint of bumping into his neighbor in the tiny hall outside their studios Ivan ended up getting to know her; she was a Spaniard of mixed blood, full of the petulance her country is known for. She soon started telling Ivan the story of her life.

While she was studying physical therapy, her mother, Liliane, a Guadeloupean from Vieux Habitants, was sent to a small thermal spa in the south of France. There, despite the pathetic sight of the obese and pallid bodies of the spa guests, she fell deeply in love with Ramon, a young Spaniard whose search for work had forced him to cross the Pyrenees. Back in Paris, she realized she was pregnant. When she finally tracked down Ramon he had married Angela, his childhood sweetheart, and emigrated to Argentina, still looking for work. She had sadly christened her daughter Ramona in memory of her father and a song that her mother would hum when she was a child:

Ramona, I hear the mission bells above,
Ramona, they're ringing out our song of love.
I press you, I caress you
And bless the day you taught me to care
I always remember
The rambling rose you wear in your hair.

Ramona had grown up in Vieux Habitants with her mother. Like her she had studied physical therapy and like her she worked at the Rehabilitation Center, The Karukera. But it was there that any resemblance between mother and daughter stopped. Whereas Liliane's only pastime was to attend mass during the month of the Virgin Mary or vespers depending on the season, roll the beads of her rosary or kneel twice a month at the altar after having duly confessed her few sins, Ramona was hot-headed and a man-eater. Very quickly she decided to get a taste of Ivan, an ex-convict perhaps but well built: over six feet tall, narrow hips, and, it must be said, an athletic build under his somewhat ungainly clothes.

First of all she invited him for a rum punch accompanied with spicy hot black pudding and nicely salted plantain chips. When that proved to be of no avail, she invited him for dinner and then a long session in front of the television. But that didn't work. Around midnight Ivan planted a chaste kiss on her forehead and returned home. One evening she could stand it no longer. She slipped on an alluring dressing gown that gaped open at all the right places and came knocking on Ivan's door. Ivan opened the door exasperated since he was in the process of sending a text message to Ivana and asked roughly, "What do you want now?"

Ramona snuggled up to Ivan.

"There's a burglar," she whispered. "I'm sure there's a burglar in my place."

With a sigh, Ivan armed himself with a broom handle and crossed the landing. Once inside Ramona's apartment it was obvious all was quiet and calm and that there was no hidden burglar. Ivan shrugged his shoulders.

"You can see full well there's nobody here."

Hurling herself against him, Ramona then smacked a passionate kiss straight on his mouth. Without losing his cool, Ivan extricated himself and made her sit down on the sofa.

"I'm going to tell you something," he gently murmured.

"Tell me what?"

"I already love a girl and I can't cheat on her," he said in all seriousness. "I can never stop thinking of her, you understand."

Ramona stared at him, her eyes wide open in stupefaction.

"What are you talking about?"

She had no idea what he was saying. She was not asking to be engaged or married. Just a bit of pleasure on the side. It wouldn't be the first time that a man in love with a woman gave way to temptation for another.

Ivan, however, managed to get out of a tight spot and went home without having surrendered to Ramona's charms. The following afternoon a police car stopped in front of CariFood and two armed police officers stepped out. They entered the facility and went straight for the corner where Ivan stacked the baby food in boxes.

"Are you Ivan Némélé?" they barked. "Ramona Escudier is accusing you of rape."

"But I never touched her," Ivan stammered, stupefied.

The other employees began crowding in and a small group was gathering at the entrance. Paying no attention to what Ivan was saying, the police officers pushed him outside and shoved him into their car. Ivan was driven to the police station in Pointe-à-Pitre where an officer charged him with the offense. He was then thrown into a cell surrounded by thick iron bars. He endeavored to think straight. He needed to get in touch with Mr. Vinteuil as quickly as possible. The latter would surely come to his aid, unless he was fed up with the constant escapades of his client. Around 6 p.m. a fat man dressed to the nines, a camera sitting comfortably on his abdomen, came to stare Ivan in the face.

"You again, Ivan Némélé. Now you're a rapist."

"I never even touched her," Ivan protested again.

The man shrugged his shoulders and without asking for Ivan's permission began firing away with his camera.

To cut a long story short two contradictory events occurred at the same time. First of all, Ivan's face was once again spread all over the front page of the local newspaper *Tropicana* followed by an article which virtually turned him into public enemy number one. Secondly, Ramona recovered her wits and withdrew her accusation. Ivan was set free. In the light of such a scandal, however, CariFood no longer wanted anything to do with him.

Is this how the world works? Ivan asked himself, as he sat devastated in the bus that took him back to Dos d'Âne. *Friends who abandon you without warning? Girls who slander you? Journalists who write lies about you? People prepared to eat you up alive? If so, give me a load of explosives for me to destroy it.*

But he had no idea how to go about it.

The grandiose landscape that the bus passed by to the left and right was of no comfort. In fact he didn't even notice it. He had not been taught to pay attention to Nature's beauty. The sea, the sky, and the trees were as familiar and indifferent to him as his own face.

At Dos d'Âne life was not rosy. Ivana was studying for her baccalaureate and virtually invisible. As soon as classes were over she would go and join a group of students who were sitting for the same examination and they would revise together until two or three in the morning. Afterwards, extenuated and exhausted, she would come and kiss her brother who was waiting for her in the warmth of his bed. Maeva, who was once so valiant, had problems standing, yet alone walking, and spent most of her time lying prostrate in bed. Her speech was incomprehensible, her eyes brimming with tears as she pointed to the Sacred Heart of Jesus above the head of her bed.

"Jesus Christ, the son of Mary, is seated to the right of the Father. Look! His heart is bleeding for all the sins we commit. One in particular makes him suffer. That particular sin, nobody dares say its name. Papa must not say that he fathered his daughter and that now he has every right over her. The brother must not think the same."

As for Simone, Lansana Diarra's silence broke her heart. She had been waiting for an answer from him for almost two years and still nothing. She imagined him giving concerts, carried away by the applause, clutching the hands of admirers, and that infuriated her. As a result, she ranted and raved against men, much to Father Michalou's disgust.

"Listen to me," he grumbled. "They're not all as bad as you say. I personally have never done you any harm. If you had let me I would have taken in your twins as my own children."

The mayor made the kind gesture of recruiting Ivan to help build the Mediatheque. Why a Mediatheque at Dos d'Âne? Why not? All the towns and villages compete with each other to have one and, although nothing much goes on there, it's the common lot. Henceforth Ivan belonged to a team of workers who broke rocks, planed beams, and mixed cement, things he had never learned to do previously. He would get up before dawn, wash with cold water in the yard then drink the coffee his mother, up very early, had made especially for him. Apparently mother and son had nothing to say to each other. In actual fact their silence was filled with soft words, full of the love and tenderness they bore for each other. Their most common expressions were weighted with meaning.

"Would you like a braided roll?"

"No, I prefer a rusk."

Ivan's work exhausted him but he didn't mind being worked to the bone. Anything was better than being confronted by a frightening tête-à-tête with his thoughts regarding the monstrousness of this world.

Suddenly everything brightened up. In the month of June the first of the extraordinary events occurred. Ivana passed her baccalaureate with flying colors. To tell the truth, nobody was surprised. She had always been first in every subject. But to see her name printed on a list of those who had passed at the Dournaux Lycée left Ivan in awe.

"There's no doubt she got all the brains," he laughed to himself. "I'm just a load of muscles."

Maeva found the strength to kneel at the foot of her bed and forced her granddaughter to do the same while reciting a dozen thanksgivings on her rosary. Deo gratias. Simone went even further. She delved into her meager savings. Since her old age prevented her from working in the cane fields she now took care of the children of a mulatto couple who lived in Dournaux. Thus she earned a little more and was able to order a crab patty as well as a marble cake from a caterer. She hung flowers around the dining room and invited a dozen young friends. They selected the best *zouk* music and danced till early morning. Nobody took offense at seeing Ivan and Ivana dance constantly together. That's how they'd always been. Everyone still remembered when they were ten or twelve and the drummers from Morne-à-l'Eau came to give a concert on the main square with Master

Lucas Carton as the star performer; during an interval Ivan had boldly mounted a drum almost as tall as himself and bid his sister dance, lifting up her skirts over her slender legs, much to the delight of the spectators.

"Who taught you how to beat the *ka* drum?" Lucas Carton asked Ivan in amazement.

"Nobody," Ivan had replied with his swaggering attitude.

Simone had flown to his rescue.

"They've got it in their blood. Their father is one of Mali's greatest musicians."

"Salif Keita?" Lucas inquired, since he knew a bit on the subject—two years earlier Lucas had been invited to a festival in Mali and had introduced a new sound from the Caribbean.

The second extraordinary event occurred when Simone finally received the answer she was waiting for from Lansana, posted from Montreal. Lansana described the tragic events that had devastated his life and explained his silence. After Colonel Gaddafi's death, gangs armed to the teeth had invaded his country and descended as far as Bamako. Based in Kidal at the Al-Akbar Mosque they claimed a change of lifestyle and a religious revival. No longer would there be prostration in front of idols or the treasuring of centuries-old manuscripts. No longer would there be dancing, singing, and performing music. Only silence would please God and be tolerated.

One day a gang of ruffians had penetrated the recording studio that Lansana had built at great expense and completely wrecked it, then pounced on the unfortunate musician hiding in a corner and left him for dead. The neighbors had been alerted and drove him to the hospital where he had spent six months while violent acts of the worst kind were being committed all over the country. Once he had recovered, the terrified Lansana had been forced to flee to Canada where he was a well-known figure. There he had been given a warm welcome. Now he wanted to leave Canada and join the resistance in Mali. He now considered his flight to Canada as an act of cowardice. He should have plucked up courage and endeavored to destroy those who were wreaking so much havoc. He had never stopped thinking of Ivan and Ivana but he was unable to bring them to Mali as long as the country's problems persisted.

"I don't know how long it will take," he wrote. "Six months, a year, two years. But I will send them two plane tickets, that's for sure."

Lansana included a photo in his letter which made Simone cry. It depicted him under different circumstances, wiry as a guava twig in his flowing *boubou*, his hair thinning and gray, portraying a wrinkled face and a sickly body, leaning on two crutches. Age had not spared him.

Lansana's photo left Ivan and Ivana indifferent. They had dreamed a lot about their father when they were small, since children imagine the family as a magic circle, designed to protect them from their fears. Deep down, they had no inclination to leave their mother, a victim of life's mistreatment. They were even less inclined to travel to Mali, a country in Africa whose religion and language they did not share. They had heard that Mali, much like the rest of Africa, didn't have one common language like France or England, but dozens, even hundreds, of dialects. One neighbor doesn't understand the next. What was the point of going to this place of purgatory? Besides, Ivana thought it was time to pamper Simone. She still couldn't manage to choose between a career in nursing or one as a police officer. Consequently, she made up her mind to pay a visit to the Careers Advisory Center in Dournaux.

The Lycée at Dournaux, unlike the school at Dos d'Âne, was lucky enough not to have been entirely destroyed by Hurricane Hugo. If that had been the case it would have been rebuilt along ultramodern lines. Such as it was, it was composed of a motley group of wooden pavilions scattered around an asphalt courtyard. Here and there a few solitary mahogany and ebony trees sadly grew. The director of the Careers Advisory Center, a young French woman, tanned from her constant sunbathing, stared at Ivana in commiseration.

"So you've never left Guadeloupe and have done all your schooling at Dos d'Âne!"

Slightly annoyed by her tone of voice, Ivana explained that trips abroad had not been lacking. She had traveled several times to Martinique, twice to Guyana, and once even to Haiti.

"But why do you limit yourself to the two careers of nursing and the police force?" the young woman continued. "With a baccalaureate like yours you could sit for the entrance exam to the prestigious higher education schools."

Ivana shook her head violently. She didn't want that sort of a career, a career of prestige. She wanted to serve, quite simply to serve those of humble origins like herself.

"I think you'd do best to choose the police force; it will enable you to discover the world around you. There are some excellent police academies in France."

Ivana then ventured that she had no intention of going to France on her own; she would be accompanied by her brother.

"Your brother?" the young woman repeated in surprise.

"Yes, my twin brother."

The young woman then made a conciliatory gesture.

"He could work as an apprentice."

"But where as an apprentice?"

"That depends on the job openings. You'd have to contact the Apprentice Training Center."

But man proposes and God disposes. The proposed appointment on the scheduled date never took place since Maeva died a few days later. She had got in the habit of asking Simone to place her chair in the yard so that she would be bathed in light and could clasp the brotherly palm of Comrade General Sun.

Returning home one lunchtime Simone found Maeva lying on the ground. Had she wanted to get up and try to walk on her own? She had stumbled against a rock and her head was lying in a pool of coagulated blood. In the time it took to alert the neighbors and dash to Dr. Bertogal's, the only physician who was not bothered about who would pay his fees, Maeva was dead, though not before having whispered in her tearful daughter's ear: "Take good care of Ivan and Ivana. I dreamt about them last night again lying in a pool of blood."

Simone was amazed she was so grief-stricken at the death of this mother she thought she had never loved and who had always frowned upon her decisions and judgment. Only their common passion for music and the beauty of the songs they sang with the choir brought them together. Likewise Ivan and Ivana were surprised to find themselves crying. Their grandmother had been the only person to treat them like potential criminals, as if they bore inside them the embryo of a crime. That, they could never forget.

At the age of fifteen, while they were lying in each other's arms, she had burst into their bedroom and violently pulled them apart, shouting, "Two cursed wretches! Two cursed wretches! That's what you are!"

"But we're not doing anything wrong," they had protested.

Maeva would hear nothing of the sort. If Simone hadn't intervened, she would have grabbed the nearest broom handle and given her grandchildren a good hiding. From that day on, they had never again slept together.

Nobody could guess the secret motivations behind Maeva's behavior nor understand why she had wanted to add "L'Aigle noir" sung by Barbara to the choir's repertoire. She, too, had been raped by her father who was neither a braggart nor a chatterbox and lacked confidence in himself. On the contrary, he was shy and indecisive with a long jet-black face and frayed trousers. Nevertheless, he had hurled himself on her when she was twelve, and a few years later on her young sister, Nadia. When he fell from the roof he was tiling; Maeva never forgave herself for feeling so joyful, which consequently dampened her later moments of pleasure. She recalled his smell of cigarettes and the burning sensation of his member. It had lasted about five years and then he had tired of the mother and her two daughters and left home.

For years Maeva had been preparing the clothes for her funeral: a black percale matador dress embroidered with white motifs, a black-and-white checkered madras head tie, and violet velvet slippers. How lovely she looked dressed in her finery, compared to the last years of her life during which she had appeared so insignificant. Death is the great equalizer since it mows down not only presidents of the republic but also street cleaners, not only the wealthy but also the destitute. Yet the manner in which each individual treats death betrays the difference in class. Simone could only afford a third-class funeral for her mother. As a result Veloxia, the undertakers, hung a collection of black rags on the door and windows sewn with the initials MN, for Maeva Némélé, and made an arrangement of white lilies which only underscored the miserable setting. The only appropriate element was the wake's thick soup prepared by Anastasia the neighbor, a tasty mix of onions, carrots, potatoes, and morsels of beef. For two days the house never emptied, since Maeva was no stranger. Not only was she member of the choir but nobody could forget the power of her visions long ago when she would sit up straight and point her fists at the sky. A group of mourners filled the small church. The mayor's homily attracted a lot of attention; he had not curbed his remorse at having evicted Simone from her council house. That was the reason he had offered Ivan the job of building the Mediatheque. He planned to have him join the roads and sanitation department since every trade has its own value and there's nothing wrong with that. But when he actually made the offer it was haughtily rejected. Ivan had no inclination to rummage in Dos d'Âne's garbage. Hadn't they recently found a baby boy a few hours old in a dustbin which sent the police hurrying from Basse-Terre? Besides, he was about to leave for France with his sister and start an apprenticeship at a chocolate factory in the Paris suburbs.

This rumor of their departure, in fact, soon turned into a certainty. The women nodded their heads with compassion: Simone would feel so isolated. But, as the English say, "Every cloud has a silver lining." Simone's condition moved Father Michalou's heart. He realized the moment had come to make an offer of living together. For the time being she was affected threefold: by Lansana Diarra's misfortunes, by the death of her mother, and by the imminent departure of her children. Old age would suddenly find her all alone.

One Sunday Father Michalou slipped on his best and only suit and went to propose to Simone what he had in mind. They had known each other now for a dozen or so years. He wouldn't be able to offer her much money, that's a fact, but constant companionship. Simone listened to him, head lowered, betraying nothing of her emotions. When he had finished she simply said, "My children are leaving at the end of August. As soon as they're gone I'll come and move in with you."

As if to conclude their agreement they then made love, not systematically or routinely as they were accustomed to, but passionately as if they were discovering and desiring each other for the first time.

He who leaves a country for good or for a long period of time undergoes a complete change of personality. A voice, which he hears for the first time, wells up from the trees, the meadows, and the shore and murmurs gentle words in his ear. The landscape is invested with a strange harmony. Ivan and Ivana were no strangers to this rule. As the date for their departure came closer they began to cherish Guadeloupe like a parent they were about to lose. They rented two bicycles from the Nestor cycle shop and cycled around the surrounding countryside for several days, usually on a Sunday when the roads were empty except for the buses. They first rode to the Commandant Cousteau marine reserve which until now they had never paid attention to. Together with a crowd of tourists, for whom Saturdays and Sundays are no different from weekdays, they climbed into a glass-bottom boat to discover the splendors of the seabed. Then they rented a traditional sailing boat and rowed to a small, flat, rocky island a stone's throw from the shore. It was called Englishman's Head after the name of the cacti which grew there in great numbers. The slit-eyed iguanas were not frightened when the visitors approached but rather stared at them scornfully. Ivana, who adored the sun's caress, took off her clothes and spread them out on the sand. Sick with desire, Ivan said to himself, "And what if I fucked her here and now!" In order to cool down he dived into the sea where a cold current flowed in from the north. Ivana would have loved to climb aboard a catamaran and sail to the islands of Les Saintes and Terre-de-Bas where they had been on so many summer camps organized by the municipality when they were young. Ivan, however, loathed these memories. He recalled the miserable wooden building where they had been parked, both humid and stuffy, the narrow cots, and the insipid food. One day when he and Frédéric, his companion in misfortune, were starving to death, he had killed one of the neighbor's chickens with a stone, skillfully plucked its feathers, and roasted it over a wood fire. The crime had been promptly discovered and he had been given one of the biggest hidings of his life. Ivan and Ivana agreed that one of the best vacations of their teens had been spent at Adèle's, their mother's half-sister, illegitimate daughter of the same absent and invisible father who nobody knew where he lived or who he was exactly.

Adèle and Simone had since quarreled for confused reasons and were no longer on speaking terms. Simone did everything she could to prevent them from going to Port-Louis where Adèle lived.

"She didn't even bother to come to Maman's funeral," she objected.

"Perhaps she didn't even know," Ivana replied conciliatorily. "She does live at the other end of the island."

"The local paper said that one of her boys had gone to prison," Simone said.

"Like me," responded Ivan. "I went in twice."

"Yes, but your case was unfair. You hadn't done anything wrong."

Guadeloupean mothers are blind when it comes to forgiving their sons for everything. In the end the two youngsters took no notice of their mother's declarations and set off for Port-Louis.

Anyone who claims that one shoreline looks like all the others doesn't know what he is talking about. Firstly, the color of the sea is never the same. Iridescent from the sun's blaze, it is sometimes violet, sometimes green like that ink they no longer make since nobody writes by hand, and sometimes pastel-colored. Likewise, the sand turns tawny like the mane of a wild animal or blond like the down of a new-born chick. Lastly, the dome of the sky shimmers differently from shore to shore.

Aunt Adèle lived at the other end of the beach. Less destitute than Simone since she was locally employed and worked for the town hall as a sweeper, she occupied a vast house together with her daughters. The youngest had just sat for her baccalaureate, but unlike Ivana she had not passed. Adèle looked like Simone. Ivan and Ivana were surprised to see traces of their mother's face mixed in with somebody else's features. Adèle's heart had been stricken with grief and she soon confided in her nephew and niece. Five years earlier her son Bruno had left to look for work in France; because of his athletic build he had been rapidly recruited by Noirmoutier as a security guard. Everything was going wonderfully! Every month he would send home to Port-Louis half of his wages. He promised Adèle and his sisters he would have them come to Savigny-sur-Orge and show them the wonders of Paris, the City of Light. Suddenly they no longer heard from him. After having endeavored to call him dozens of times in vain, Adèle vaguely remembered an unemployed cousin living in Sarcelles and begged him to help. The cousin called on Noirmoutier who informed him that Bruno had not turned up for work. Since he wasn't at home either, his friend Malik Sansal became alarmed and alerted the police, who had not exactly moved heaven and earth to find him. He had been gone for three years now. Vanished! For the second time Ivan came up against this word, this barbed-wire wall as frightening as death itself. First Miguel. Now Bruno. What became of people who disappeared? Where did they go? Ivan imagined them in a cold and icy limbo.

"You can't imagine the handsome little boy he was," the aunt said, totally absorbed in her grief. "He was so fond of me and his two sisters, especially Cathy, to whom he was godfather."

Ivan shivered as he listened to her quavering voice. He heard himself promise to track down Bruno as soon as he arrived in France. The mater dolorosa immediately went and fetched the photo album she kept among her worthless treasures.

"He took this one a few days after he had started work at Noirmoutier," she explained. "And this one's on his wedding day. She's the girl he married: Nastasia, an Algerian."

"An Algerian!" Ivan exclaimed. "Perhaps he's quite simply in Algeria with his wife's family."

Adèle shook her head.

"His wife's family lives in Aulnay-sous-Bois where they emigrated in the 1950s."

"Where is Nastasia? I'll get in contact with her."

"Nastasia has disappeared as well," Adèle said. "She was a very bad influence on my son. He became a Muslim because of her."

All of this reminded Ivan of Monsieur Jérémie's story.

"We should not convert to Islam," Adèle said categorically. "We Guadeloupeans have been raised as Catholics. We know there is but one God in three distinct persons: the Father, the Son, and the Holy Spirit."

"One God! He doesn't do much for us," Ivan couldn't help mocking.

Adèle's eyes immediately brimmed with tears.

"You're right! What have I done to deserve to suffer so much?"

Bruno's disappearance was the subject of every conversation in Port-Louis, as Ivan and Ivana realized on entering the bar on the corner. A certain Jeannot, who had been his closest friend and paid him a visit just before he disappeared, lamented:

"I took him some rum. Good rum, Damoiseau and Bologne. He calmly emptied the bottles down the sink telling me he no longer drank that sort of poison. Likewise, he no longer listened to music despite the fact we had once created an ensemble together in Port-Louis. He had completely changed."

"I think he left to wage jihad in Syria," exclaimed another young man.

"Syria? Why would he go over there?"

The group broke up without agreeing on Bruno's possible motivations.

Jihad! There's a word that Monsieur Jérémie didn't like and which made him angry, Ivan recalled. Jihad! Jihad! Every religion proselytizes. We tend to forget the Inquisition when heretics were burned by auto-da-fé at every crossroad.

Back in Dos d'Âne, Ivan was kept awake at night thinking of his future. A certain Sergio Poltroni, originally
from Italy but settled in France, owned a chocolate
factory in Saint-Denis and was hiring an apprentice.
Thanks to the government's generosity, Ivan would
receive a modest sum every month. This was not exactly
to Ivan's liking since he had no intention of becoming a
chocolate maker. First of all, he didn't like chocolate and
secondly the idea seemed ridiculous. He reassured himself by saying that in one respect he was lucky since
he could accompany Ivana to France. Otherwise, what
would become of him without her?

To her surprise, at the beginning of August Simone
received a heavy, registered package containing a letter
from Lansana and two airline tickets for Ivan and Ivana
Némélé, issued by Jet Tours. Jet Tours was a low-cost airline proposing a complicated itinerary. First of all, a
three-hour stopover in Paris then an entire day in Marseille and another in Oran before arriving in Bamako,
from where they would finally reach Kidal. Three days'
traveling was a lot! Lansana explained that he had
returned home earlier than expected as the political
situation in Mali seemed to have calmed down thanks
to the efforts of a foreign power. The latter had pushed
back the invaders to the north and everyone was trying
to lead a normal life again. But now that he was in such
poor health and virtually penniless he could no longer
take care of two seventeen-year-olds without jobs, as he
had once intended. For that reason he had found them
each an occupation: Ivana would work in an orphanage
which took in children whose parents had been killed
during the war against the horde of attackers. As for
Ivan, he would become a member of the national militia
whose patrols protected the country. Ivan and Ivana

pouted in disgust on receiving the letter. Firstly, the length of the journey put them off. Then, as we have already said, they were not particularly interested in seeing their father. As for the jobs he was offering, there was nothing attractive about them. Why travel so far to do subaltern work?

Simone, however, went into a rage. It was not for nothing she had asked for Lansana's help. Ivan and Ivana had to go to Mali and postpone their plans for France which anyway had nothing worthwhile about them. Okay, perhaps for Ivana, but did Ivan really want to become a chocolate maker? As for Father Michalou, he sided with the twins; all you saw on television were terrible pictures of Africa. There was one war after another, refugees were fleeing in every direction, and some countries no longer had a government. Simone persisted and ended up having the last word. With a heavy heart the twins had to obey her. With the same aching heart they embraced their mother. Of course, she had been devilishly strict and often finicky, but her love and devotion for them had remained unquestioned.

Since the Jet Tours flight left at four in the morning they had to travel to Pointe-à-Pitre the day before and stay with a relative, Aunt Mariama, who lived on the Morne Verdol, a densely populated neighborhood filled with children of every age and every color. Opposite her house the general hospital loomed up, on whose facade the three letters CHU glowed red. Ivana felt a deep regret at the thought she would never work there, dressed in the comely uniform of a nurse. Aunt Mariama had done her best and cooked Creole rice, slices of avocado, and a fricassee of curried pork.

"What are you going to do in Africa?" she asked. "I hear the people over there are savages."

"We're half African," Ivan replied in a mocking tone of voice. "Don't you know our father comes from Mali?"

You can judge from this conversation that neither Aunt Mariama nor the twins were conversant with the origins of the Guadeloupeans. They were ignorant of the fact that the peoples of the Caribbean were shipped from Africa in slave ships and were prepared to return to Africa to seek their ancestry. In their defense it must be said that they had heard very little about the raids on the African coast. Like most of their fellow islanders they believed the blacks were native inhabitants of the Caribbean. It was during the pale light of the predawn hours they took off with Jet Tours. Although they had just enough time to change planes in Paris, in Marseille they had an entire day to kill. What can you do in a strange city when you have so little money to spend? Ivan and Ivana roamed the Old Port, then wolfed down a sandwich in one of the numerous cafés while enviously watching the expensive restaurants that boasted to be offering the best bouillabaisse. After their frugal lunch, Ivana suggested they visit the Château d'If. Such a suggestion didn't interest Ivan at all since he had never heard of Alexandre Dumas or the Count of Monte Cristo. They both agreed, however, to climb up to the basilica of Notre-Dame de la Garde, thinking how overjoyed their mother would have been if she had been with them. For the first time they were alone, free to act as they pleased. They sensed they were entering adulthood, which aroused in them a delicious feeling of trepidation.

They did not like Oran, where Ivana searched in vain for the memory of Albert Camus and his necessitous childhood. As a result of a car bomb the streets were under the tight control of armed soldiers who inspected the shopping bags of women returning from market, stuffed with innocent victuals. All these assault weapons seemed dangerous and could easily be pointed at passersby should the military take it into their heads. Why was there a bomb attack? Ivan and Ivana realized they knew nothing of the world around them. Despite their poverty and the anxiety it had caused them back in Dos d'Âne, they had been living in a cocoon.

They finally reached Mali and landed at the airport in Bamako.

IN AFRICA

Mali occupies a proud place in history books. Nobody has forgotten the famous pilgrimage by Emperor Kankan Moussa, who distributed so much gold on his way to Mecca that the price of the precious metal collapsed. Likewise, everyone has read the book by Djibril Tamsir Niane, *Sundiata, An Epic of Old Mali*, which narrates the exploits of Emperor Sundiata, who despite a difficult childhood was destined to become a hero:

> Listen then, sons of Mali, children of the black people, listen to my word for I am going to tell you of Sundiata, the Father of the Bright Country, of the Savanna, the ancestor of those who draw the bow, the master of a hundred vanquished kings.
>
> I am going to talk of Sundiata, Manding-Diara, Lion of Mali, Sogolon Diata, son of Sogolon, Nare Maghan Djata, son of Naro Maghan, Sogo Sogo Simbon Salaba, hero of many names.
>
> I am going to tell you of Sundiata, he whose exploits will astonish men for a long time yet. He was great among kings, he was peerless among men, he was beloved of God.

History tells us also of the splendor of certain king-doms, like the one of Segu which has caused so much ink to flow. Oddly enough it was the Tukolors waging jihad to impose their one and only god who laid waste to the region and made it ripe for colonization. Ivan and Ivana knew nothing of this past. In fact all they knew of Africa were the negative images they saw on television: coups d'états perpetrated by loutish soldiers, famine, and Ebola epidemics that without foreign aid the Afri-cans are incapable of curing. They were surprised to find Bamako such a pleasant place. The avenues crisscrossed at right angles under the shade of magnificent trees. They stopped short in front of the main market, which was surrounded by a wooden fence carved with all sorts of animals. They admired the fabrics and the rugs in the Pink Market. Inside, they were amazed at the vivid col-ors and size of the fruit: mangoes, guavas, and cherries. They didn't dare taste or buy them, however, since they instinctively felt they shouldn't run the risk. Lansana had sent them the address of a restaurant owned by one of his sisters (same mother, same father, he indicated) called Délices du Sahel; it was nothing but a modest shack whose walls were made with woven straw. Aunt Oumi was a large woman, badly rigged out in her indigo wrapper, but welcoming. She embraced them affection-ately exclaiming, "You're genuine Diarras. Both of you look like your father."

Thereupon she introduced them to the few customers present and explained, "These are my brother Lansana's children. They live in Guadeloupe with their mother. Now they've come to live with him."

Live with him! Ivan and Ivana didn't dare protest. Upon answering the question "What would you like to drink?" with "A beer please," the aunt's face fell.

"We don't serve alcohol here," she said severely. "Otherwise, you can have anything you want. Hibiscus flower juice, *bissap*, for instance. I make it myself."

Suddenly the restaurant was swarming with men in military attire. They all wore the same red-colored fez, like the former Senagalese infantrymen, and the same bottle-green uniform.

"Who are they?" Ivan asked intrigued.

"They're the militia," the aunt explained. "Last week there was a terrible bomb attack at the Metropolis hotel: over twenty-seven dead. A state of emergency has been declared and there's talk of imposing a curfew, which will be bad for business."

"Another bomb attack?" Ivan repeated in amazement. "The same thing happened in Oran."

The aunt shrugged her shoulders.

"A bunch of individuals thought the West was having too much of an influence on us and claimed to remedy it," she continued. "According to them, our education system must be totally overhauled and religion made all-powerful. The same thing's happening in Lebanon and Cameroon, not to mention Syria and Libya."

As the days went by, ever since they had left Guadeloupe, Ivan and Ivana found themselves thrown into a strange environment, riddled with a tension they were incapable of deciphering.

Finally, around five in the afternoon, they had to head for the airport again to fly to Kidal, less than an hour's flight away. The sky was streaked in scarlet. They flew over regions of the same reddish-brown color, where there was no apparent sign of life—not a tree, dwelling, or animal in sight—to the great surprise of the twins, who had so far never seen the desert. Lansana was waiting for them at the airport, surrounded by a dozen boys and girls whom he pushed forward as he introduced them one by one.

"This is your brother Madhi," he said. "This is your brother Fadel, this is your sister Oumou, and this is your sister Rachida."

The introductions lasted almost an hour. Ivan and Ivana were astonished, since they thought they were Lansana's only children. They did not know that the terms "brother" and "sister" also applied to first cousins, second cousins, nephews, and nieces—in short, every possible relative. Lansana must have once been a strong, handsome man. Now he was wizened and thinner and limped, leaning on two crutches.

Ivan and Ivana were surprised they felt nothing on this, their first meeting. Ivan even found him disagreeable with his stingy face, his narrow eyes, his balding head, his yellowed teeth, and the gray hairs that poked out of his nose and ears. Well, he said to himself, perhaps affection grows on you as the days go by.

Outside the air was dry and burning, the heat stifling, even more so than in Bamako. Night had fallen unnoticed, a jet-black darkness the likes of which they had never seen before and from which all sorts of spirits could emerge. Childhood fears suddenly awoke in them. It was probably on such a night that Ti-Sapoti grabbed his victims who were mesmerized by his tiny body and dragged off to their death.

Following Lansana as he limped on his crutches, they arrived at a compound which once upon a time must have been grandiose. A wall encircled half a dozen huts that had been wrecked by the incursion of the jihadists. They had wreaked havoc, especially on the music building which, apart from a collection of precious musical instruments, housed a state-of-the-art recording studio.

Mats had been laid out on the ground in the yard and everyone sat down to share the dinner that was served in a huge communal dish. Ivan and Ivana, who had never eaten with their hands, did the best they could to imitate the other guests. The meal was almost over when a short, stocky man with braided hair under his helmet emerged, dressed in a soldier's uniform and with a gun swinging by his side.

"This is Madiou," Lansana said, introducing him to Ivan and gesturing him to sit next to him. "He's the commander in chief of the militia, in charge of security not only for our town but also for the entire country. You will work under his orders."

After having swallowed several mouthfuls, Madiou motioned to Ivan to follow him into a corner of the yard. There he looked him up and down.

"How tall are you?" he commanded.

"One meter ninety-two," Ivan answered, surprised by the question.

"How much do you weigh? Almost a hundred kilos I can guess. I bet you think that's all it takes. Unfortunately, it's not the muscles that count, it's the brain. It's the brain that makes decisions, drives you to act, and combats fear."

The disagreeable impression Madiou immediately made on Ivan only worsened the following morning when he went along to the Alpha Yaya barracks. Madiou was nationally nicknamed El Cobra like in an American film. A batch of stories circulated about him. He was a callous ruffian. He had spent several years with the Foreign Legion until he was expelled for a dubious affair. It was whispered he had raped a small boy, a case rapidly hushed up by the authorities. Everyone was astonished and amazed when he was appointed commander in chief of the national militia. From the very beginning he made his authority felt, selecting Ivan for the most dangerous and singular missions. Sending him, for instance, into the middle of the desert to monitor suspicious comings and goings; asking him to attend the mosque on Fridays to study the faces of the worshippers after the imam's preaching, something Ivan couldn't understand since it was given in a foreign language, such as Bambara, Malinke, Fulani, or Soninke; or demanding he burst into the Koranic schools to ensure the children were chanting the suras in rhythm with their nodding heads. After a few weeks of this Ivan was fed up and confided in his sister.

"I'd do better to go to France," he declared. "To learn how to make chocolate. If he goes on like this, I'll end up giving this Madiou a good punching."

Ivana listened to him in amazement. Ever since she had arrived in Kidal, on the contrary, she had been overjoyed and fallen in love with her surroundings: first of all the landscapes, these vast, wonderfully fawn-colored expanses of semi desert; and then the people whose beauty and elegance transformed their humble clothes. She who was keen on music was fascinated by the chants of the griots and attended classes by a pupil of Fanta Damba, whose great voice we have now lost. She learned the national languages and was already capable of babbling in Bambara or Fulani. She loved her work. The Sundjata Keita orphanage where she worked housed a mere twenty or so children, for African families are tightly knit and refuse to abandon those children whose parents have perished in a bomb attack. Here an uncle, there an aunt or cousin would fight to take charge of them.

In the morning Ivana would wash the infants, feed

them, teach them how to keep clean, and above all sing them the nursery rhymes that she had grown up with: "*Savez-vous planter les choux à la mode de chez nous,*" or else "*Frère Jacques, frère Jacques, dormez-vous, dormez-vous, sonnez les matines, ding, dang, dong.*"

"Please," Ivana begged her brother. "Be patient. Think how hurt Maman would be if we left Mali now. If you are just as unhappy in a few months we'll see where we stand and make a decision."

Ivan, who couldn't deny his sister anything, resigned himself to staying in Kidal where he soon made two friends despite the circumstances. The first was called Mansour. He was the son of one of Lansana's sisters who had died during a particularly painful childbirth. Everyone made Mansour responsible for her death and the poor boy never managed to get over it. He was the compound's whipping boy: puny with a dour expression and hardly affable, afflicted moreover by a high-pitched voice which made most people shriek with laughter. Because of a heart condition he had been rejected by the militia, which didn't exactly enhance his reputation. He was also blamed for being a good-for-nothing. For the time being he was working in a restaurant in the town center, Le Balajo, a kind of modest café-bar owned by a French couple who allocated him the dishonorable job of dishwasher.

Ivan and Mansour hit it off straight away. They immediately sensed they were carved from the same wood that made them losers for life. In fact Ivan had hardly made any friends, so obsessed was he by his sister. He discovered the pleasure of finding someone who had similar reactions, concerns, and opinions. He surprised himself by talking to Mansour about his childhood, as he had always thought his childhood to be of no interest to anyone. He was not at a loss for words when describing his island, his mother, or his grandmother, as well as a thousand small events which suddenly emerged and filled his memory. In the evening, Ivan and Mansour drew their folding chairs up close and chattered well into the night. Usually silent when confronted with the jibes he was regularly showered with, here Mansour kept up a constant string of words. He liked to repeat: "We must get out of this country. It's one of Europe's vassals, where nothing original is created and nothing good can emerge. We must go to Europe and strike the heart of capitalism."

Ivan listened to him, not entirely convinced. But he was no more interested in making chocolate than he was in participating in this violence. Go to Europe, yes, he was prepared to do that, but not to destroy capitalism. In order to find a better life, better than the one in Guadeloupe or Mali. Sometimes Mansour uttered serious accusations that Lansana was a drunkard, a marabout-cognac.

"A marabout-cognac?" Ivan repeated in amazement. "Why do you say that?"

Mansour lowered his voice.

"You only have to watch how he behaves when he returns home in the evening. He walks askew, then locks himself up in his room and doesn't come out till early morning. It's because he's drunk and has to sleep it off."

By dint of hearing such comments, Ivan set about watching his father whom he was not overly fond of. He very quickly realized that Mansour was entirely mistaken; it wasn't alcohol that Lansana locked himself up with in his room, but women of whom it seemed he could never get enough. Women. All kinds of women. Some were married and looking to make ends meet.

Others were naive young girls who were impressed by the prestige of this man twice their age. Finally, there were the professionals, specializing in love with a price tag. Ivan was horrified by this debauchery since the love he bore his sister protected him and made him chaste. For him the body of a woman was sacred. He could not imagine possessing a woman without love. The hypocrisy of his father, an arrant sermonizer constantly quoting the Koran, disgusted him.

More and more Ivan detested the compound and found his father's authority increasingly difficult to tolerate. Lansana ordered him around as if he were a ten-year-old kid and didn't hesitate to take him down a peg or two in front of witnesses. He had nicknamed him "the guy who walks without knowing where he puts his feet." Ivan didn't understand why it made everyone laugh and constantly wondered whether he was conceited, reckless, or simply a blind fool.

One evening Mansour drew up his chair even closer. You sensed he was racked by a deep emotion and on the point of confessing something terrible.

"Yesterday I met a certain Ramzi," he whispered. "A smuggler from Lebanon. Together with a group of other boys he will take us to Libya then Europe, the very heart of all the terrorist attacks. Do you want to join us?"

Since Ivan remained speechless, he insisted.

"It will only cost you five hundred Malian francs, as Ramzi is not doing it for money. He has the faith. We must destroy this world of ours that has been reduced to the status of a vassal."

Ivan shook his head and apologized. He could not leave his sister behind all alone in this compound where she knew very few people and set off for another life.

A few days later Mansour disappeared, leaving Ivan

his copy of the Koran as a souvenir; it bore the dedication: *We will meet again one day. Your brother who loves you now and forever.* Once Mansour had gone, a lot of stories were rumored about him. Just imagine, at La Balajo he gave himself to foreigners, tourists obviously, who paid dearly for the possession of his body. According to intelligence the police had received, Mansour had left for Belgium to join a group of terrorists who were planning an attack. Unfortunately nobody in the compound could provide any information or confirm the rumors.

Ivan often thought about Mansour. Since he had left, the compound seemed even emptier. There was nobody to speak to. The endless nights were pierced by the shrill refrains of the singers gathered around Lansana's hut. He always had the same nightmare: he saw his friend muffled up, wearing a woolen bonnet, setting off bombs in airports and shooting bullets from his Kalashnikov at customers sitting on the terraces of cafés. He admired his courage, nevertheless, and constantly regretted his friend's departure.

It was then that Ivan met a second friend, different from Mansour yet subtly similar. He was a member of the militia going by the name of Ali. He was handsome, a giant over six feet tall, and light-skinned since his mother was a Moor. Yet he was constantly attacked and cruelly mocked by the other members of the militia who were jealous of his noble ancestry. He was the son of a well-known scholar of the Koran and a singer who some compared to the great Umm Kulthum.

Their friendship began when they were both assigned the same mission. They were ordered to go to Kita, a small village fifty kilometers away from Kidal, where some farmers had been killed and their herd of goats carried off.

"This mission is one of the stupidest I've ever heard of," Ali declared, sitting down in the military jeep next to Ivan. "If in all likelihood the terrorists *are* responsible, by this time they must have safely hidden most of the herd and roasted the rest in the shelter of the cliffs."

"You shouldn't say things like that," Ivan commented. "You never know into which ears your jibes will fall. This camp is full of guys only too keen to denounce the slightest gossip to the commander in chief in order to make an impression."

"You're not one of them," Ali assured him, starting the engine. "I've been watching you for weeks. What's that place you come from? I know you're a foreigner."

"I come from Guadeloupe," Ivan replied. "It's not really a country; it's a French overseas department."

"A French overseas department!" Ali guffawed. "What does that mean?"

Ivan attempted to explain the strangeness of the place he came from and found himself repeating the words he had heard from the mouth of Monsieur Jérémie. He depicted a dilapidated land and an unemployed youth reduced to drug trafficking and violence.

"Well I never," commented Ali. "Here's one more place to be liberated."

After a few moments of silence he continued.

"If we drive straight ahead we'll soon come to Algeria. There, we'd have no problems taking a plane to France or even better, to Belgium."

"France? Belgium?" Ivan exclaimed.

Once again he heard talk of Europe as a place where you could start life over again.

"Why do you want to go to France?" he insisted.

Ali didn't answer.

The village of Kita numbered around a hundred or so

souls. The streets were deserted. Inside their houses the women whose husbands had been assassinated were sobbing their hearts out.

"We've lost both our husbands and our herds," they lamented. "What have we done to deserve such a fate?"

"You have probably offended God," Ali replied drily.

He soon invited Ivan to his house in Kidal. Within the genuine palace where his parents lived—tapestries, silk drapes, thick-pile woolen carpets and deep-sunken sofas—he had arranged for himself a narrow room with a low ceiling, rudimentarily furnished with a bed and some brown leather ottomans. Ivan quickly understood why his three younger brothers had nicknamed him the ayatollah. He did not drink, did not smoke, dutifully said his five prayers, was the first at the mosque on Fridays, and finally, as soon as he had a moment to himself, he fiddled with his string of beads chanting suras. He only allowed himself two things: food and, like Lansana, women. He had a Moroccan cook at his service, a sort of hunchbacked gnome, who prepared succulent dishes for him such as tajines, guinea fowl cooked in honey, and stuffed squash on a bed of herbs and spices. As for women he had two or three spend the night fondling him every evening.

One evening, right out of the blue, he asked Ivan, "You're a virgin, aren't you?"

Ivan blushed and was incapable of giving an answer.

"I've never seen you interested in a woman," Ali continued. "Or get excited about one. It's as if you don't notice them."

Ivan, who had somewhat gathered his wits about him, launched into a complicated explanation.

"It's because I'm deeply in love with a girl I left in Guadeloupe. If I looked at another, I'd get the impression of having betrayed her."

"You can't pull that one on me," Ali chuckled. "Every man has in mind an ideal woman he respects and adores. That doesn't prevent him from taking his pleasure with other mere mortals. So that fine instrument you have down front has never been put to use? Hard as a spur it has never penetrated a woman's secret cocoon and made that delicious marine water well up? Unbelievable."

The day following this conversation Ali invited three women to dinner who were visibly destined for his friend Ivan: Rachida, Oumi, and Esmeralda. They were lovely and wasp-waisted, showing much cleavage and with buttocks that curved provocatively under their wrappers. Although Rachida and Oumi were home-bred, Esmeralda was an Indian from Kerala. She had spent seven years in a temple studying lovemaking techniques more daring than the sexual positions of the *Kama Sutra*. One of her specialties was called "the nibble," where the caress was so insidious it drove those on the receiving end out of their mind. Another one, using small rings, we do not dare describe here.

As soon as they had downed the last bite, Ali got up and suggested to the women:

"Tire him out. Spare no effort regarding your techniques. Give him all you've got: fondle him, suck him, sodomize him. Devour him with kisses. Leave no inch of his skin untouched."

Thereupon he closed the door behind him and disappeared. This first night of initiation aroused in Ivan a sensation of indescribable pleasure as well as a deep feeling of shame. He compared the moaning, groaning, and shouting of his body to that of a swine wallowing in its mud. Once it was over, having lasted several hours, without troubling to thank the three women, Ivan dashed home. He would have liked to rush into Ivana's arms and beg her forgiveness. But she was out of reach since she slept chastely in the compound reserved for girls. Consequently, he threw himself into the wash room and soaped himself from head to foot so as to wash away the memory of these disgusting acts.

The following morning a battle began which he had not foreseen.

"You must become a Muslim," Ali shouted at him sharply. "You must convert to Islam."

"And for what reason?" Ivan responded. "One must remain faithful to your mother's religion in which she brought you up and to the society you belong to."

"There's no question, you must convert," Ali insisted. "I'm thinking only of your own good. If you die while fighting, you'll go straight to the Garden of Allah. There you'll have seventy-two virgins to deflower while houris with their long black hair dance around you."

"Who's talking about fighting?" Ivan asked.

Ali went back to his office and pulled out a bundle of documents.

"We must leave this country which, under the pretext of being Muslim, is merely subject to the diktat of the West: this same West which has transformed your country into a French overseas department. Everything is written here. We'll go to Amharic in Algeria and from there to Iraq."

Ivan then brandished his ultimate argument.

"I cannot abandon my sister. We arrived together in Mali. We'll remain together. We'll leave together."

Ali turned red with anger.

"Your sister couldn't care less if you left. It's come to my knowledge that El Hadj Mansour has fallen in love with her and asked your father for her hand."

Ivan hurled himself on Ali as if to strangle him.

"What are you saying, filthy liar?"

"I'm only telling you the truth," Ali stammered, struggling to free himself.

Ivan dashed outside into the thick black of night. He made straight for the house of El Hadj Mansour, the imam of the Kerfalla Mosque. But the imam was at somebody's deathbed, the servants said. Ivan then headed for the Sundjata Keita orphanage where he knew his sister was working even at this late hour. In actual fact, in the bedroom allocated her she had just taken off her white uniform bordered in red and was standing bare-breasted, dressed only in her panties. Ivan shouted at her.

"What do I hear?" he screamed. "El Hadj Barka Mansour wants to marry you?"

Ivana clasped Ivan in her arms and showered him with kisses.

"That's his problem if he's in love with me," she said softly. "He has in fact asked our father for my hand but I refused since you know full well I only love you."

Ivan returned her kisses passionately, pressing his body on fire against her nakedness. That evening they were both very nearly consumed by love.

Once they had left the orphanage and reached the main square they witnessed a surprising sight. A group of armed men masked in black were climbing out of two or three jeeps. Terrified, the twins plunged into a side street and managed to get home. On waking they learned that a commando of terrorists had killed thirty or so men and women during the night, shooting haphazardly at innocent customers sipping their mint teas outside cafés, and setting light to several neighborhoods in the town.

Ali was brought before an exceptional military tribunal presided by El Cobra. He was accused of being an accomplice and having aided the terrorists by shooting down innocent tea-drinkers. After less than an hour's deliberation, he was sentenced to punishment by the sun's rays, which dates back to the time of Emperor Kankan Moussa (yes, him again), whereby an individual is tied up and abandoned totally naked to the sun's violent rays in the desert until the veins in his head swell up and burst. El Cobra ordered Ivan to bring back the bloodied corpse of his friend to Kidal which was then thrown into a common grave without further ado. Ivan thought he too would die. Risking retaliatory measures he never again set foot in the Alfa Yaya barracks. All day long he lay prostrate on his mat incapable of feeding himself. He only emerged from his torpor to answer Lansana's stupid comments.

"He deserved everything he got, this Ali. He was a traitor and a terrorist."

Relations between Ivan and his father worsened. Certainly they had never been as cordial and affectionate as the bond between Lansana and Ivana. Nevertheless, father and son had always displayed a facade of being on good terms. That was now over. Lansana grumbled to anyone prepared to listen: "He's an ex-prisoner. His mother hid that from me. He's been in prison twice."

As for Ivan, he told everyone that Lansana was nothing but a product of the West and that his music came nowhere near the genius of Ali Farka Touré and Salif Keita. The major bone of contention was that Ivan refused categorically to return to the barracks. Furious, Lansana belched, "You can't expect me to keep this good-for-nothing who won't lift a finger."

One evening while Ivan was idling on his mat as usual they came to inform him that a visitor was asking for him. A small man with a shaved head was waiting for him at the entrance to the main hut.

"My name is Zinga Messaoud," he introduced himself. "Let us not stay here, for the walls have ears."

It was only once they reached the street that Zinga made up his mind to speak.

"You were a great friend of Ali Massila, weren't you?"

"He was my brother," Ivan replied, holding back his tears.

"There are many of us who cannot tolerate what they did to him," Zinga continued. "And we are resolved to avenge him. Please follow me."

Zinga guided Ivan to a secluded neighborhood of public housing all of which looked the same. Once they arrived in front of one of the buildings Zinga preceded Ivan up to the third floor. There he took a tiny instrument out of his pocket and whistled three times. Then he knocked twice against the wooden door. After a while the door opened from the inside and they entered a meagerly lit living room where a forty-year-old man was waiting for them. The latter stood up, walked around his desk, and held out his hand to Ivan.

"Call me Ismaël," he declared.

Ismaël was originally from India and came from the Muslim village of Rajani. He had a crown of smooth hair and wore flowing dark-colored clothes.

And that's how Ivan was recruited into the Army of Shadows. They called the Army of Shadows those recruits who as members of the official militia had nothing better to do than thwart the plans of their military command and put a spanner in its works. Ivan therefore had to put on his uniform again and, pretending to eat humble pie, return to the Alfa Yaya barracks. On his return he was greeted by El Cobra in person and by his venomous smile.

"You've regained your senses."

"Forgive me if I've been stupid."

El Cobra's smile broadened.

"I don't hold it against you," he said. "It's not your fault. This Ali managed to dupe you sexually. Rachida, Oumi, and Esmeralda described to us the whole affair. Esmeralda had a camera hidden in her clothes and we were able to witness the crime."

"Rachida, Oumi, and Esmeralda are spies then!" Ivan exclaimed in amazement.

El Cobra looked pleased with himself.

"They work for us. Let's say they'll service you the same way but this time it'll be free."

In the meantime El Hadj Mansour, the imam of the Kerfalla Mosque, was determined to marry Ivana. He already possessed three wives and seven children, which should have satisfied any man. But this chick from far away who babbled a bit of Bambara with her adorable accent and stretched out her long, naked legs in her white cotton shorts, that no woman in Mali would be seen wearing, got his blood flowing. It wouldn't be the first time that a young beauty, having refused a suitor, changes her mind, provided the spurned suitor knows how to make her reconsider her decision. El Hadj Mansour could count on the help of Garifuna, a *dibia* from the Igbo country, who had been dragged to the outskirts of Kidal by the fortunes of life. His reputation was well established. He lived ten or so kilometers away on a semi-barren plateau where his mud-brick hut rose up, strange and mysterious. He was not a sorcerer, or an evil creature who unleashes the worst catastrophes on individuals provided he is paid to do so. He was rather a man who worked with both hands, the right and the left, the good and the bad. In other words he did both good and evil. In the midst of the cacti and wild grasses around his hut were jars of every height in which he locked up the spirits of the dead before they were allowed to slip inside newborn infants.

El Hadj Mansour arrived at nightfall, as certain deals are best made in darkness. Garifuna had no trouble recognizing him.

"You again! What brings you here this time?" he cried out.

"I need a woman."

"Another one!" Garifuna guffawed. "You're collecting them."

El Hadj Mansour made a sweeping gesture with his hand.

"That's life! Women are our only consolation on this earth inhabited by the wicked. That's what the Koran teaches us."

Thereupon he handed the *dibia* a sample of white percale and kola nuts he had brought by way of payment. Garifuna grabbed them then poured a concoction of plants he had taken from the jars on the shelves into a calabash, carefully washed his face, especially his eyes, lit seven candles, a fateful number, and began to chant softly a string of incomprehensible words.

After half an hour of this he gave a start, looked straight at El Hadj Mansour, and cried out, "This woman of yours is totally possessed by another man."

"That doesn't bother me," El Hadj Mansour retorted. "That's why I've come to see you. You're clever enough to solve this problem. I trust you entirely."

Garifuna relit two of the candles that had gone out and once again carefully washed his eyes. After a while he continued, "What I don't understand is the nature of this man. He is not an ordinary lover. He was born with her and shares the same life."

He remained silent, and once again peered into the invisible. Suddenly he uttered a cry.

"Does she have a twin brother?"

El Hadj Mansour didn't have a clue. He had sometimes caught sight of Ivan in Lansana Diarra's compound but had no idea of his relationship to Ivana.

"This business of yours seems extremely complicated," he told El Hadj Mansour. "Make inquiries and come back to see me in four days' time. There will be a full moon then and I'll take advantage of the vapors transmitted by its light. I'll know exactly what to do."

"How much is all that going to cost me?" El Hadj Mansour asked worriedly.

"A lot," Garifuna declared, lighting an oil lamp set on a low table. "As I said: it's complicated."

El Hadj Mansour traveled the ten kilometers back to Kidal lost in his thoughts. The moon which sat pale and imposing in the middle of the sky was not yet full. Its light transformed the dunes and cliffs into prehistoric animals that seemed about to pounce on travelers. But the imam was not afraid. He was too absorbed in his thoughts. He didn't understand a thing. How could a sister be fully possessed by her brother? What did Garifuna mean when he said he shares the same life?

El Hadj Mansour was not naive. It's just that in Mali incest is unknown and they are not used to the wild theories of psychiatrists and psychoanalysts.

He reached the gates of Kidal safe and sound. While driving past Lansana Diarra's compound he caught sight of a small crowd at the entrance guarded by armed militia. He made inquiries and learned that the famous jazz singer Herbie Scott was singing together with Lansana and backed by the Grand Orchestra of Cairo. These types of musical fusion were hardly to El Hadj Mansour's liking as he considered all music to have a distinct, particular, and foreign voice that does not necessarily match up with those of others. He parked his car, however, and entered the compound so as to observe what was going on. Refusing to sit in the VIP section, he chose a more discreet place from where he could watch the youngsters crowded to the left of the stage, including Ivan and Ivana. He had never noticed how alike those two were: the same sparkling, black, almond-shaped eyes, Ivana's slightly more languishing; the same full lips, Ivan's slightly pulpier; the same dimpled chins, Ivana's slightly rounder. What was striking was that the twins moved in the same way, making identical gestures and expressions. At that moment the annoying El Hadj Amadou Cissé came and sat down presumptuously beside El Hadj Mansour and started up an insipid conversation. El Hadj Mansour was at his wits' end and interrupted him.

"Lansana must be glad to have such lovely children."

El Hadj Amadou Cissé made a face.

"He's not as glad as all that, believe me. His son is a good-for-nothing. He refuses to go with the militia to the North where he'll get better pay. Poor Lansana has to double his musical engagements in order to survive. Believe me, those twins are by no means a blessing."

That was exactly what El Hadj Mansour wanted to know.

When the concert was over the audience gave the musicians a standing ovation. It was not a sign of appreciation, El Hadj Mansour thought, always prepared to criticize; the spectators simply wanted to show they had adopted Western ways.

Four days later El Hadj Mansour went back to see Garifuna. He found the dibia sitting outside his hut staring at the flames of a blazing fire.

"I've understood everything," he said. "Bring me a spotless white hen and a red-feathered cockerel. Neither of them must be older than five months. I'll work on them and probably make a purée you'll mix with a pigeon pâté. You'll serve them up to Lansana and his children when you invite them to dinner at your place, which shouldn't be difficult."

The time needed to obey his directives was fairly long, as was the time it took to convince Lansana and his children to come for dinner. In the meantime, Awa, El Hadj Mansour's first wife, his *bara muso*, who was in charge of cooking the meal, threw out the jar her husband had given her because she didn't like the color of the pâté. The affair therefore was a complete failure.

Ivan now had an excellent reason for never leaving Kidal or his father's compound, where he was unhappy and fed up with this batch of brothers and sisters. The recruits of the Army of the Shadows, who deceptively wore the uniform of the militia, would meet every evening in the vast courtyard behind Ismaël's lodging and were lectured to by a number of teachers. Ismaël was unquestionably the most brilliant of them all. His tone of speech was both smooth and peremptory.

"We are blamed for not liking music and outlawing it. That's not true. We prize above all the silence which allows us to hear the voice of God. And any noise or sound that interferes must be silenced."

Listening to Ismaël, Ivan recalled the words of Monsieur Jérémie and blamed himself for not paying more attention at the time. He had probably still been too young and too immature. The recruits sat down under a blue tarpaulin and took notes in identical notebooks.

Standing on a small platform Ismaël and the other leading lights addressed them through a microphone and illustrated their talks by drawing on a blackboard that was, oddly, painted green. The topic of the first lesson was the Crusades. Ismaël demonstrated that they were the fundamental aggression committed by the West against Islam. The individual whom the West venerated as a martyr, King Louis IX of France, also known as Saint-Louis, was in fact the first agent of imperialism: an imperialism that has, since, constantly threatened the peace of the world.

The subject of the second lesson was slavery. Of course the Arab sultans also practiced slavery, filling their harems with black beauties bought for fabulous sums, but their slavery was not dehumanizing and could not be compared with the brutality of the Atlantic slave trade, which reduced millions of Africans to the state of commodities and wild animals. Ismaël described the conditions on board the slave ships: the stench of the hold and the repeated rape of women and prepubescent young girls. He handed around engravings illustrating the slave markets on the islands of the Caribbean where the teeth of the slaves up for sale were examined, their testicles weighed, and the insides of their anuses checked to make sure they were not hiding any contagious disease.

These lessons began after the last raucous call of the muezzin and ended at 10:30 p.m. Around 9 p.m. refreshments were served. Always the same smoked fish, hard-boiled eggs, and millet couscous. Oddly enough this frugality had nothing monotonous about it. On the contrary! It sharpened the brain, and a host of questions inundated Ivan's mind. Why did the Age of Discovery result in the marginalization of and contempt for millions of human beings? Why did the conquistadors rapidly turn out to be ruffians and assassins? Ismaël calmly explained: the discovery of the New World had not been an age of lively interest, tolerance, and communion. The Discoverers had come to plant their flags, and to grab and control anything that differed from them.

One evening Ismaël took Ivan familiarly by the arm and dragged him into his office.

"I'm extremely satisfied with you. You should become one of us and convert to Islam."

"Convert to Islam?" Ivan cried out. "Why, for God's sake? I would be betraying my mother and grandmother who have been so loyal to the Catholic religion."

"It's because they have been misled by the myths and the lies and never been made aware of the truth," Ismaël retorted. "If you become a Muslim, you will be our true brother. You will strive to make great and powerful our wonderful religion that has been so disparaged, so misjudged."

All night long Ivan turned these words over and over in his head. Ismaël's words had one good thing going for them: if he converted, he would be closer to his father and his extended family, and at the same time fool El Cobra and other fault-finders.

In the morning he had made up his mind. Although Lansana was overjoyed at the news (at last, this rebellious boy was giving in to him), this was not the case with Ivana. When her brother confessed his intention she firmly shook her head.

"I will not follow you along this path. This religion disgusts me. Look at what's just happened in Nigeria: girls kidnapped from their school and sold as wives or concubines to men they don't even know, and boys massacred."

It was the first time they had thought differently. Cut to the quick, Ivan clarified his thoughts: to become a Muslim was merely a way of integrating into a society which in actual fact he rejected. Once their differences had been ironed out the twins embraced each other, glad they were both of the same opinion.

Nothing is more different from a Catholic baptism than a Muslim baptism. A Catholic christening is all pomp and finery. Near the baptistery the infant in the arms of her godfather and godmother wears a gown of white lace whose train is sometimes as long as a wedding dress. The priest can hardly be seen amidst the clouds of smoke created by his choirboys in red surplices swinging their censers. Then he utters a long homily where he compares the faithful to Christian soldiers. The Muslim ceremony on the other hand is short and sweet. The neighborhood imam shaves the head of the baby and repeats his name. It only lasts a few minutes. But Lansana acted otherwise.

He invited the numerous Diarras to come to Kidal. They came in crowds, dressed in their finest attire. Among those present were the Diarras from Villefranche-sur-Saône, where the start-up they had created had made them millionaires. However, the guy who got the most attention was unquestionably El Cobra, wearing his combat uniform and with his Kalashnikov swinging from his hip. He smiled left and right, swaggering and showing off. This little man symbolized all the duplicity of a power structure that knew his reprehensible violence only too well but exploited him for its own security. He was accompanied by a young mixed-blood guy with languishing eyes that looked like they had been made up with kohl like those of a woman, and who claimed to be his adopted son. People whispered it was nothing of the sort, and that in reality he was his lover, proof by nines he was hiding something. How could we know the truth? Nevertheless, he appeared to be on the best of terms with Ivan and Lansana, whose music he claimed to adore.

The next day when Ivan attended the meeting of the Army of Shadows, Ismaël once again put his arm familiarly around Ivan's shoulders and dragged him inside his office.

"We are very glad you made this decision. As a way of showing his satisfaction the commander in chief of the Army of Shadows is giving you the honor of eliminating El Cobra."

"Eliminating? What does that mean?" Ivan stammered in fright.

"It means," Ismaël explained, "eliminating physically —murder, assassination."

Ivan was not exactly fond of El Cobra, but to assassinate him was another matter! Moreover, the time had long gone when the idea of possessing a gun intoxicated Ivan. Ever since he had handled Kalashnikovs and repeating rifles in the militia he had been frightened by their power of destruction.

"Why me?" Ivan murmured in dismay. "I'm a new recruit in the Army of Shadows. Couldn't you find someone older and more capable?"

Ismaël shook his head.

"I repeat, it's a great honor we are doing you. We all agreed about your intelligence and bravery."

Ivan protested weakly, "But I have never killed anyone."

Ismaël gave him an affectionate dig in the ribs.

"Well, it's never too late to start and, you'll see, you'll take a liking to it!"

He then turned serious.

"You've got four weeks to do it. You can of course enlist other recruits from the Army of Shadows to assist but you realize it must remain a secret."

Ivan returned to the compound trembling and weak-kneed. In his worst nightmares he had never imagined such a situation. Now he had four weeks to put to death a man of flesh and blood like himself. He thought about running away. But where? He was as vulnerable as a prisoner locked in his cell. He spent the following days elaborating plans which seemed more and more ridiculous. As a last resort he decided to ask his friend Birame Diallo for help. He had noticed Birame, not because of his amazing athletic build and muscles, something rare for a Fulani, but because at every session he would frown and bombard Ismaël and the other leading lights with questions: "What should we think of Christopher Columbus? Was he a bastard too?" Or else: "Does Eric Williams's book *Capitalism and Slavery* have the place it deserves in the school syllabus?"

Ivan came and sat beside Birame during lunch at the Alfa Yaya barrack's canteen and managed to whisper, "I need to talk to you. But nobody must overhear us. Where can we meet in secret?"

Birame looked doubtful. After a while he declared, "I can see no other place but my house. My mother died last year. My two older brothers have gone to France to look for work. I live alone with my younger brothers who are never home."

Ivan went to join him the same evening at his mud-brick house situated in a crowded neighborhood. After drinking his mint tea he explained his problem. Birame listened to him without saying a word, then whistled at length through his teeth.

"Well, that's a real ultimate initiation test they are having you take."

"Ismaël never stopped telling me that the military command was doing me a great honor," Ivan explained.

The two boys snickered in unison.

Then Birame declared, "Let me think it over. I'll get back to you when I come up with an idea."

A week went by before Birame invited Ivan to his place again. This time he offered Ivan a ginger beer, and after careful consideration said, "Prepare yourself for a mass killing, since El Cobra always travels with a bunch of bodyguards, friends, and relatives."

"A mass killing!" Ivan shouted. "What do you mean?"

"I mean you'll need several people to help you. You can count on me as well as my young brother; we hate El Cobra and his clique. I have a plan. El Cobra is fond of techno music and every Saturday he goes to the Ultra Vocal concert hall which specializes in that type of music. After half an hour he gets up and begins to dance on his own. That's when you have to shoot him."

"I still don't understand. What do you mean by mass killing?"

Birame looked Ivan straight in the eyes.

"I mean you'll not only have to aim for El Cobra but also for his bodyguards, his relatives, and friends who make up his followers and accompany him everywhere."

Ivan remained speechless, both flabbergasted and scared. Birame went on with his explanations regardless.

"We shall have to be masked so that none of the survivors will recognize us. We might also have to wear a special belt and blow ourselves up once we have accomplished our mission. You know in that case we'll go straight to Paradise."

Ivan refrained from shrugging his shoulders. This business of Paradise, he didn't believe a word.

Two weeks went by before he accepted the proposed plan. And finally he made up his mind to act. Birame had spared no detail and arranged to meet him at 9 p.m., the time when the concert would begin. In order not to attract attention, each of them would enter the Ultra Vocal separately and sit down several rows apart. They would join up only when El Cobra began to dance on his own. They would then slip on their masks, and fire, conducting their mission of death.

The Ultra Vocal concert hall had been built in the '80s by a French businessman, a homosexual who loved techno music. It was a plain building but had perfect acoustics. It had hosted groups from all over the world but its biggest success was a Japanese ensemble who combined melodies from East and West.

That evening, Saturday February 11th, a crowd began to assemble on the Place de l'Amitié, where the Ultra Vocal concert hall was situated, composed of young girls and boys, some in short trousers, for only the under-eighteens liked techno music in a vague desire to rebel against their country's traditions. Cherishing such music, which came from the United States of America, from Detroit, was a pledge of their modernity. Nobody stopped to suspect the four armed militia men who mixed in with the concertgoers. On the contrary, their presence was reassuring. The hall rapidly filled up.

At 9:10 p.m. the concert began, slightly late because one of the musicians had been taken ill with violent diarrhea and had to relieve his intestines. Moreover, he was too weak to continue and had to go home, and thus escaped the massacre that was to follow. At 9:37 p.m. El

Cobra got up and climbed the few steps leading from the spectator's pit to the stage where the musicians were seated. He began to dance with his eyes shut, somewhat clumsily like a bird without wings. Nobody understood what was happening when he fell to the ground smashing his head, while blood spurted from his forehead like a geyser. Nobody understood either why the spectators covered in blood began to collapse left and right while the militia assembled at the back of the hall systematically fired their weapons. Birame's two younger brothers playfully tossed a grenade, which hollowed out a monstrous hole among the spectators. Without running the slightest risk, the gang of four withdrew, pushing open the heavy armored doors, removing their masks, and while crossing the lobby deciding on a whim to kill the old guard who was asleep. They walked out and crossed the Place de l'Amitié. It was then that panic broke out in the Ultra Vocal concert hall and the spectators began to run out screaming. It was too late. The four militiamen had only to quicken their step and take refuge inside Birame's house close by.

A few hours later a communiqué claimed responsibility for the attack. It was signed: *The Army of Shadows. We will never leave you in peace.* This communiqué threw the country into a state of incomprehension and panic. Who was this Army of Shadows? What did they want? Everything had seemed to be going so well. The Moors who were siding with the terrorists had recently rallied behind the government while the latter had decreed a Persons and Family Code, which earned them much praise from the West.

The government declared a state funeral for El Cobra. He was taken to be buried at the Rawane cemetery. His adopted son walked in tears at the head of the procession surrounded by some of the regime's most eminent personalities. He was followed by a dense throng who had traveled from Timbuktu, Gao, Djenné, Segu, in short from every corner of Mali. Some had even been bold enough to travel to Kidal either on those small Moorish stallions whose hooves raised clouds of dust or on camels walking at a slower pace. It was a beautiful ceremony without a doubt, and El Cobra, so denigrated while he was alive, became a legend: at the age of ten he had killed a lion and, making the tail into a belt, had knocked on the door of the hut where the elders were debating the welfare of the tribe. At the age of fifteen he had killed the man who had tried to rape his sister, and when the court released him the villagers had carried him in triumph through the streets, and so on and so on.

As for Ivan, he was worked up into a somber excitement. It was as if the blood he had spilled, at first reluctantly, suddenly and amazingly had invigorated him. He had fallen prey to a transformation out of his control. The Koran, which he had read up till now as an act of conscience, came back to haunt him and he could quote from memory entire suras. He was constantly preoccupied by the idea of God and walked with renewed authority around the compound. He openly confronted his father: "We ought to say our mea culpa," he argued. "Perhaps we deserved this dramatic event."

Lansana threw a fit of anger and shouted, "What are you talking about? You're crazy. This government is by no means perfect but it's doing its best. The rebellion in the North has been quelled. The family code has stipulated that a polygamist can only have two wives. What more can it do?"

Ivan went to find Ivana who, on the contrary, never

stopped crying as she had lost two of her best friends in the Ultra Vocal attack. He told her quite plainly that she should no longer wear the white canvas shorts which she so liked and which showed off her legs.

"No longer wear my shorts?" she exclaimed. "But why not?"

He looked at her with a sense of importance.

"They excite men's desires and, in doing so, the wrath of God."

"They excite men's desires," she repeated in amazement, "and, in doing so, the wrath of God. You speak like a sanctimonious old man."

"I am a sanctimonious young man," he coldly corrected her. "Do not take umbrage, but certain details of your behavior must change. You do not take God into enough consideration."

She stared at him open-mouthed.

"Which God are you talking about?" she retorted. "I'm not a Muslim and have nothing to do with Allah's precepts."

This was the second time their opinions had diverged. Ivan realized in terror that a crack was becoming apparent in the beautiful edifice of their love. Consequently he drew her into his arms, showered her with kisses, and said not a word more.

A few days later the government named El Cobra's successor, Abdouramane Sow, an impeccable choice, a former blue helmet who had been assigned to the MINUSTAH peacekeeping mission in Haiti. The very next day he assembled the militia. According to him, the recent attack was an inside job. Without a doubt the national militia was harboring traitors, assassins, and friends of terrorists. The Army of Shadows was inserted into the very heart of the militia. Such lucidity surprised more than one, starting with Ivan.

Ever since the attack they had committed, Ivan and Birame had become very close friends. At noon they sat side by side in the barrack's canteen eating their miserable lunch. In the evening Ivan drank his mint tea with Birame, had dinner at his place, spent the night there, and finally ended up moving in with him. Ivan, who loathed the pile of relatives crowded into Lansana's compound and the inevitable promiscuity it entailed, loved Birame's three dilapidated huts, now deserted since Birame's younger brothers, busy with mysterious jobs trafficking both soft and hard drugs, regular visits to the prostitutes in the Tombo neighborhood, and gambling, returned home only in the early hours of the morning. Ivan spent his nights in the hut that had belonged to Birame's mother. Through the open window he could watch the fluctuations of the moon. He took delight in smelling the droppings and manure from the goats raised in the backyard and listening to the cackling of the chickens, while a red-feathered rooster swaggered around three gray-plumed hens.

Two or three weeks had passed when one evening while he was lying naked in bed due to the heat, Birame burst into his hut, forced himself onto Ivan, and struggled to penetrate him. Ivan had enough strength to push his assailant back against the wall.

"Are you mad!?" he shouted.

Although taken by surprise Ivan was by no means naive for he had often seen this same desire mirrored in the troubled waters of other men's eyes because of his muscular build and had had to defend himself against their advances. But this time he had not seen it coming.

Birame did not lose his cool. With a visible erection and heaving chest he declared, "You don't like girls, everyone knows it. So I thought you were like me and you liked boys."

"You swine," Ivan roared. "How long have you been practicing this vice?"

"It's not a vice," Birame replied. "Nobody is responsible for their sexual orientation. You have to put up with it, that's all. When I discovered at the age of twelve that I was homosexual I wanted to kill myself. Then one of my father's shepherds took my virginity and ever since I have gone with the flow."

"Gone with the flow?" Ivan said, horrified by his cool.

Birame shrugged his shoulders.

"You've no idea how many respectable heads of family are in fact homosexual. El Cobra being the first. Haven't you heard all the stories that are being rumored about him?"

After such a misadventure there was no question of whether Ivan would continue his friendship with Birame, or stay in his compound. He returned to Lansana's place where crowds of relatives from the towns and villages in the North were piling into the mud-brick huts, tired of being threatened by terrorists and seeking safety. Ivan nevertheless found room to unroll his mat near a group of gray-haired men who claimed to be uncles. One of them was describing the latest attacks they had suffered.

"It happened during the wedding of my niece Lalla with Mossoul," he said. "We had known them since they were knee high. That day everyone was overjoyed. Everyone was singing and dancing when suddenly three armed, masked men burst in. But this time our guards knew how to handle them. They jumped on the new arrivals and pinned them to the ground. After that I rounded up my family and fled."

Ivan was ecstatic to find his sister again.

"I'm so glad you've come back," she said, embracing him. "Our father is very strict, it's true, but he loves us and he's not a bad sort."

"He's not a bad sort," Ivan retorted. "Yet he offends God in everything he does. He smokes Job cigarettes and leaves his cigarette butts just about everywhere. Night after night he invites women to the house, sometimes very young girls, still prepubescent."

"But nowhere in the Koran does it say a man must not frequent women. What are you blaming him for? Is it your job in the militia which has changed your character? You've become radicalized."

She used the word for the first time. Up till then she had not been aware of how her brother had changed. Suddenly she realized how much.

The compound was undergoing great upheavals. First of all, Lansana was living openly with Vica, a Haitian singer with a lovely contralto voice whom he had met at a concert in Rotterdam. Vica had lost her husband and six children in the last earthquake in Port-au-Prince. She had remained almost a week under the rubble until some rescuers had pulled her out to a cheering crowd. She now had one foot in the supernatural and spent most of her time singing traditional Haitian melodies:

Twa fey / twa raisin / jeté blyé ranmassé songé / mwen gen basen twa / mwen twa fey tombé ladan'n / chajé bato z'anj la.

Vica and Ivana got on like a house on fire, speaking Creole and whispering little secrets.

Lansana also got it into his head to regulate the status of the griots. Since the noble families were no longer capable of ensuring their subsistence given the insecurity which prevailed in the country, many of the griots were often reduced to begging. They would turn up uninvited at baptisms or weddings, croaking a song of praise in exchange for a plate of *fonio*. Why couldn't the state pay them an allowance and hire them as civil servants like Sékou Touré did in Guinea?

This idea by no means met with general approval. Its critics claimed that what happened in Guinea would happen in Mali, i.e. the griots would sing a lot of rubbish praising the merits of the regime and the grandeur of its ministers. It should be remembered that originally the griot cared little for fortune or power and praised virtuousness. They were masters of eloquence for those who deserved it. None of these objections bothered Lansana. Despite the squabbling, the griots emerged out of every crack and cranny and dashed to Lansana's place so as to be acknowledged by their benefactor.

Finally, as if these innovations were not enough, Lansana created an ensemble which he called The Voice of God out of provocation, for he was intent on showing everyone that music is a noble expression and must be safeguarded at all costs. Ivan thus found himself marginalized since his sister was monopolized by Vica and even more so by her father. In the evening, armed with a computer, she made a list of all the names of the griots, their addresses, their favorite instruments, and their repertoires.

Lansana organized more and more concerts and meetings throughout Mali, one of which was to be performed in Timbuktu, a decision which was by no means a coincidence. Timbuktu, the Pearl of the Desert, much praised by René Caillé, had been occupied militarily by the jihadists for many long months. They had destroyed its mausoleums and endeavored to lay hands on the rare manuscripts owned by the mosques. Thanks to the intervention of a foreign power they had been chased out, but still remained present in the surrounding desert and continued their reign of terror over the population. Ivan insisted on accompanying them so as not to be separated any further from his sister. The voyage was planned in two phases. First of all, by road to Gao on the banks of the Niger River, and then on to Timbuktu by boat. Lansana therefore had bought four seats on the deck of the *Capitaine Sangara*.

"Why do you need a cabin?" he drily asked Ivan, who was complaining bitterly. "A seat on the deck is quite sufficient. The voyage only lasts two or three days."

If it hadn't been for the resentment he felt towards his father, Ivan would have found the trip on the waters of the Joliba quite charming. When you opened your eyes in the morning you were plunged into a fluffy whiteness. Not a sound. Draped in mist the Somono fishermen were already casting their nets. The boat glided over the water, and the huge shapes of animals asleep in the fields could be seen. When the sun dawned it immediately began its ascension in the sky. There then followed the heat which gradually seeped over the land while the tightly shut doors of the huts slowly opened like large frightened eyes. Children set off for school while the infants stretched themselves in the relative cool of the morning. At noon everything fell calm and silent. At dusk singers and musicians emerged from every corner of the boat, which became a floating orchestra.

When they arrived at Timbuktu, night was about to fall. The sky was streaked in red and the roughcast white of the huts was turning blue. Timbuktu was in a state of siege as the jihadists had threatened an imminent attack. The streets were deserted. Only black-and-white soldiers could be seen patrolling on foot or in military jeeps. They would roughly pull over the rare passersby and ask for their identities. To Lansana's surprise nobody had come to meet them at the landing stage. No matter, they knew where to go and they set off on foot for the house of El Hadj Baba Abou, an Arab, who had been the former rector of the Sankoré Mosque. He had been blinded in both eyes for refusing to hand over the rare manuscripts in his library to the jihadists. Despite this disability, he remained affable and courteous. He conveyed his concern about the rumor that the concert would be canceled because of the state of emergency.

"The concert canceled?" Lansana cried. "That's exactly what the jihadists want. Their intention is to force us to obey the diktat of the irascible and evil God they have fabricated and destroy everything that is good and beautiful in life."

"What is good and beautiful in life?" Ivan asked sarcastically.

"Creating music and literature, that's what's good and beautiful," replied his father.

El Hadj Baba Abou held out a calming hand to cut short this burgeoning quarrel and sent one of his servants out for news. He returned shortly afterwards to announce that the concert had truly been canceled. Lansana then went into a fit of rage which only he could justify and, without saying a word, downed in next to no time the delicious meal prepared by El Hadj Baba Abou's cook. He then rushed out dragging Vica along with him.

A few moments later, since El Hadj Baba Abou had buried his nose in the Koran, Ivan had nothing left to do but accompany his sister to the women's compound where she was to spend the night.

"What a rude lout our father is!" he ranted.

Ivana shrugged her shoulders leniently.

"El Hadj Baba Abou and Lansana have known each other for years, ever since they were students. Don't meddle in their affairs."

Their stay, however, was not lacking in charm. Kidal couldn't hold a candle to Timbuktu, which is a literary icon. Ivan had never seen such a countless number of mosques and shrines, masterpieces of African art. He peeked into Koranic schools where young students wearing white caps chanted verses from the Koran. His heart skipped a beat. And what if God really did exist? And this life on earth, so precarious and disappointing, was merely preparation for the splendors of the after-life? In the evenings he would wander the narrow, winding streets in the dark. Night-lights twinkled here and there. All you could hear were the pounding feet of the soldiers on patrol. He was not frightened. On the contrary, he felt safer since the city seemed better protected than Kidal.

Every evening he set off to look for Lansana, who disappeared mysteriously with Vica as soon as dinner was over. Unfortunately Ivan could never find him. As a rule he ended the night at the Albaradiou caravanserai where three Fulani acrobats could usually be seen clowning around.

Aware of the prejudice the cancellation of the concert had caused Lansana, the governor-general of Timbuktu had him driven back to Kidal with his family in a car which belonged to his personal fleet: an ostentatious Mercedes 280 SL, blue as the sky. This gave Ivan food for thought. Do the governing classes get all the pleasures on earth? Women, villas, cars. While El Hadj Baba Abou, the remarkable man Ivan had so admired because of his bearing and knowledge of the suras, possessed nothing at all, this obscure governor-general seemed to be living in the lap of luxury. It merely confirmed Ivan's opinion that the world was not made right, and half-heartedly he found his way back to the Alfa Yaya barracks.

We now begin a chapter of our story which is not reliable. We have no proof of what really happened and must rely on suppositions that cannot be trusted.

Every town has its immigrant neighborhood. Whether they come from Burkina Faso, Benin, Ghana, or Congo, men leave their country in search of that rare commodity: work. As a rule, they leave their wives and children behind. The immigrant neighborhoods are miserable, poorly maintained, and often outright insalubrious. Cafés, restaurants, bars, dives, or joints—call them what you want—swarm along every street. Kidal was no exception to the rule. Its immigrant neighborhood was called Kisimu Banco. On several occasions the government had threatened to raze it but never did.

Why was Lansana such a frequent visitor to the Etoile des Neiges, a low dive owned by a Moor, El Hassan, a kind of whorehouse where they traded in feminine flesh? It was said that Lansana was in his element in such a place and had numerous partners, sometimes very young. It was even claimed that he had relations with girls as young as twelve or thirteen. Who took offense at his behavior? The fact remains that Lansana was stabbed to death coming home from the Etoile des Neiges. Did a quarrel with an unknown rival degenerate into a brawl? Did he fall victim to a jealous husband or a father angered at seeing his daughter deflowered? Or to a hooligan, a thief, or a thug who was roaming freely through the streets at that time of night? As usual, there were different versions. Some said Lansana had collapsed at a crossroads, others claimed he was killed not far from his home. Another version was that he had been murdered in his bed and the crime had been made to look like a suicide.

His death caused a huge sensation throughout the country. The griots came from all over to sing the praises of his family, the Diarras, who had once governed Segu so masterfully. They did not fail to highlight the talent of this son of royal origin who had not been ashamed to devote his life to music. For days his compound was a throbbing heart from which a range of sounds could be heard.

The police conducted a thorough inquiry. They arrested all those who had quarreled with Lansana, and God knows there were quite a few. Nevertheless, they did not arrest Ivan, who quarreled with his father for no reason at all, as parricide is unknown in Mali. To plunge one's knife into the blood of a father is a madness common only to Westerners.

Lansana had kept his little secret well hidden. He had amassed the royalties from the sale of his records in Japan, where he was very popular, in an account in Switzerland. Consequently Ivan and Ivana both had the same idea: bring their mother over to Mali. Without a doubt it would be a pleasant surprise as Simone had never left the Antilles. She had been separated from her children for so many months now. To their amazement they received a negative answer to their offer. Even more surprising, Father Michalou and Simone were getting married and intended to renovate Father Michalou's house at Pointe Diamant, and as such had no time to waste traveling.

For Ivan and Ivana, Simone's reply was a slap in the face, although Ivana endeavored to console herself by imagining that her mother would not grow old alone and could lean on a companion.

Vica was the second sensation. She began to emerge from her hut at night dressed only in a pair of red briefs. For hours on end she would utter incomprehensible words while downing small glasses of a liquid at regular intervals from bottles marked *Rhum Barbancourt*. Any attempt to get her back to bed usually ended in a fistfight interspersed with screams. After two weeks of this little game she packed her bags and left on a plane for Port-au-Prince.

"This compound has a bad smell," she had screamed before she left. "All night long I see Lansana marching up and down. A crime has been committed and we'll never know who did it."

Vica had scarcely turned her back than the malicious gossip began to flow. She had gone back to a man, a man she had never broken up with, a man almost twenty years younger than her. The same one who had spent the last rainy season locked up in her hut, a poet, a certain Jean-Jacques, nicknamed the Batrachian because of his two huge eyes like those of a toad. Very popular in Haiti, he would spout his texts day after day for hours over the state radio. Shortly after she left, Ivana received a package from Vica containing a letter carefully sealed inside a bistre-colored envelope. It contained a small collection of poems entitled *Mon pays verse des larmes de sang* (My Country Weeps Tears of Blood). Here is the text of the letter Ivana received.

My dear little sister,
I miss you so much and I remember our long conversations at my place when we discussed our dreams. I found my island again both monstrous and magnificent. On the sidewalks around the Iron Market there are piles of naive

paintings. Some are real works of genius depicting *loas* descending from heaven on golden swings. There's music and singing everywhere.

But my people are too poor and still housed in torn canvas tents. The children are running around bare-bottomed, famished, with their willies out. There's no other place in the world so desolate.

I'm enclosing the collection of poems by a young man who is more than a brother to me. Savor every drop of this magic potion.

With love and kisses,

Your sister Vica

Unfortunately Ivana appreciated only what she did not understand. That's why she was mad about René Char. Consequently she never opened the book, and *Mon pays verse des larmes de sang* remained untouched. If we may take this opportunity to give our point of view, Ivana was wrong not to leaf through the poems, for they contain some real gems. For example, the poem on page ten begins in French with a reference to the great Aimé Césaire: *Blood! Blood! So much blood in my memory. My memory is filled with blood.* But on the very next line he differentiates himself from his model and writes in Creole: *Pigé zié, pigé zié* (Weep, Weep). The poem then becomes a composition worthy of the best of Sonny Rupaire, our national poet.

As for Ivan, he was increasingly determined to leave the compound. It was not only because it was overcrowded, swamped with false relatives, useless mouths to feed, and the professionally unemployed. It was not because it was bombarded with evil spirits, as Vica claimed, but because rumors, malicious rumors, had begun to circulate. When Lansana was alive, his presence had muzzled people's mouths. Once he was gone, mouths opened and guffawed. Why? Judge for yourselves. What was the mystery behind this boy built like an athlete who never screwed around? He had no known mistress, whereas at his age he could easily have been the father of one or two sons. What was he hiding? The explanation of course was plain to see. As a result, beautiful young men began posturing and showing off their attributes in front of Ivan. Momo Diallo, the well-known playwright, nicknamed Tennessee Williams, wrote to Ivan inviting him to be the guest of honor at the first Gay Parade in Bamako. Much more serious was the fact that this malicious gossip forced open the doors of the Alfa Yaya barracks and swept inside. Ivan was given a nickname which we translate as best we can to: "He who doesn't know how to use his tool cutter." Instead of handling their Kalashnikovs, the recruits started mimicking gay behavior. One day the commander in chief of his division locked Ivan in his office and threw himself onto him.

"I don't like boys," Ivan protested, about to burst into tears.

"That's a likely story! Perhaps you prefer them younger, less beefy than me."

Bullied, Ivan was at a total loss. What was to become of him? The idea haunted him. Then something only a homosexual could come up with so he wouldn't be outed: take a wife. Yes, he needed to take a wife and show the entire town. But where should he look? He imagined in disgust the body of one of these females pressing up against him.

After days of hesitation, he set his heart on a close friend of Ivana's, which was perhaps also a way of remaining close to his sister. Aminata Traoré was not yet twenty. Everyone agreed she was lovely, with her curious little straight nose and her fiery eyes. Her young years had not yet fully formed her personality and she radiated gentleness. Employed like Ivana at the Sundjata Keita Orphanage, she adored the little children in her charge. Seducing her was no trouble at all: a few well-turned words, a few smiles, and some presents such as *rahat lokoums*, which she was mad about and which could be bought on the black market in town.

Then the moment arrived, the moment of conquest. Aminata Traoré lived not far from the Diarra compound. Once the mint tea had been downed, Ivan had no trouble shutting himself up with her in his room. Utterly lacking in desire he made his move towards the pretty body which was to be his. First of all he feared he would make a fool of himself. Fortunately nature came to the rescue and he managed quite well.

"This makes me so happy," Aminata moaned, once the act had been consumed. "I never thought that one day I would be so happy. I've been watching you for some time now and I'm not the only one. But you seemed out of reach and inaccessible."

Annoyed by this verbiage, Ivan found nothing to say. Unexpectedly he was ashamed of himself and had the loathsome impression of being a seducer. He rapidly took his leave and returned home.

The night was jet black, which added to his feeling of having committed a despicable crime. Very quickly, however, the news of his relationship with Aminata made the rounds of the compound.

One evening Ivana rushed into his hut.

"I've just heard the news and am so glad," she cried. "I hear you want to marry my friend Aminata Traoré?"

"Marry?" Ivan groaned. "That's saying a lot."

"What exactly do you intend to do?" Ivana asked severely. "She's young and innocent and deserves to be your wife."

Her insistence was not entirely without reason. On learning of her brother's liaison, Ivana had cried a lot. That brother she believed was hers ever since they were born. Her brother who some called her lover. Then she blamed herself for being jealous, which was uncalled for. Her brother was not her property.

"I'll make no bones about it," Ivan explained. "Men have certain desires unknown to women."

He then hugged his sister passionately, which only increased tenfold his indifference to fondling Aminata. The hollow between his pectorals was made for Ivana to nestle her head. Her legs were designed to wrap around his. Her sexual desire, ah her sexual desire, Ivan didn't dare think of it. Seeing as Aminata's mother and young sister had moved house to God knows where, Ivan soon moved in with her. Living with her had its positive side. She polished and shone the buttons on his militia uniform. She made him long flowing boubous so that he could relax coming home from the barracks. She waxed and polished his shoes and fitted him with oriental slippers to rest his feet. All these considerations, nevertheless, irritated him. Was that all a woman was good for? He compared her with his sister who was independent, spoiled by her mother, and hopeless at housekeeping. Yet she had read André Breton, Paul Éluard, and René Char and was cultivated.

Ivan was bored in Aminata's company. Once the evening meal was over he would read his Koran, noting down the particularly difficult passages so that he could ask Ismaël, his superior in the Army of Shadows, for an explanation. Meanwhile Aminata would watch stupid programs on the television, a habit he had not taken the trouble to cure her of since at least during that time she wasn't talking.

One evening she came over to him with a winsome expression, which made him fear the worst. She crouched down at his feet.

"I have a wonderful, big surprise for you," she said. "The Lord has blessed our union. I'm carrying your baby."

Pregnant! Already! Ivan thought, horrified. They had only been together three months. She continued, little doubting the reaction her words echoed in him.

"Tata Rachida felt my stomach and she thinks it will be a boy. You must be so proud."

The following day at the barracks Ivan returned from practice, scarcely recovered from his emotions, to the announcement that someone was waiting for him. It was Ivana, overexcited.

"She's pregnant," she cried. "You have to marry her."

"Why?" Ivan calmly retorted. "Did Lansana marry our mother when she discovered she was pregnant? Was Maeva, our grandmother, married? I won't be the first man to father a bastard."

Thereupon Ivana went into a violent fit of rage, which Ivan of course could not resist, and the wedding was decided. From the information we have, we can safely say that Ivana's anger was pretense. Thanks to the tearful explications of the innocent Aminata, Ivana knew all about her brother's behavior: a reluctant lover, little prone to caresses, preferring to snore with open mouth rather than fondle the naked body cuddling up to him.

"He turns his back on me in bed," Aminata moaned. "He turns his back on me and I have to sleep beside this mountain of indifference."

Ivana knew her empire was intact. This liaison was nothing but a sham designed to hide a passion that was unshakeable.

Ivan's wedding was twice as splendid as the celebrations for his baptism. Not only did the Diarras, the Traorés, relatives, and friends crowd into town from all over Mali, but also from every corner of this earth where they had scattered to find a living. Everyone lamented Lansana's absence. How happy and proud he would have been to see his son married and throwing down roots in the soil of Mali. Ivan had come back home.

Nevertheless, the glitziest guest was Aminata's sister, cousin, or aunt—you never know what to call them— Aïssata Traoré, who taught at McGill University in Canada. She had had to leave Mali in a hurry after publishing her first book, *Africa up for Auction*, and regularly printed scathing political pamphlets in which she criticized Africa in general. She was a very pretty woman. It was said she lived with a Canadian but had been careful not to bring him with her. Those who passed her in the street lingered to watch her, intrigued by her dress: baggy *sarouel* trousers usually worn by men, and a military-style tunic. Aïssata kept open house at the Three Aces bar in the center of Kidal where dozens of youngsters, skipping classes at the teachers' training college, gathered to listen to her. For the very first time, Ivan found himself uncontrollably attracted to a woman. He liked the shape of her face, her graceful and well-proportioned figure, but above all her biting and scornful frame of mind. When he accompanied her back home of an evening Ivan imagined he could spend the night with her, chatting or necking, he didn't know which. He was not surprised, then, when Ismaël asked him to convey an invitation for her to give a lecture for the Army of

Shadows. Aïssata first of all tried to be difficult and she only agreed at the last minute, the day before she was due to leave for Canada.

When she arrived at the Army of Shadows headquarters, the courtyard was packed with people. Extra benches and chairs had to be added. Aïssata was seated on a platform surrounded by the entire staff of teachers. She began her speech in her pretty foreign accent.

"I am not endeavoring to make apologies," she said, "but to understand. Jihadism is the result of centuries of oppression and exclusion. It did not emerge from the Gulf War, and the Bush family, both father and son, are mere puppets. It took root in colonization and perhaps even before that."

She suddenly raised an avenging fist.

"But the jihadists are only intent on killing and killing. Death is not an answer. What we need is to engage a new type of dialogue between peoples so that there are neither oppressors nor oppressed."

Listening to her, Ivan's entire body began to tremble. Did she realize where she was? Did she know the true nature of those around her? All it needed was for Ismaël to signal to the many militants carrying Kalashnikovs and roaming at liberty for her to be gunned down.

But the evening went off without a hitch and ended with a standing ovation. Then Ismaël and some members of his team took Aïssata to dinner at La Criée, a seafood restaurant owned by a Frenchman from Marseille who boasted that he had spent fifty years in Africa and never been put off by the numerous terrorist attacks. They were served oysters flown in overnight, which they downed with ginger beer since most of the guests were Muslim and didn't drink alcohol.

In the early hours of the morning Ismaël asked Ivan to

accompany Aïssata back home.

"Take good care of her," he smiled. "You know at this early hour anything can happen."

The streets in Kidal were in fact jet black, and the street lamps set at irregular intervals lit up just a few squares of sidewalk. Apart from these small patches of light, they were wrapped in dense darkness. With beating heart Ivan took Aïssata's arm and they arrived home safe and sound. Moments before entering her bedroom Aïssata grabbed his hand and drew him close to her whispering, "You want it as much as I do. Why should we deny ourselves?"

The next morning Ivan woke up all alone in his bed, half-covered with a crumpled sheet. He tried to stand up but his legs were shaking. Why were they shaking? It was as if a fire was raging inside him and had drained him of all his strength. He managed to walk into the next room where Aminata, in tears, was embracing Aïssata who was formally dressed in a navy-blue suit and carrying her coat over her arm while the concierge was loading her luggage into a taxi. Ivan couldn't understand what he was feeling. Had he imagined the passion and frenzy of the night he had just spent? How had he managed to get back into bed with his wife? In the meantime, Aïssata and Aminata were holding each other in a passionate embrace. As Aïssata dived into the taxi, Aminata again burst into tears.

"She didn't stay long enough," she groaned.

Ivan was at a loss for words. Had he really dreamed it all? Every morning after that he began to look for the mailman's bicycle hoping for a letter from Aïssata, but he never heard from her. He even went so far as to buy her latest book, *The Rape of a Continent*, but he could never make it past page ten.

Gradually he fell into a rut of boredom. Aminata no longer felt like making love or begging for meagerly dished-out kisses. She was only concerned with the movements inside her body, running her husband's hand over her belly so he could feel the frolicking of her fetus.

"It's a boy," she said. "Look at the shape of my belly. What's more, the doctor said so after my last ultrasound. We'll call him Fadel. I've always loved that name. It was the name of a little boy turned into a bird by the magician Soumaoro Kanté. He managed to escape from the cage where Kanté had locked him up. Do you know this story?"

Ivan, who had heard this story over a hundred times, politely shook his head. Sometimes he caught himself crying without understanding why. The only consolation could have been to throw himself into the arms of his sister and be devoured by her kisses. But Ivana was invisible. Courted by half a dozen suitors, she spent most of her time fighting off their advances. In short, life for Ivan had become insipid. It was then that an unexpected event of a very serious nature occurred.

One morning the militiamen were summoned to one of the rooms in the Alfa Yaya barracks. Those who were due to go on exercises stayed behind, those on leave were called back, and those who patrolled in the North seeking out terrorists were brought back to town by the truckload. At the end of the morning, in front of an assembly of officers in full uniform, Abdouramane Sow took to the floor, speaking in a solemn tone of voice. The ballistic tests conducted in Germany had proved today that the attackers of El Cobra, responsible for the massacre at the Ultra Vocal concert hall, were not jihadists but members of the militia.

"There were four of them," he hammered out. "Two armed with Kalashnikovs, whose numbers we have, and two others armed with Lugers which they must have procured from an arms trafficker. Soon we will know the names of these scum. We'll arrest them and inflict on them the punishment they deserve."

Ivan managed to make it home, where he learned, thanks to the television which was left on all day long by Djenaba, the little servant, that a curfew had been declared. A curfew! This meant that nobody was allowed out of doors after 10 p.m. and identity checks would start at 8 p.m. Aminata was not home to discuss these terrible events and was probably busy talking about the contents of her womb with one of her friends.

Anyone who has not experienced the fright of their lives has no idea how a human being reacts at such a moment. The blood becomes more intense, more alert, and flows faster. A series of rapid decisions run through the brain and one has to weigh the arguments for and against in next to no time. In other words, one's intelligence is galvanized. Ivan immediately realized that he was in terrible danger and had to flee as quickly as he could. Leave town. Leave the country. He wrote a letter to the only person who counted in his eyes, his sister Ivana, and rapidly described his plan. He would not travel north, east, or west, all of which were bristling with militia patrols. He would take the southern route and make for Gao where it would be very easy to reach Niamey in Niger. Once there, since his French passport was still valid, he would have no difficulty in taking a plane to France. As soon as he was settled in Paris he would have her come over. Once he had finished writing his missive, a thought crossed his mind. Would he need money? He knew that Aminata distrusted banks, for some unknown reason, and kept sums of cash in the chest of drawers in the bedroom. He dashed in and, after emptying some of the drawers, laid hands on the treasure and pocketed it without remorse. As a precautionary measure he decided it was better to leave the house and run to the Cheikh Anta Diop hostel, where all sorts of homeless converged. A young girl wearing a thick scarf in jihad fashion sat at the reception. She examined him from head to foot.

"You homeless?" she said jokingly.

Ivan invented a preposterous story on the spot: he had quarreled with his wife and did not want to spend another night with her under the same roof. The young girl shrugged her shoulders signifying she did not believe a word he said, but nevertheless allocated him a bed in an overcrowded dormitory.

He couldn't sleep a wink all night, constantly disturbed by the chattering and comings and goings of those who claimed they were looking for sleep. From the open window came the meowing of cats squabbling over a quarry or territory, and the sound of rats scampering after each other.

At five in the morning Ivan was already at the bus station. Alas, all the bush taxis for Gao had already left and he had to make do with a bus which served the neighboring localities. He set his sights on El Markham, a small town situated five kilometers from Gao according to the tub-of-lard bus driver who was scraping and polishing his teeth. Ivan sat right at the back and wrapped a sort of keffiyeh scarf around his face so as to hide his features. They reached El Markham only at nightfall.

If Ivan had been in another frame of mind he would certainly have noticed the splendor of the landscape around Kidal, where the desert edges into a realm of fawn-, ochre-, or mauve-colored sand, depending on the whim of the sun that sat in the middle of the sky like an unblinking, wide-open eye. Gradually a landscape of stone reappears and sharp, jagged cliffs emerge. They stopped to eat at an inn owned by a couple of Italians. The menu consisted of vegetable soup, chicken, and a delicious polenta. Ivan would have liked to ask these two jovial and smiling Italians why two Westerners had left behind the splendors of the Capitol in Rome and the Leaning Tower of Pisa to end up in this godforsaken hole.

Apart from the moiré silk of the river winding as far as the eye could see, the village of El Markham was not much to look at: two or three streets intersecting at right angles and lined with corrugated-iron and mud-brick shacks. The village was swarming with men of all ages, including human smugglers, recognizable by their superior airs, riding on spluttering motorbikes.

Ivan was shivering in his cotton shirt, for the night was cold. In order to warm up he entered La Bonne Table, a dirty, cramped little restaurant, as unappealing as the rest of the place. A tiny television set was crackling in a corner. It wasn't long before a young man came and sat down at his table and began talking.

"I'm sorry," Ivan replied. "I don't speak your language."

"It's Bambara, brother," the young man said in surprise. "You must be a foreigner. Where are you from?"

This innocent question brought back memories of the years Ivan had lived in Guadeloupe. He forgot the dark side of those years and embroidered them with nostalgia. It was a time when it seemed he had been happy and carefree. Above all he thought of his mother.

"Don't call me brother," Ivan replied drily, since he had taken an instant dislike to the expression when he lived in Lansana's compound. "Let me tell you, I come from far, far away, from the other side of the world. And how about you? Are you from El Markham?"

Instead of answering, the young man pointed to the bag set down beside him.

"Is that your bag?" he asked. "Is it well locked? Is the key in a safe place? Around your neck for example?"

"Why are you asking me all these questions?" Ivan said, exasperated.

"It's because El Markham is a dangerous place. It's a nest of thieves, crooks, and con artists. I know what I'm talking about. My name is Rahiri. My brother and I have a jeep and we've been smuggling travelers for five years. We know all the border points and all the customs officers."

"You own a jeep?" Ivan interrupted him, suddenly interested. "Could you take me as far as Niamey or even to Gao? I have a valid passport and I'm looking for an airport where I can fly to Europe."

The young man made a face.

"Niamey's too risky, too many police officers over there," he said. "Well, we'll think it over once my brother is back, since he's the one who decides."

While they were finishing their meal of mutton stew a man burst in, a fat, fleshy, bald individual whose clothes were too tight for him. Rahiri suddenly got up and ran towards him.

"This is Ousmane," he exclaimed. "My older brother. Have you had a good journey?"

Without answering, Ousmane held out a limp hand for Ivan and sat down at their table. Rahiri explained the conversation. With a negative grimace Ousmane shook his head in turn.

"Niamey is too dangerous," he repeated. "But we'll talk

about it tomorrow. I've just driven five hundred kilometers and I'm dead tired. First of all let us get some rest."

The three men went out into the night lit only by the glimmer of a new moon. They walked down the main street until they reached a kind of square, where they skirted the men who were lying on public benches, mats, or even on the stony ground.

Standing in front of a shack with the notice *Rooms to Let*, Ousmane drew a key from his pocket and they went inside: three filthy bedrooms, a bathroom hollowed out in the center, and a Turkish-style toilet. A powerful smell of urine and excrement caught Ivan's throat. Nevertheless, he told himself that under the current circumstances he couldn't be too difficult. Consequently he entered one of the bedrooms and lay down without a word of protest on the inflatable mattress Rahiri had designated. Despite the stink and the mosquitoes he immediately fell asleep.

He had been asleep one or two hours when the door opened gently on its hinges. A woman entered wearing a heavy navy-blue burka. She sat down beside Ivan, and good-humoredly, it seemed, began to nibble his ear. Then she moved down to his mouth and gave him several kisses. Ivan was amazed at her audacity. But he was too exhausted to resist.

"Take this burka off," he told her. "It's ridiculous."

She obeyed him, threw off the heavy blue veil in which she was wrapped, and he found himself in the arms of a skeleton. Terrified, he ran to switch on the light. The squalid room was empty. It was merely a dream. A bad dream.

When he awoke the second time, the window was streaked with light. He called out to his companions but there was no answer. The shack was deserted. Rahiri and Ousmane had vanished. As well as his bag, he realized. He ran outside. The sky was now bluish. The men who were sleeping on the square had rolled up their mats and were washing their faces in the public fountain. One of them, his cheeks covered in foam, was shaving while he whistled. No sign of Rahiri. No sign of Ousmane. As fast as he could, Ivan ran to La Bonne Table where he had dined the night before. The restaurant was closed. He shook the metal shutter furiously with his foot but nobody responded to the din. Still no sign of Rahiri or Ousmane. Ivan ran back along the road he had just taken and ventured down the neighboring streets, one of which was comically named General de Gaulle. After a while he had to resign himself to the fact he had behaved like an idiot. He had been taken for a novice. The two men had stripped him of everything he owned.

What do you do when you find yourself without ID, without money, and without friends, miles from home? You cry. That's all you can do. Sitting on a public bench, Ivan had no idea his body could weep so many tears.

Gradually, however, he found enough courage to act before considering himself beaten. Rahiri and Ousmane had not disappeared into thin air. They must have left clues. Someone must know them in the neighborhood. Last night at dinner the waiter spoke to them as if they were regular customers. Resolutely, Ivan stood up and made his way back to La Bonne Table. As he approached, a man, a white man, drew up level with him, came to a standstill, gaped on seeing him, and grabbed him by the arm, whispering, "Don't stay here, come with me."

Ivan tried to shake him off.

"Are you crazy? Take your hands off me!"

The man looked left and right and, lowering his voice,

asked, "Aren't you Ivan Némélé? I've just seen you on television. You have a price on your head."

"What!" Ivan shouted, immediately regaining the use of his legs, and began to run hand in hand with the stranger.

The two men climbed into a dilapidated jeep parked nearby.

The white man was skinny, ascetic even, with vivid blue eyes set in an emaciated face. His long graying hair curled down to his shoulders. A genuine Jesus Christ, you might say. With a roar of the car's engine he shot off at top speed.

After a while he held out his hand to Ivan.

"My name is Alix Alonso," he introduced himself. "I hear you are responsible for the attack that killed a certain Boris Kanté, otherwise known as El Cobra."

Outside the car the décor was picture perfect: a blue sky in which the sun was slowly settling into place; the river sparkling without a ripple between reddish stone cliffs; and, inside the car, a feverish conversation between two overexcited men.

"Me?" cried Ivan. "Never in my life. I never committed such a crime!"

He knew that one must always proclaim one's innocence, even under the worst circumstances.

"You'll be safe with us," Alix continued. "I live alone with my wife and nobody ever comes to visit."

For ten or so kilometers the car traveled alongside the river. Suddenly it turned its back, veered left, and set off along a rough stony track. They drove under an arch where the following words were written: *The Last Resort*. However hard Ivan searched his memories from school, he could not understand what those words meant.

At a bend in the road, a stone house appeared, spacious

but plain, surrounded by a wide terrace shaded by yellow striped parasols. A woman could be seen lying on a deck chair, her back resting on a pile of cushions. Her feet were wrapped in navy-blue woolen slippers without a sole, as if she never walked in them.

"This is my wife, Cristina," Alix explained. "She's disabled."

Cristina had the same blue eyes as her husband and her smile was marked with a singular grace. Her face fell when her husband explained the circumstances in which he had met Ivan and who he was.

"You have nothing to fear with us," she reassured him. "Alix must have told you we never have any visits."

Thereupon Alix took Ivan familiarly by the arm and led him inside. The minimal furnishing was not lacking in charm. Alix preceded Ivan and opened the door of a comfortable bedroom that looked out onto a section of the garden.

"Feel at home here," he repeated with a wide grin.

Ivan discovered in astonishment that Alix and Cristina seldom left The Last Resort. They had no friends, and no servants working for them. In order to entertain Cristina, Alix had bought a gigantic, ultramodern television set which broadcast the most unlikely channels, such as the one from Wallis and Futuna. You could watch endless programs where the king decorated a number of his subjects. It was thanks to this television that Ivan was kept up to date about the tsunami which had swept over Kidal after he left. Birame and his two younger brothers had been arrested in Djenné, where they had taken refuge at a relative's place. Oddly enough Ismaël had been left untroubled, as had every member of the Army of Shadows. What broke Ivan's heart and made it bleed was the fact that both Ivana and his wife, Aminata, had been arrested. What he didn't know was that they hadn't stayed very long in prison, since both of them had foolproof alibis. On the evening of the attack that took the life of El Cobra, the nurses at the Sundjata Keita Orphanage swore that both women were giving the infants their baby food and putting them to bed. There was also another story that was badmouthed around: apparently Abdouramane Sow was in love with the lovely Ivana and wanting to take her as a second wife, he had rapidly liberated her together with her sister-in-law.

"Don't take any notice of all this agitation," Alix advised Ivan. "When matters have blown over I myself will go and fetch your sister in Kidal. I'll drive her here and then you can both take a flight from Niamey, which is only about five hundred kilometers from here."

"You forget I no longer have a passport," Ivan groaned.

"I'll find you another one," Alix promised jokingly. "Which one would you like? Libyan, Lebanese, or Syrian? Nothing works better in this country than the trafficking of false passports."

Cristina squeezed Ivan's hand and softly inquired, "Ivana's your twin sister, am I right? Just like I'm Alix's twin."

Ivan had but one regret. Why hadn't he made love to Ivana before being separated from her? All these years of platonic passion were ridiculous! When they're reunited he will take his revenge. He'll make her howl and scream and writhe beneath him! But will he ever see her again? Perhaps he was being punished because of his real or imaginary misdemeanor with Aïssata. There were moments when he sobbed bitterly.

Alix Alonso and Cristina Serfati had known each other from the cradle for they were the offspring of two families of acrobats who performed at the Seventh Wonder circus. They had been born on the same day in the same year which allowed them to think that not only were they simply made for each other but they were one and the same person. They got married at the age of eighteen, unable to postpone any longer the merger of their two beings.

The Seventh Wonder circus had been founded in Bordeaux in 1758 by Thibault de Poyen. We know for a fact that he was of mixed blood: the son of a woman from what later came to be known as Nigeria, and Aymery de Poyen, a French man who hunted slaves in Africa. Little Thibault was brought to France when he was very young, and we have all the letters his mother, Ekanem Bassey, wrote inquiring about his condition. We don't know, however, the reasons why the circus was created. Was it Thibault's yearning for his mother or his lost homeland that drove him, on reaching his majority, to collect wild animals, lion tamers, acrobats, and dancers of all sorts? Whatever the case, the Seventh Wonder circus became increasingly popular. In summer it entertained children in the South of France. In winter it traveled to the French-speaking regions of Africa. The two countries where it met with its biggest successes were Algeria and Mali, where it set up its colorful tents near Bamako.

Unfortunately, colonization, which destroys everything in its path, destroyed it along with all the rest, while the popularity of the circus throughout the world diminished and disappeared.

When the Seventh Wonder circus finally closed its doors in 1995, Alix and Cristina had no difficulty finding work with the Barnum circus in the United States of America. Unfortunately, the day before they left to go and work for Barnum, during a farewell gala, Cristina, who was performing one of her acrobatic numbers, had a terrible accident. She survived but remained paraplegic. Alix and Cristina decided to sell everything they owned in France and go and live in Mali where they had grown up with their parents.

The first few years were not rosy. They disliked the town where they were living, a mixture of parochial traditions and the extravagance of a consumer society. Moreover, Alix was working himself to death, torn between his job in a cosmetics factory owned by some Germans and the constant attention needed by Cristina who Alix jealously guarded for himself. After a few years he got lucky; it happens sometimes. He discovered a formula for making shea butter and sold it to his bosses for a small fortune. Together with his wife he bought a patch of desert and turned it into an oasis. By dint of Alix's love Cristina managed to regain use of her arms, but that was about all.

Ivan had never been close to white folk. It was a species he saw only from a distance in Guadeloupe. In fact he had nothing against them, as despite Monsieur Jérémie's lessons colonization for Ivan remained an abstract concept. Much more often, it had been people with the same color as himself who had brought about his misfortune, Ivan felt. White folk were simply mysterious beings who spoke French with a strange accent. Eager for the sun, this sun which does so much harm, they crowded along the beaches at all times of day and lined up on the sidewalk to watch the carnival processions. Now, for the first time, Ivan found himself in close contact with a white couple.

At first Cristina felt uneasy with Ivan. She would jump at the sound of his voice and his rare bursts of laughter. Once a week Alix went to El Markham to stock up again with provisions, and Cristina didn't like staying alone with Ivan. Gradually, however, the ice melted and she warmed to him. Ivan caught himself finding her beautiful with her milky-white complexion, her extremely slim figure, and her hair, not marred by a single white streak, which flowed brown down to her shoulders.

Leaving Alix to take care of Cristina's intimate needs, Ivan began to feed her and help her drink like a baby. He peeled her fruit. He pushed her wheelchair onto the terrace and went down into the garden to have her admire the flowers which had just bloomed. During the afternoon siesta, unaware of his ancestral gesture, he would fan her to keep her cool. His feelings for Cristina were a mixture of tenderness, compassion—she must have suffered so much—and also desire, yes desire, when she revealed velvety patches of her skin.

He leafed through their shared photo albums, which portrayed her when she was an acrobat, her black leotard enhancing her magnificent body.

"I can't tell you what I felt," she said, "when I was up there at the top, the circus ring sparkling with lights down below my feet. I imagine that's how you feel at the moment of death: the soul flies away and leaves the body behind, a rough, unwieldy sheath. I felt like a goddess."

It would be an understatement to say that Alix and Cristina worshiped each other. They were one and the same: brother, sister, father, daughter, and lover, achieving the deep fusion that Ivan had dreamed of attaining with Ivana.

One afternoon while they were taking in the cool air, Cristina declared, "You are the son Alix and I could never have. You are everything that's missing."

Ivan burst out laughing.

"Your son? Me, a black guy? And you, both white?"

She looked him straight in the eye.

"Black, white! What does that mean? They are words which divide, invented by humans to cause harm. Color doesn't exist. I repeat, you are our son, full stop."

Night flung itself voraciously over The Last Resort. It was the same psychodrama every day. The sun, mortally wounded, ran to take refuge in a corner of the heavenly canopy, not without having first spilled long scarlet streaks. And its rival, the moon, never managed to replace it; however hard it puffed itself up, it always petered out and then darkness set in.

Cristina often had herself pushed along the river that flowed nearby. She watched for its swirling waters, convinced they were caused by the combat of the great manatees swimming down from the cold waters of the North, and remained hours looking at them. Alix had a great deal of trouble getting her to come home, insisting he disliked the way the impenetrable darkness wrapped itself over everything. Once back at the house, as a rule before going to bed, the trio would drink a sweet-smelling tamarind herb tea prepared by Alix. Then he and Cristina would each plant a kiss on Ivan's forehead and make their way to their bedroom. As for Ivan, he would head up to his room under the roof.

One evening the routine changed. Alix pushed aside his half-filled cup and declared, "Let's stop pretending. Ivan, you're coming with us."

Thereupon he stood up, pushing Cristina's wheelchair in front of him. Ivan was frank enough to confess that he had been waiting for this moment. Without uttering the slightest protest he stood up in turn and followed in their footsteps. We can hear the criticism of the righteous, who claim to be shocked by this ménage à trois. But they have no idea how those moments were immersed in poetry; how so much tenderness was applied by so many hands. Cristina's body was that of a young girl, her breasts uplifted, her stomach flat, and her legs as graceful as the columns of a temple. Alix's body was powerful and heavyset. As for Ivan's, he was built like a young bull capable of satisfying the entire human race. They made love until the morning hours without managing to satisfy each other's hunger. Henceforth it became a habit.

Confined to her invalid's wheelchair the entire day without being able to move her legs, Cristina dreamed at night of a whole different life from the one she was actually living. Every morning she would describe her dream to her two lovers who were also her two sons and offered them the tenderness of her surprisingly young and firm breasts.

"My body was floating like the cotton fibers of the silk cotton tree," she said. "I zigzagged across the sky. Sometimes I sat on a cloud and swung back and forth. From my swing, I could see the earth parched by the sun. I liked to float down and land at the top of a tree. I was particularly fond of flame trees and jacarandas. I also loved the perfume of the ylang-ylang and the scent of the cayenne rose bushes and arum lilies. Sometimes I floated even further down and took it into my head to race the humming birds. I was always last even though they stopped to gather nectar from every flower."

When he found himself alone with Ivan, Alix often burst into tears.

"It's my fault. I'm to blame for what happened to her. I shouldn't have left her for a second. Instead of which, I let her experiment in the air on her own."

Ivan dried Alix's tears.

"Don't say such nonsense. What happened was surely not your fault."

One day Alix looked him straight in the eye.

"I haven't told you what happened during that gala evening when she had her terrible accident. We were supposed to climb up together to the top, glide through the air, and shower the spectators with red rose petals. But just before our number I felt dizzy, so I let her go on her own. So you see, it's all my fault."

Disconcerted, Ivan clasped Alix in his arms, unable to find any words of comfort.

Four weeks passed in perfect bliss. Ivan got the impression that Cristina represented for him a mother, a sister, and a lover, whereas Alix was his somewhat scary double, exciting the brutality of his desire. Only Ivana was missing. Oh, if only she had been present, it would have been happiness fulfilled, utter perfection.

Nobody expected Alix to discover the trail of Rahiri and Ousmane again. It happened quite by chance. One Tuesday while he was at the market in El Markham he caught sight of two men near the second-hand clothing stands who perfectly matched Ivan's description. He threatened them with the Mauser he carried constantly under his shirt. In actual fact this weapon was illusory; Alix was against all forms of violence. In May 1968, while the riot police and students were waging a war to the death in the streets of Paris, Cristina and Alix had created an association called On the Trail of Mahatma Gandhi. They were also fiercely opposed to the war in Algeria and had sided with the draft dodgers. The Mauser, however, produced the desired effect.

Rahiri and Ousmane sat down and confessed they had robbed Ivan. They had sold his suitcase and his clothes, which were of good quality, but kept his French passport, which they hoped to sell for a small fortune. Rahiri and Ousmane agreed with Alix that they shouldn't involve the police, and in exchange for his silence they offered to drive Ivan as far as Niamey. They knew places along the border where there were neither police posts nor customs checkpoints.

On hearing what they had said, Ivan leapt up.

"They'll have nothing better to do," he cried, "than to hand me over to the militia and pocket the reward."

Alix firmly shook his head.

"I'm sorry to disappoint you but they know nothing of what you did in Kidal nor that you're wanted by the militia. People watch television without recalling what they've seen. They'll take you as far as Niamey, where you'll easily take a flight for France. Once you've arrived you'll write to your sister and have her come and join you."

Contrary to appearances, the trio was devastated. Ivan was going to leave. What would Alix and Cristina become, deprived of his youth, his beauty, and his ardor? The time left to them was spent sunk in deep despair.

The day before Rahiri and Ousmane were to come and pick him up, Alix took Ivan into a small, padlocked room at the back of the house. He slid open a panel and revealed a veritable war arsenal of machine guns, rifles, and revolvers. On seeing Ivan's amazement, he explained.

"You know I'm against all forms of violence. But I wasn't going to live in such an isolated spot all alone with a handicapped wife. In the event of an attack, I have to at least make a pretense of being able to defend myself."

Thereupon he handed Ivan a Luger which Ivan carefully replaced in its black leather holster.

"Take this, too," he continued, handing him a heavy envelope. "You'll need it."

The envelope contained a bundle of dollars. Ivan wondered how he could find words to thank him enough. He understood now what Adam must have felt when he was chased out of his earthly paradise. The Last Resort had been a haven of peace from which fate was now shouldering him out to continue down the chaotic and grim path of his life.

During these four weeks Ivan had been on intimate terms with two exceptional individuals and lived together a deep and complex relationship. Alix and Cristina knew nothing about him and yet they had opened their arms to him. Would he ever see them again? Perhaps never on this earth. Perhaps in that invisible other world religion promises us.

The following day Rahiri and Ousmane knocked on the door of The Last Resort at four in the morning. In spite of his grief, Alix in his generosity had made them sandwiches for the road. Cristina was sobbing and showering Ivan's cheeks with kisses.

Alix, however, had got it thoroughly wrong. Rahiri and Ousmane knew perfectly well who Ivan was and were fully aware of the rich reward for his capture. As soon as they had traveled a certain distance from The Last Resort they grabbed Ivan, savagely tied his wrists and heels with strong hemp cords, slipped a thick woolen hood over his head so that his shouts couldn't be heard, and headed for Kidal to hand him over to the militia.

Little did Alix know, moreover, that these two crooks planned to reveal the hiding place where Ivan had taken refuge and had made a perfect sketch of The Last Resort for the benefit of Abdouramane Sow.

And what about Ivana, you are asking? What has become of her? We haven't heard from her for some time. Forgive me, dear reader. It's because she is not involved in this business as much as her brother. We were afraid that the description of her schedule at the Sundjata Keita Orphanage would make boring reading: Six in the morning—wake the infants and potty practice. Breakfast—millet cereal and sorghum biscuits. Followed by long, stimulating exercises to awaken the children's intelligence. Lunch—millet cereal, smoked fish, hardboiled eggs, and ginger-flavored drink. Afternoon siesta and then educational games. Children's book-reading session. Free time. 8 p.m.—bedtime.

You see, this routine is not very appealing. Yet on second thoughts we realize there are a number of things missing from our description. For example, we haven't mentioned Ivana's reaction to Lansana's death. Unlike her brother, Ivana was very fond of her father. She had even come to realize that his absence during her childhood had made her feel vulnerable and insecure and had cast a shadow over those years. Whereas Ivan had left the house whenever he liked, to go and play games with ruffians like himself—games that lasted hours, after which he would come home covered with cuts and bumps and torn clothes—she had stayed home with her mother, quietly reading books borrowed from the school library. Likewise, she considered Ivan responsible for the state of her mother, who came home from work exhausted and, with heavy legs, slumped into a chair to get her breath back before busying herself to get dinner ready. All this bitterness, all this tension, had vanished when she saw Lansana at the airport and he had tenderly called her "my daughter." From that moment on, her sole concern was to remain loyal to what he expected of her. Consequently when Lansana died she cried a lot and was deeply moved by the condolences from friends and family.

By way of a tribute she decided to continue his work, and with the help of the Jean Belucci Foundation, named after the Swiss philanthropist who had bequeathed his massive fortune to the country, she created the audio archives known as Sounds of Mali. It involved not only identifying the living griots and listing their most successful praise songs but also researching the dead griots who in their time had made a lasting impression on their community and created works of importance. In order to do this, Ivana traveled to remote villages and endeavored to flush out any hidden talent.

We didn't say much about Ivana either when her brother decided to move in with Aminata Traoré. Like everyone else, she had heard the rumors going around about Ivan and had suffered a lot. She knew full well he was by no means a homosexual and could have explained the reasons for his behavior towards women. She was, however, obliged to keep silent. In fact, what is more reprehensible for the common mortal? To be homosexual or incestuous? Hypocritical are those who claim not to know that every family is a knot of vipers, as François Mauriac so justly wrote. The father covets and rapes his daughter. The brother lusts after his sister. As for the mother-and-son relationship, everyone knows about that. The decision to live with Aminata seemed to Ivana to be an effective subterfuge and left her in peace and happiness for a few months.

When her brother decided to marry Aminata, although she had encouraged him to contract the marriage, Ivana thought deep down that he was going too far. The fact that Aminata was pregnant, it seemed, was not a deciding factor. At Dos d'Âne one child out of two did not know their father. If a child did know his name, he was like a god worshiped from afar.

The fatal blow came when she discovered that Ivan had become a terrorist and had probably taken part in the assassination of El Cobra.

Suddenly everything turned to ashes. Where was Ivan? Where was he hiding? Had he managed to reach Niamey so he could get to France, as he said in the letter he had scribbled her? In utter despair she went to see Malaika, a well-known clairvoyant, so as to penetrate destiny's secrets. Malaika lived in the Kisimu Banco neighborhood, a district we have already mentioned, and came from Benin, a country known for its seers and sorcerers. She had lived for a long time in the Paris suburbs and attended to the careers of famous right-wing politicians. When they were beaten in the last elections, she had found herself in dire straits and had to come and live with her sister in Mali. Malaika was a woman with an ample figure, no less than a hundred kilos, but nevertheless one who moved with an agile grace.

Like all those who claim to penetrate the secrets of the invisible world, she lit a good dozen candles, remained silent for a moment, then declared, "I can see only blood, blood all around me. In order to know where it comes from and why, you must bring me some money."

Thereupon she announced such a large sum of money that Ivana jumped. How could she manage to collect such an amount? She only knew down-and-outs and penniless griots, rich merely in musical chords. She stumbled out of Malaika's hut determined never to approach her again.

We have already described the Kisimu Banco neighborhood as being filthy, overcrowded, and noisy with all sorts of music from the Third World. You could hear reggae and salsa mixed in with snatches of hip-hop and gloomy rap recitations. Men in search of a one-night stand solicited this pretty girl who seemed unafraid of the night.

It was the following morning that the police came to arrest Ivana. Very politely they took her to the SUV where Aminata was already sitting. The two women hugged each other in tears while Aminata whispered, "Aïssata told me not to trust him because he kept company with the wrong type of people."

On the afternoon of her arrest, while Ivana was languishing in her cell, in burst Abdouramane Sow. She knew Abdouramane. She had done nothing to attract the attention of this admirer who already had two wives, one of whom was very pretty and came from Mogadishu. One day when she had gone to the Alfa Yaya barracks to admire the militia's military exercises, she had caught his eye. He had insisted on inviting her together with her brother Ivan to have a glass of *bissap* fruit juice at his place, full of luxurious furnishings: white leather sofas mismatched with purple leather sofas as well as rich tapestries hanging from the walls.

"He's one of our best recruits!" Sow had said at the time, casting a flattering eye at Ivan.

Ivana, who was only too aware how much her brother loathed military postures, was surprised by this remark. But Abdouramane Sow had already jumped to another subject and was describing the years he had spent in Haiti.

"It's a wonderful island," he declared, "whose creativity is a constant delight. In the markets of Port-au-Prince they sell naive paintings. Have you heard of naive art?"

Neither Ivan nor Ivana could find an answer to this question. In Guadeloupe they had rubbed shoulders with a good many Haitians who were not painters but miserable wretches, exploited and humiliated by their leaders and forced into servile jobs in order to survive. Vica, Lansana's companion, had also described to them a picture of her people's suffering.

Abdouramane continued.

"In Haiti, art is a magic potion which, despite the ups and downs of life, provides strength and courage to those who drink it."

Despite her not saying a word during this visit, Ivana had become an object of passion for Abdouramane. He had even gone so far as to ask for her hand from Lamine Diarra, who since Lansana's death served as elder in the compound.

The evening he entered Ivana's cell Abdouramane looked extremely serious.

"You are free," he told Ivana, pointing to the door of her cell.

Free? She looked at him in amazement. Staring at her with blazing eyes, he went on, "I love you too much to hurt you. Go home."

"Does that mean my brother is innocent?" Ivana asked.

Abdouramane shook his head in all seriousness.

"No, he is guilty and we have proof."

Ivana then returned to the Diarra compound where nobody was expecting her and where some were already overjoyed at her imprisonment. From that moment on she lived in limbo, dressing mechanically, eating likewise, and looking after her infant charges without seeing them. In order to share her solitude, every evening she would dine melancholically with Aminata, who now attributed every virtue to Ivan. Going by what Aminata said, Ivan was affectionate, considerate, and always ready to make love. Ivana, who knew perfectly well this was all a pack of lies, didn't even trouble to contradict her. Assailed by a host of other thoughts, she ended up asking her, "Did you notice any change in his behavior? Did it seem he was becoming more radical?"

Aminata gestured her ignorance.

"Radical? What does that mean? He conducted himself like a good Muslim, that's all. He never missed a prayer. He would read the Koran. If you could only see the comments he made on the copy he left behind. He didn't smoke, he didn't drink, and he gave to charity. Is that being radical?"

Ivana was none the wiser. She would walk back home through the dark, deserted streets and arrive late at the Diarra compound, which never sleeps. Until the early hours of the morning it throbbed with life and noise. Some would play the kora to accompany their traditional songs. Others played checkers or card games such as belote. High-pitched exclamations would fly through the air.

"Belote! Rebelote! Hearts are trumps!"

Others sadly discussed the topic which was on everyone's minds: the flight of migrants to Europe given the state of Africa.

"And while they welcome some with open arms," they moaned, "they want nothing to do with us. They claim our countries are not at war. But what's the difference between being killed by bombs that drop from the sky and starving to death? It's racism over and over again."

All these conversations stopped when Ivana appeared because some of them cherished her and felt sorry for her. Unfortunately she was insensitive to these marks of respect and affection. All she wanted to do was shut herself up in her room, to wait for the burst of thunder that would once again devastate her life. And that's what eventually happened.

One evening she returned home earlier than usual,

went to bed without dinner, and tried to get to sleep. For her, sleep provided neither rest nor relaxation. It was merely a hedge against the terrible suffering she endured day in, day out. It must have been around midnight when Magali, her servant, came into the room, lit the bedside lamp, and, leaning over her, whispered in an urgent voice, "Sister, sister, wake up. Monsieur Abdouramane Sow is here asking for you."

Stupefied, Ivana sat up, opened her misty eyes, and stammered, "Abdouramane Sow? Did you say Abdouramane Sow?"

The servant nodded.

"What shall I tell him, sister?" she asked.

"Go and see what he wants," Ivana said, bewildered.

But she didn't have time to slip on her dressing gown or get up before Abdouramane had already forced his way into her room and shoved Magali out. For the first time, Ivana saw him without his military uniform, dressed in a white gandoura which hugged his athletic build. A silky beard covered his cheeks. His hair curled slightly, the probable legacy of a Tuareg ancestor. He was undeniably a very handsome man, she realized.

"I have your brother on my hands," he said.

"My brother!" Ivana exclaimed, dumbfounded.

"Two crooks have just called to say they captured him while he was trying to escape to Niamey. They'll hand him over in exchange for the ransom that was promised. Then I'll give him to the militia who will inflict the punishment he deserves. Is that what you want?"

Ivana burst into tears and shook her head.

"No, of course not; you know full well that's not what I want."

"So? What do you want?" Abdouramane asked, shooting her a jet-black look.

Once again we have very little reliable information as to what happened next. Ivan and Ivana's departure from Mali is the subject of so much hearsay and fabrication that it's impossible to get a clear picture. What we do know for certain is that on the morning following this visit Abdouramane Sow did not turn up at the Alfa Yaya barracks, which was hardly surprising. It was a Friday and we know that on mosque days he spent several hours praying, reading his Koran, and making rounds in the poorest neighborhoods to distribute alms. In the early afternoon, three or four jeeps loaded with armed militia drove off on one of the southern routes. Passersby anxiously gazed after them. Where was this convoy going? To fight the jihadists? Did we have to expect yet again more dead?

The day after, in the predawn hours, it was the turn of Barthélemy, Abdouramane's personal chauffeur, to take the southern route as well, at the wheel of a Range Rover. Since the car windows were tinted you couldn't see who was inside. Nevertheless, we are certain it was Ivan and Ivana.

Barthélemy was not only Abdouramane's personal chauffeur. This Haitian had been in Abdouramane's service ever since he had worked for the MINUSTAH in Port-au-Prince, and had carted along his mistresses and delivered the young girls he had coveted. He had followed him when Abdouramane had returned to Mali.

Barthélemy and his mysterious cargo, although not mysterious to us, drove for three or four hours, before stopping to sleep in one of those rudimentary caravanserais which provide travelers with a basic meal. The customers stared at Ivan, wondering where they had seen that face. Nobody could say they recognized him for sure. Consequently, the mustache, beard, and sideburns he had grown were of little use, if only to give him the look of a pimp, much like Sese Seko in *A Season in the Congo* by Aimé Césaire.

Strangely enough, Ivan was deeply disappointed. He would have loved to strut about and boast to everyone that he was the one who had dared attack El Cobra and flout the entire country. The fact he was forced to hide deprived him of the bravery and audacity of his act.

Our three travelers crossed the border at the Kifuma checkpoint where the police and customs officers stamped their laissez-passer nonchalantly. From there, they reached Niamey in a few hours. Unlike Timbuktu, the Pearl of the Desert, Niamey had never been a major stopover for the caravans. It had never seen long lines of camels, their flanks loaded with treasures destined for the sultanates of North Africa. In fact, its recent prosperity was barely a century old.

The Range Rover headed for the airport as Abdouramane had urged Barthélemy to put Ivan and Ivana on the first plane to Paris. Alas, they were met with an unpleasant surprise. Air France, true to form, was on strike. You know when a strike begins but you never know when it will end. Our three travelers, therefore, had to take refuge in the so-called Waterloo Hotel, a one-star, shabby-looking edifice that matched their modest means.

We haven't described Ivan and Ivana's behavior since their reunion because there is nothing extraordinary to tell. After so many weeks of separation and anxiety, after so much repressed desire, their happiness at being reunited overwhelmed them. Their only reaction was to hug each other and reel off a rosary of sweet nothings in each other's ears. Barthélemy, who knew nothing of their liaison, took them to be a couple of lovers in the early stages of their passion. Ironically, he recalled a well-known song from the Caribbean: "Beware of Falling in Love on This Earth for When Love Vanishes Only Tears Are Left."

Beneath their mutual raptures, however, Ivan and Ivana were suffering the martyr. On the one hand, Ivana was forced to give in to Abdouramane in order to save her brother. She blamed herself for the pleasure he had dragged out of her and the moans and cries she had uttered, albeit unwittingly, during these moments of carnal passion. *How vile and wretched is the human body,* she constantly repeated to herself. At night she had trouble getting to sleep. On the other hand, Ivan was unable to forget the time he had spent with Alix and Cristina, whose memory was encrusted in his flesh.

The Waterloo Hotel had a shabby dining room where you could down a frugal breakfast every morning. For three days our friends stood around waiting, wondering when the wait would be over. On the morning of the fourth day, a newspaper seller came in. The *Niamey Matin* posted a headline that drew Ivan's attention: "Spectacular Military Operation: Ivan Némélé's hideout discovered". There followed an article describing how Abdouramane Sow's militia had launched an attack on The Last Resort where two foreigners, Alix and Cristina Alonso, had hidden Ivan Némélé for several weeks. The two wretches had received the punishment they deserved and been slaughtered.

Ivan's hands trembled so much he let the newspaper fall to the ground. Racked with grief, he collapsed onto the table, shaking with raucous, painful sobs like a child's.

"Why? Why did they kill them?" he stammered. "Alix and Cristina were non-violent, they had hearts of gold, they were tender and understanding."

Barthélemy picked up the paper and handed it to Ivana who read it in turn.

The assassination of Alix and Cristina brought on a fit of anger in Ivan, beyond anything he had previously known.

If you ask my opinion, I would say that it was at this precise moment that Ivan became radicalized, as they say. All the horror of the world was revealed to him. The world seemed to be divided into two camps: the West and their lackeys, and the rest. The former claim they are victims and are attacked for no reason as they have done no harm and are fervent defenders of free speech, every type of gender, love between people of the same sex, and adoption of children by homosexuals. In actual fact, this is not true. Both camps are playing games of massacre and each is as savage and implacable as the other. Both have no other solution but to respond to violence with violence. No finger is lifted to engage a dialogue or invent a compromise. Peace conferences open in Geneva and result in nothing and still the bombs keep coming.

It was then, I believe, that Ivan decided to destroy this rotten society that stretched out around him. In my opinion this is when he resolved to change the world. How? For now, he had no idea.

The Air France strike ended after a week throughout which the unfortunate passengers had piled into all the available hotels. Those who couldn't afford to delay their business any longer had endeavored to reach Europe by every possible means. The day before their departure Barthélemy invited his travel companions for dinner at the well-known Trigonocéphale restaurant, for the three felt a strange affinity towards each other. The trigono-cephalus or pit viper is a small, poisonous snake endemic to Martinique. Why this name was given to a restaurant owned by a French couple from Strasbourg is a complete mystery.

"It's big brother who's inviting you," he joked. "I'll find a way to get him to pay for the dinner."

Ivan had no inclination to follow him. Ever since he had learned of Alix's and Cristina's deaths he had lost interest in everything. Memories of them constantly came back to haunt him and almost suffocated him. He was obsessed with the idea of making a final pilgrimage to The Last Resort, drinking in with his eyes what remained and losing himself in the memory of those who had disappeared. But the banks of the Joliba where The Last Resort was situated were at least five hundred kilometers away and he didn't dare ask Barthélemy to drive such a distance, something he was sure to refuse. Moreover, Ivan had no intention of taking advantage of their executioner's generosity. It took all of Ivana's persuading, her arms locked around his neck, for Ivan to follow his companions to the restaurant.

Despite its weird name the Trigonocéphale was a magnificent, welcoming establishment located a little outside town. It was the place to be for the Niamey elite. It was known for its professional artistic turns between dishes: belly dancers from Turkey and Egypt, acrobats from Ukraine, knife throwers who seemed to aim straight for their partner's heart, jugglers, and ventriloquists. The high point of the dinner, however, was performed by the fortune-tellers. Their heads wrapped in turbans, and dressed in sparkling colors, they grabbed the hands of the diners and claimed to read the future. One of them plonked herself in front of Ivan, who nonchalantly held out his palm. No sooner had she taken a long look at him than she stepped back in fright.

"Who are you?" she asked. "I see only rivers of blood, tears, and assassination where you are concerned. Aren't you one of these fearsome terrorists?"

Ivan replied quite calmly.

"I am what I am."

Thereupon he swiftly handed over the bank note he had prepared for her.

The following day at 5 p.m. brother and sister took the plane to Paris. The rays of the setting sun drew great scarlet Vs across the sky: V for vengeance. *Yes, thought Ivan, Alix and Cristina had to be avenged. But how?*

OUT OF AFRICA

Ivan and Ivana disembarked at Roissy Airport, still dazzled by the colors of Mali, on a morning which to them appeared gray and dirty. Although we were only in the early days of September the weather was quite cool. Fortunately one of their "mothers" in the Diarra compound had knitted soft pullovers for them, unfortunately in a shocking spinach green for Ivan and salmon pink for Ivana. Hugo, one of Father Michalou's cousins, who for years had tightened bolts in the car factory on the Île Seguin and now enjoyed a meager pension, had come to meet them. He was very proud to own a car, an antiquated Ford which still hummed along intrepidly. Exiting the airport they drove along a road cluttered with cars. At the end of a tunnel they entered Paris. Ivan and Ivana had never seen such tall, massive buildings forming a sooty black wall along the sidewalks. Set apart at regular intervals the street lamps gave off a ghostly, yellowish light. Despite the early hour the streets were by no means deserted. Men, women, and even children headed down into the metro while vehicles as gloomy as hearses revved impatiently at red lights. Ivan's heart sank at the sight of this hardly welcoming atmosphere. Ivan had never liked Kidal but now he felt he wouldn't like Paris either. Why was it named the City of Light? He recalled that Father Michalou compared it to a lovely odalisque who struck dumb those who admired her.

They drove for miles across Paris and then exited the city, for Hugo lived in Villeret-le-François, a suburb that to the two new arrivals seemed miles away from anywhere. Hugo proudly insisted that in Villeret-le-François there were people of every nationality.

"We have Indians," he said. "Pakistanis, and even Japanese. Soon the Whites will be in the minority compared with those who come from elsewhere."

He had kept a strong Guadeloupean accent, and on hearing him Ivan relived his childhood and those moments of happiness.

After an endless journey the car finally reached Villeret-le-François. It stopped inside a somewhat shabby-looking housing estate in front of four or five multistory tower blocks surrounded by a peeling wall.

"Here we are," Hugo said. "This is the André Malraux housing estate. There was a time when they called it the Mamadous. Chirac was very proud of it. He went straight ahead and installed electricity and running water for the garbage collectors he recruited from Africa."

"What!" exclaimed Ivan, climbing out of the car, "He had Africans come over to empty the garbage of the French!"

Apparently Ivan had never heard of the famous song by good old Pierre Perret:

> They thought she was fairly pretty, Lily
> She was a Somali
> Who arrived in a ship full of émigrés
> Who came of their own free will to empty the garbage bins
> in Paris!

Hugo did not seem to be at all shocked.

"Chirac pampered his garbage collectors like they were the apple of his eye. Today everything's dilapidated. The elevators no longer work. A pack of dealers sell drugs in the stairwells."

Hugo shared his two-bedroom apartment and his life with Mona, an ageing woman from Martinique who still cut a fine figure and had once sung at La Cigale club in Paris. She had even been highly successful singing Luis Mariano's famous hits.

> Life is a bouquet of violets
> Love is a bouquet of violets
> Love is sweeter than these flowerets
> When happiness chances by, beckons, and stops
> You must take it by the hand
> And not wait for tomorrow.

At present she worked at the Villeret-le-François school canteen and could go on forever about the students' deplorable behavior.

"They're impolite," she would say. "Aggressive and always prepared to answer back. It's not surprising they end up going to Syria and elsewhere to do their jihad."

The next day, while Ivana was anxious to get to the police training school where she was registered, Ivan reluctantly set off for the establishment where he was to do his apprenticeship. During the months he had spent in Mali, the prospect of such an apprenticeship in a chocolate factory had seemed incredible and somewhat ridiculous. Since the establishment was located in another suburb, he had to take the regional express metro, which to his amazement was crowded with a foul-smelling humanity. The day before in Hugo's car he had been spared the smell of these unwashed bodies as well as their brilliantine and cheap perfume. Men with crimson-colored faces trying to look natural took advantage of the crush to squeeze up against young women's curves. What struck Ivan was the number of Arabs—the girls wearing dark headscarves over their hair, the boys growing curly beards over their cheeks. What a surprising change of face France had undergone, he said to himself. He wondered whether one day there would be room for him.

The buildings of the Crémieux chocolate factory founded in 1924 by Jean Richard of the same name were not visible from the street, even though a strong smell of chocolate swept over the sidewalk. You had to enter along a corridor and then cross a paved courtyard where overflowing garbage bins stood guard. In the meagerly lit entrance hall Ivan introduced himself to the receptionist, a disagreeable man who searched in vain for his name in the register.

"You're not here," he concluded drily.

Ivan explained he had been registered as an apprentice for over a year now and that the management had consented to delay his apprenticeship. Since he had no letter or document whatsoever to prove it, the man shook his head and pointed to a chair.

"You'll explain yourself to Monsieur Delarue," he said.

Ivan sat down. Gradually the hall filled up with men of every age sharing the same lack of confidence.

Are these the people I'm going to work with? he wondered. The prospect discouraged him. He felt as though he was a prisoner deciphering his death sentence on these faces.

After waiting for an hour he unconsciously got up, went out into the courtyard, and found himself on the sidewalk. It had started to rain, a gentle, penetrating drizzle which added to the gloom. Was this what he had left Guadeloupe and then Mali for?

Once again he sat down in the express metro and returned to Villeret-le-François, where he took a walk to get to know the neighborhood. What he saw was not exactly heartening: nondescript buildings which all deserved a good touch of paint; public squares covered in seedy-looking grass, and a patch of wasteland where some children were playing football. He got slightly lost in the maze of narrow streets as he walked back to the André Malraux block. Hardly had he set foot in the hall of Tower A than he bumped up against two rapidly approaching colossuses.

"Who are you? Where are you going?" one of them asked him in an arrogant tone of voice.

Ivan's answer was evidently not to their liking for they indicated coldly for him to follow them.

"You're going to have to explain to the boss what you are doing here."

Ivan had no choice but to follow them and climb up the dusty stairwell. The two men preceded him into an apartment on the third floor and pointed to a chair for him to sit down. After almost an hour a door opened and Ivan found himself face-to-face with the last person he expected to meet: Mansour. His friend Mansour who had lived in the same compound in Kidal. Mansour was totally unrecognizable, dressed like never before. At one time always so badly dressed in faded gandourahs and sarouel trousers he had now become a genuine fashion plate. He was wearing a dark-blue suit. His neck was clasped by a white high-collar and now that his hair was better combed it seemed thicker. In short he might have looked like an African version of Karl Lagerfeld. Mansour and Ivan threw themselves into each other's arms.

"Mansour, Mansour," Ivan shouted. "What are you doing here? I thought you were in Belgium."

Mansour shook his head.

"Yes, I did go, but I didn't stay. Nothing good, nothing lucrative to be had there. Nothing like I expected; I was so disappointed. I landed in France, and here I found what I was looking for. But what about you? Tell me about yourself. Apparently you've become what they call a terrorist. I thought you were locked up in a prison in Kidal. Tell me more."

Ivan gave an evasive wave of the hand. He didn't like referring back to that part of his life which forced him to wonder about his sister's behavior. How had she obtained his liberation?

"But what are you doing in Villeret-le-François?" Ivan asked.

"Listen to me carefully, if you do what I tell you to do, you'll do as well as I have done."

From that day on Ivan worked for Mansour. Well, work is one way to put it! Judge for yourselves. He got up at noon and, since he slept on a mattress spread out in a corner of the dining room, Hugo and Mona had to use elaborate tactics not to wake him while they ate their breakfast. Then he went into the tiny bathroom which he flooded with water and never thought about mopping up or cleaning. After which he, too, dressed like never before. Whereas previously he had always taken little notice about what he wore, now he began to imitate Mansour: bow ties, neckties, polka-dot or striped ties, slim-fitting shirts, and Giorgio Armani suits. He began taking a liking to Tergal, salt-and-pepper fabrics, and linen, and making comparisons between these different yarns. That's how he treated himself to a red leather jacket, which he wore like a toreador, together with a black leather ensemble that could have passed him off as a homosexual. You might well ask where he got the money from to dress so ostentatiously. It was because money now flowed endlessly between the hands of Mansour and Ivan.

His work consisted of filling little sachets with a drug which arrived in packs of four or five hundred grams and delivering them in exchange for a small fortune to a bar called La Porte Étroite, owned by Zachary, a Serbo-Croat. Zachary would then hand over small cases full of carefully pre-counted bank notes which Ivan took back to Mansour. No credit cards, no checks. Cash, and cash only. The barons of this drug trafficking remained invisible and stayed safely hidden, probably in their luxury apartments in Paris or the wealthy suburbs. Ivan did his best, having only one hope in mind: earn enough money to find an apartment where he would live alone with Ivana as Mansour had promised him.

Ivan's attitude regarding drugs was steeped in indifference. He was totally unaware of the harm he was doing by becoming a drug trafficker. He had no idea that this white powder, apparently as inoffensive as the wheat flour in Simone's pastries, was capable of liberating the imagination, arousing death wishes, and destroying individuals. He carried out his smuggling without the slightest remorse or guilty conscience.

In the evening he would follow Mansour. For someone

like him, who neither drank nor took an interest in girls, the charms of this night life were extremely limited. Mansour regularly visited La Baignoire, a night club in the center of Paris that was once a meeting place for famous homosexuals. It was said that Marcel Proust loved to swim in the pool on the lower third floor where he organized sumptuous parties with his one-night stands. Mansour was extremely busy making off with numerous maidens, preferably blonde and buxom. It was amazing when you think of how the girls in his own country used to treat him. The money he now flouted in Paris gave him direct access to and possession of the bodies of these lovely foreign girls.

Ivan, who at first was bored to death at La Baignoire, gradually took a liking to gambling. He was no longer content to sluggishly pull the slot machines on the first floor. He began playing roulette and especially baccarat. He liked the aristocratic charms of the rooms where the tables were laid out; the unexpected turn of events for the gamblers excited him. The croupier's somber, fateful voice seemed to utter the diktat of destiny. All around him the gamblers were an eccentric lot. For example, Ivan became friendly with an old penniless countess, who called herself Gloria Swanson, as well as her lover, Hildebert, a house painter, forty years younger than her. The countess and Hildebert often invited him to their apartment on the boulevard Suchet to down a glass of champagne, since they knocked back a case a day. Even though Ivan didn't drink alcohol he was fond of their company. Unfortunately all that didn't last. After a few months of this frequentation the countess fell into an alcohol-induced coma from which she didn't come out alive and Ivan had to follow her to the Père Lachaise Cemetery along the alleys lined with graves bearing all sorts of names. Here he thus discovered it was possible to brave death's anonymity. Ivan had never heard of some of the names engraved on the tombs. Who was Jim Morrison? What had he done to deserve such a long epitaph? When Hildebert explained to him the whys and wherefores, Ivan was bombarded with a new idea. Why couldn't he too overstep his destiny? It's true he was neither a musician nor a painter or writer and that he had no talent. But he could be the author of an extraordinary act which would shake the world and thus avenge Alix and Cristina. The death of Alix and Cristina was constantly on his mind and it repeatedly came back to haunt him. At certain moments he told himself it was his fault and that he had poisoned their generosity. Then his heart would break and he'd burst into tears.

One day coming out of La Baignoire in this depressive condition, Mansour questioned him, intrigued.

"What's up? Why are you crying?"

Ivan told him of the episode at The Last Resort. When he had finished Mansour shrugged his shoulders.

"This Alix and Cristina were white folk, weren't they?"

"Why are you asking me? What do you mean?" Ivan asked.

"I mean they belong to a different species to us. If I saw some Whites fall into the water, I'd help them drown."

It was against such inept theories that Alix and Cristina had struggled. In their eyes there was no such thing as color. Yet Ivan did not say a word; he knew Mansour wouldn't understand.

When the yellowish light of dawn rose over the roofs of Paris they would breakfast as a rule in a bar called L'Éteignoir. Ivan would down cups of coffee while listening to Mansour recollect his memories.

"In Belgium I was a member of the H4 unit in charge of

preparing attacks in the airport, the railway stations, and the metro. Finally, killing people for no reason at all while the world made martyrs of them seemed senseless. From that moment on I refused to obey instructions and I was considered a coward. I had to flee to France to save my life and there I met Abou, a drug trafficker: an African like you and me, no more, no less. He opened my eyes to the way the world works. Money rules the world; you've got to make money by every means possible."

Ivan devoted Sundays to his sister, whose well-ordered and studious life was totally different from his. She was already up, washed, and dressed at seven in the morning. At eight she climbed down the stairs of Tower A and walked briskly across the dismal patch of wasteland to the street. There, she took her seat in the regional express metro and got off at boulevard Brune in Paris where she was studying to become a policewoman, the career she had always dreamed of. The teachers, charmed by her pretty little face, couldn't stop praising this lovely girl from Martinique (the French have always mixed up Martinique and Guadeloupe, you have to forgive them), who was so talented and would go far.

When Ivan entered her bedroom on Sunday mornings she was already seated at her desk, preparing her classes for the following day. She never failed to lecture her brother in a serious tone of voice.

"You gave up your apprenticeship," she said, "and it's a shame. Maman and I are brokenhearted. Be careful Mansour doesn't drag you down into his dark dealings. I've heard he's mixed up in drug trafficking on the estate. That's where his money comes from."

Ivana had not exaggerated. Simone had gone into a fit of rage on hearing Father Michalou's indiscreet remarks that her son was a drug dealer. Her son a drug dealer! Never on her life! She planned to travel to France herself to lecture him and make him ashamed of his behavior. She stormed on until Father Michalou became tired of listening to her and ended up giving her a piece of his mind.

"What would be the purpose of such a trip?" he asked. "That boy has never listened to you and has always done exactly as he pleases. Keep calm, it's a good remedy, as the saying goes."

Henceforth Simone no longer talked about taking a plane. She merely dispatched a daily dose of threatening and despairing emails and telephone calls to her son.

On Sundays Ivan invited his sister for lunch at his favorite restaurant, Le Pré-Catalan Lenôtre, situated in the middle of the Bois de Boulogne. This elegant pavilion was built in 1920 and its specialty was butterflied sea bream served with chestnut purée. Sometimes he invited Hugo and Mona, although they didn't get along very well together and made no mystery of their opinion that Ivan was mixing with dubious, even dangerous, company. This Mansour was a notorious drug dealer wanted by the police.

These events lasted around three months. Deep down Ivan was increasingly dissatisfied. What was to become of his ambitions, his dreams, and his future plans?

One afternoon when he arrived at Mansour's as usual to pick up his load of drugs he found the apartment empty, the doors wide open, the furniture overturned, and the contents of the drawers strewn over the floor like in an American crime thriller. He dashed down to the ground floor for an explanation. The entrance hall was empty. Nobody. *What had happened?* he asked himself. He then got it into his head to run to La Porte Étroite, and in his haste knocked over two children who were playing ball at the foot of the tower blocks. The bar's metal curtain was lowered, which was strange since it was after one in the afternoon. Fortunately for Ivan he knew the entrance to the storage room that served as a back shop. At the third ring, Zoran, Zachary's cousin, finally opened the door.

"You! What the hell are you doing here?" he shouted, his eyes wide open in stupefaction.

"I want to see Zachary," Ivan answered feverishly.

Zoran stared at him, wide-eyed in amazement.

"Haven't you heard? The police came to arrest Mansour at dawn. They are certain to hunt down his ring of connections. Consequently, Zachary is lying low. At this time Mansour is probably at the Fleury-Mérogis prison."

In actual fact Zoran was mistaken. Mansour had been taken to La Santé prison. Weak-kneed, Ivan returned to the André Malraux housing estate convinced that at any moment the police would swoop down to arrest him.

But days went by and nothing of the sort happened.

You are probably wondering why Ivan wasn't arrested as well. We have no idea and cannot provide a reasonable explanation. Nevertheless, he remained at liberty despite the fear that gnawed at him and forced him to hole up at Hugo's.

It was then he received a letter from his wife Aminata Traoré, whom he had totally forgotten. She informed him that his son had been born and was called Fadel, such a handsome little guy. Did he have a computer or an email address where she could send photos of this marvel they had conceived together? She had moved heaven and earth to find his address and was getting ready to come and join him as soon as she had the means. This merely sent Ivan even further into the panic stations in which he was already living. What would he do with a wife and a baby, he who possessed nothing? Where would they live? How could he feed them? Money ill-gained has the odd particularity of being spent immediately. Ivan had kept nothing of the considerable sums that had slipped through his fingers and was reduced to living off his sister, who received a grant from Guadeloupe due to her brilliant studies. Mona had found him a job. Pathetic, it should be said! Dishwasher at the school canteen. Despite his revulsion, Ivan told himself that if his situation didn't improve, he would have to resign himself to accepting the offer.

Come December, winter arrived with a bitter cold. The patchy-looking grass of the André Malraux housing estate was covered with a thick white carpet while a violent, ice-cold wind blew between the tower blocks.

Children no longer played ball in the parking lots. Muffled up to the eyes, they crowded into the entrance halls desperately attempting to keep the doors closed to protect them from the cold. Except for Mona and Ivana nobody left the apartment. In an effort to battle his depression Hugo downed glass after glass of neat Depaz rum and, half drunk, began chattering away, out of character with his usual taciturn self. He told Ivan, who also hadn't set foot outside, that it reminded him of the terrible winter of 1954. When he was still young and working in the factory on the Île Seguin. Frozen birds would fall from the sky between the feet of passersby. This was when the Emmaus charity was founded and Abbé Pierre, a young unknown priest, became the spokesperson for the homeless. As for Mona, she was happy because it was the holiday season and she was setting up a Christmas tree for her three grandchildren. The stars and colored lights reminded Ivan of the warm

Christmases of his childhood. He would accompany his mother and grandmother to the church at Dos d'Âne whose ugliness briefly faded and which turned into a throbbing vessel. Dressed in white, the members of the choir who had rehearsed for weeks sat down in the pews to the left of the altar, holding their children between their knees. Under the vaulted ceiling "O Holy Night" burst forth and filled the congregation with its fervor.

"Why did you convert to Islam?" Mona often asked Ivan while she decorated her Christmas tree. "Our religion has such lovely ceremonies."

Ivan confessed he no longer remembered what had made him convert. Islam today had become an integral part of his life. He who seldom opened a book never tired of reading and rereading his suras.

"It's because I believe Islam to be tolerant and generous as well," he said gingerly.

Mona looked at him slightly scornfully.

"That's true of every religion," she affirmed.

She was probably right.

They had a white Christmas. Oh, those white Christmases when Bing Crosby's melody floats furtively in the air:

I'm dreaming of a white Christmas,
Just like the ones I used to know,
Where the treetops glisten
And children listen
To hear sleigh bells in the snow.

For Christmas Eve, Ivana put on a dress by Jean-Paul Gaultier that her brother had given her when he was in the money. How pretty she was, dressed in all this red and gold! She was much lovelier than Mona's daughter-in-law, a Kabyle who took herself very seriously because she had studied to be a nurse and was now working in a famous hospital. Mona had gone to a lot of trouble. She herself had made a joyously spicy blood pudding, accras, salt fish fritters, meat patties, and, marvel of marvels, a mutton pot patty, a specialty from Martinique made from sheep's offal. This sumptuous meal was naturally accompanied by a great variety of rum punches and lasted until the early hours of the morning. Everyone laughed and joked, especially Mona's son who had come especially from Montpellier where he lived with his family.

Only Ivan felt forlorn and was unable to share in the general mood of good humor. Moreover, he didn't eat pork and didn't drink alcohol. More than ever, the memory of Alix and Cristina haunted him. He thought he could breathe in their scent and imagine himself deep in the delights of their beings. He felt a painful premonition coming on, as if destiny was granting him one last chance before dealing him a fatal blow. *What did the future still hold in store for him?* he never stopped anxiously asking himself.

Two days later the postman handed him a registered letter. It was an urgent summons from the director of La Santé prison to present himself together with his ID. Let's take this opportunity to take a closer look at this somewhat surprising missive. It was typewritten on ordinary stationery and bore a large seal by way of a signature. What did it mean? What did they have against him?

"Nothing," Hugo assured. "If they had wanted to arrest you because of your ties with Mansour they would have done it a long time ago. The police would have swooped down and taken you with them."

According to Nathaniel Hawthorne, prison is the black flower of civilized society. The prison of La Santé does not fit this description at all. Located at the very heart of the fourteenth arrondissement in Paris, it is a vast, featureless construction. Its thick flint walls are appropriately whitewashed. A vaulted door opens onto a large paved courtyard. Despite this nondescript appearance Ivan's heart beat faster with a deep sense of foreboding. He felt the forces of evil were waiting for him, hidden inside this building; like a beast about to pounce on him and tear him to pieces. He was shown into an office where a photo of the president of the republic was majestically on display. Three men were waiting for him. Two of them were uniformed police officers, their faces pale and arrogant beneath their flat caps. The third man was a civilian with a pleasant face, slightly dark-skinned under a head of curly brown hair, and an affable smile. He introduced himself.

"My name is Henri Duvignaud. I'm Mansour's, your cousin's, lawyer. My father was from Guadeloupe, like you," he added.

Cutting short this show of politeness, one of the police officers with the same arrogant look picked up a blue folder and opened it.

"We have some very bad news for you. We took our time contacting you because we first tried to track you down in Guadeloupe and then in Mali."

The second officer took over and with eyes lowered, declared, "Your cousin, Mansour Diarra, committed suicide in his cell. He left a letter for you."

Suicide? Ivan refused to understand the meaning of such a word. Here is the text of Mansour's letter to Ivan, which we finally discovered after much research. It's not very long but loaded with emotion:

My dear Ivan,

Do you remember what I told you? That all you need is money and that you have to make money by every means possible?

Well, I was mistaken because here I am at the end of the road. Perhaps you were right. In order to change the world we need to attack people's hearts and minds. But how?

The hearts and minds have become as hard as stone and are hidden deep inside the body.

I'm writing to you because you mean more than a brother to me, you are the only person on this earth who granted me your esteem and admiration. I am sure we will see each other again somewhere.

Yours affectionately,

Mansour

We will not dwell here on the painful formalities Ivan had to confront. We will highlight rather the extreme despondency which took possession of him. He wandered around like a zombie. If it hadn't been for his sister's tenderness and the consideration of Mona, who beneath her looks of a harpy hid a motherly heart of gold, he would have probably gone out of his mind.

The most painful moment was without doubt the burial of Mansour, who they threw into a common grave at Villeret-le-François's municipal cemetery. Henri Duvignaud had insisted on attending. Although he never failed to allude to his origins, he had not known his father and had never been to Guadeloupe. He had grown up with his mother in his maternal grandparents' luxurious apartment. For generations the Duvignauds had been business lawyers whose rich clients had paid them in hard cash. They married gifted women: pianists, violinists, and cellists who were content to play for friends of the family. Only one of them, Araxi, an Armenian who set ablaze the heart of Joseph Duvignaud, eighth in line, had made a name for herself and been invited to play violin solo at Carnegie Hall. Henri was the first of the Duvignauds to become involved in social issues. He had created an association to defend the growing numbers of undocumented migrants.

After Mansour had been buried, he put his arm familiarly around Ivan.

"Can I see you again?" Henri asked, using all his charm.

It was rumored he was a homosexual and often became the lover of those he defended. It had never been proven, however. Ivan, who was stumbling along in a thick fog, gathered his wits about him and had the strength to answer.

"I shall be only too pleased to see you again."

Henri Duvignaud, therefore, slipped him his business card. He worked together with two other lawyers, who shared his interest in social topics, at their office on Place du Châtelet. Ivan turned up the next day.

"How are you feeling?" Henri asked, still just as affable. "What I'm about to tell you is extremely serious. I don't believe your cousin committed suicide as the police claim. But rather that he was tortured and died from his wounds."

Ivan recovered his wits enough to shout, "Tortured!"

"Didn't you see the bruises all over his face and the massive badly patched-up wounds on his head?"

No, Ivan hadn't noticed anything of the kind since he was blinded by grief. Henri continued, burning with enthusiasm.

"You have no idea how these interrogations take place. The police don't care a damn for minor drug dealers such as your cousin. What they want are the names of the drug lords and barons who ship in their merchandise from abroad and smuggle it around wherever they want. The police will go to any lengths to get what they want."

Ivan had the impression of listening to a crime thriller.

"What are we going to do?" he stammered.

"For the time being, try to find proof," Henri replied. "I'm asking you to find witnesses who can testify to your cousin's gentle character. Everyone must be made to realize that he was a victim who was led to the slaughterhouse."

Once this conversation was over, Ivan found himself on the banks of the Seine beside a secondhand bookseller who sold first editions of André Gide's novel *Les Nourritures terrestres*. How had he got there? How had his body managed to obey him, avoid all the traffic, and unconsciously make it over the pedestrian crossings? It was as if he had received a blow to the head that had left him half dead.

As usual the day was gray and rainy. Ivan sat down on a crowded bus which, after numerous stops, was to take him to the boulevard Brune. Remembering his mother's advice on manners he gave up his seat to an old lady bent in two whom nobody took notice of.

"Thank you very much," she said.

Then, sadly shaking her head, she continued:

"People didn't used to be so indifferent, selfish, and devoid of compassion for those around them as they are today. As soon as they saw me they would get up and offer me their seat. Nowadays people don't know which way to turn … with all these bomb attacks."

Ivan had no time to answer since he was pushed further along by a young woman entering the bus victoriously with a stroller.

Every time he had been hurt, his sole refuge had been

the arms of his sister. The police training school on the boulevard Brune was housed in an elegant, modern building, all glass and concrete. Ivan crossed the lobby, whose walls were covered with photos of police officers going peacefully about their daily duties such as helping children cross the road, pushing the disabled in wheelchairs, and assisting families as they climbed into small boats during floods. There was even a photo of a group of officers playing in an orchestra.

Upon hearing the reason for his visit the eyes of the wishy-washy white receptionist lit up and he complimented Ivana Némélé for being so charming and so well-mannered. After a while Ivana in person appeared and it's true she looked gorgeous in the dark-green bubble jacket she wore over her uniform.

"Life is treating you well, Snow White?" the receptionist asked her, smiling smugly.

"Very well, thank you," Ivana replied, taking the arm of her brother, who, amazed, lowered his voice to ask her, "You let him call you Snow White?"

"It's an in-joke," she explained calmly. "It's quite innocent. You mustn't make the mistake of seeing racism everywhere."

She led him to a bar close by called Le Bastingage (The Ship's Rail). Once inside, the meaning of such a strange name became evident. The walls were covered with photos of happy, smiling travelers standing on the decks of ocean liners as they passed on the open sea. In fact Le Bastingage belonged to a former employee of the Compagnie Générale Transatlantique, who had opened it on retirement. It was filled with regular customers. Some were playing darts, others were playing cards or dominoes. This family atmosphere reminded Ivan of the bars in Dos d'Âne where the regulars used to slam down their domino pieces on the deal tables.

A waiter asked Ivana if she wanted a coffee: "What will it be? A little black one as usual?"

This time Ivan didn't even bother to take offense and kept his thoughts to himself. He described as best he could the conversation he had just had with Henri Duvignaud. After listening she firmly shook her head.

"Above all don't get mixed up in this business," she urged. "I immediately saw through that lawyer, whose only ambition is self-promotion and who risks dragging you into dangerous territory. Tortured? Whatever next? You'd think we are in the middle of the Algerian war when the police followed the orders of a panicky government who didn't know which way to turn. On the contrary, the police are here to support and assist the destitute and protect them from danger."

Ivan didn't dare protest, for ever since they had arrived in France he felt he and his sister were growing apart. She was increasingly occupied by her studies, her new colleagues, and her new lifestyle. Whereas he was left to his own devices, his hands filled with ashes.

After a while a trio entered the bar: two young guys and a young girl dressed like Ivana, all in dark-green bubble jackets over their uniforms. They sat down at the twins' table without asking for permission and Ivana introduced Ivan to them.

"So you're the famous twin brother?" Aldo, one of the guys with a large square face under a head of straight, brown hair, asked. "I, too, have a twin sister but our story is quite different. We loathed each other ever since our mother's womb, so to speak. At the age of sixteen she met an Indian from Goa who had come to Paris to perfect his French. She married him and they left together. I can't get it out of my head that she didn't love him and merely wanted to put an ocean between me and her."

Everyone burst out laughing. The conversation then turned to small talk about the school. The students were all excited about the simulation of an attack they had just practiced.

Ivan tried to show an interest. But what they were talking about was not for real. It was pretense, fiction, a game. Mansour's death was well and truly for real. Nothing would bring him back.

One of the members of the group proposed going for dinner in a local Korean restaurant. They entered a plain dining room crowded with customers who were visibly concerned about expense. Simple pleasures for simple people. Ivan, who had known ultra-sophisticated restaurants, found the food tasteless. He was obliged, however, to pretend he was enjoying his meal and join in the general conversation. Deep down, he felt that Ivana was being treated with a shocking, patronizing familiarity. Aldo openly flirted with her, and Ivan suffered no end from being excluded by this intimacy, from not understanding the jokes, and not laughing at the innuendos.

Around 10 p.m. he returned home on the regional express metro with Ivana. Men and women slept on the seats, tired out. Was this the life he had dreamed of? Oh yes, the world had to be destroyed and started all over again.

If Ivana hoped, however, that Ivan would get rid of Henri Duvignaud, she was mistaken. Two days later the lawyer telephoned Ivan to invite him to go together to the refugee camp in Cambrésis. For years Cambrésis, like Calais, had been an open sore on the face of France. Right- as well as left-wing governments had tried to eradicate it to no avail. Crammed in together, Eritreans,

Somalis, Comorians, and West Africans were all galvanized by the dream of reaching England, where they believed they would find work and lodging.

"Why do you want me to come with you to such a place?" Ivan asked in surprise.

Henri Duvignaud remained unruffled, and explained, "The government has got it into its head to evacuate the camp and transfer it to a tent city a few kilometers away. There, it claims everyone will be safe, with schools for children and a dispensary. Those who are asking for political asylum in France will be given work. They claim this new village will be more fitting for genuine human beings."

"That sounds great," Ivan exclaimed. "What's wrong with that?"

"I want you to see for yourself the divorce between words and actions," Henri hammered out. "The police will be in charge of evacuating the migrants at Cambrésis whether they like or not. Forcefully, if need be. So you will understand that what happened to your cousin is not the fruit of my deranged imagination."

Ivan preferred not to tell Ivana of his plans and, after a sleepless night, he decided to accept Henri Duvignaud's invitation. The lawyer came to pick him up at eight in the morning at the wheel of a Renault Mégane, dressed to the nines as usual and wearing a dark-gray fedora. Duvignaud took the opportunity to accept a cup of Jamaican Blue Mountain coffee from Mona, who claimed it was the best in the world. As usual, she didn't fail to recollect her past. Draped in her yellow striped kimono she dwelled at length on the glory of her younger years and even went so far as to sing one of Francis Cabrel's songs: "La dame de Haute-Savoie." When she decided to end it, Henri Duvignaud showered her with compliments.

They finally managed to take their leave.

"I hate motorways," Henri declared, driving out of the parking lot. "The byroads will take longer but be less monotonous."

Ivan didn't mind as he hadn't once left the Paris region since his arrival. Despite himself he was overjoyed at this unexpected excursion. Although it was winter some of the trees were still draped in green. The towns and villages they drove through seemed poor but nevertheless welcoming. Exceptionally, it wasn't raining. An unexpected sun shone in the midst of a pale blue sky.

Shortly before noon they reached Cambrésis. Suddenly the wind got up and blew away all the clouds. Cambrésis was nothing more than two or three parallel streets lined with dilapidated building facades. In the distance you could make out a flat, languid sea whose waves rolled up and died along kilometers of beach strewn with sagging dunes like the breasts of ageing women. By comparison Ivan remembered the sunny, lively beaches of his childhood to which he had paid so little attention. Alas, that's how he was. He attached no importance to what he possessed. Because of his carelessness and recklessness Alix and Cristina had been killed. Sometimes he remembered Cristina's body welcoming him into her arms and he too wanted to die.

Once upon a time the refugee camp at Cambrésis consisted solely of two gymnasiums kindly lent by the municipality. Now it spread for miles and miles and nothing seemed to stop its advance. Under the winter sky rows of patched-up wooden and corrugated-iron shacks sat lopsided along the narrow alleys awash with a reddish mud that stuck to the soles of your shoes. The migrants were dressed in odds and ends visibly supplied by the goodwill of their sympathizers. Just as many police officers paraded back and forth with a threatening air. Nevertheless, Ivan did not witness any act of brutality. The police behaved rather like mentors, carrying young children in their arms and helping the old to walk.

Henri Duvignaud and Ivan soon began to attract attention.

"Who are you?" one of the police officers asked, rushing up to them. "This is no place for journalists."

"We are not journalists," Henri protested, and explained he was the founding president of La Main Ouverte, a humanitarian charity.

La Main Ouverte's headquarters was situated on a small square, oddly named Aux Bourgeois de Calais. In a rudimentarily furnished room, a group of French people sat among a handful of migrants on chairs placed in a semicircle around a long table. On seeing Henri Duvignaud, one of the French guys, with white hair and a Father Christmas beard, quickly stood up and said in a reproachful tone of voice, "We were expecting you much earlier. Most of our migrants had to obey orders and have already left the camp."

Henri Duvignaud sat down behind the table and began to speak.

Constantly haunted by the feeling of being excluded, Ivan found a chair at the back of the room. He had no idea what was going on around him. Suddenly a young man sitting next to him introduced himself with a smile: "My name is Ulysses Témerlan. And you?"

"Ivan Némélé, and I come from Guadeloupe."

"Guadeloupe? Are there migrants from Guadeloupe?" Ulysses asked. "I'm from Somalia. I come from a village called Mangara. My father was the school principal, which explains why my name's Ulysses and my brother's Dedalus."

The names Ulysses and Dedalus meant nothing to Ivan, who had never heard of James Joyce. He was struck by his neighbor's handsomeness. Ulysses was over six feet tall, and the regular features of his face were crowned by a head of curly hair. Despite his wretched attire, a kind of beige-colored parka and a pair of trousers too short for him, he looked radiant. Since Henri Duvignaud never stopped talking of incomprehensible matters and kept opening numerous files, Ivan and Ulysses preferred to go outside. Ulysses ordered a beer in a bar next door.

"You drink alcohol?" Ivan said reproachfully. "You're not a Muslim then?"

Ulysses shrugged his shoulders.

"Sure I'm a Muslim but, you know, I don't go for all this holier-than-thou business. I'd very much like to visit Guadeloupe. You'll never believe me but when I was small I had an elementary school teacher who came from Vieux-Habitants. She had us learn by rote: 'I was born on an island in love with the wind where the air shimmers with sugar and cinnamon.' Or something like that. Do you know that poem?"

No, Ivan had never heard of Daniel Thaly. Ulysses, however, was not listening since he was an out-and-out chatterbox and lost in his recollections.

"Mangara, the village where I was born, is a genuine marvel. It dates back to the sixteenth century. I still dream of it at night. Imagine houses hollowed out from the cliff and donkeys carrying their loads up the steep lanes. On Saturdays there was a cattle market, and as children we used to go and tease the huge cows with reddish eyes.

"Unfortunately, when I was ten my father died. They say he was poisoned by jealous neighbors. I'll never know the truth. All I know is after that my mother, who had no means of her own, had to leave for Mogadishu and take refuge at her sister's. That's when the nightmare began. My brother, cousins, and I attempted to make money by every means imaginable. We stole anything we could. Once, we robbed a group of foreigners who were sailing round the world in their luxury yacht and had stopped off following an engine breakdown; they had taken pity on us and regularly bought our fruit and vegetables. Tired of living a life of misery, my cousins emigrated to Europe. After two years of tribulations they miraculously reached England and invited us to join them since they had found work. Work! From that moment on, my brother and I took it into our heads to leave.

"Dedalus and I set off for Libya, where we were told there were hundreds of boats leaving for Europe. Alas, Libya was in a state of chaos. Coming out of a bar during a brawl, my brother was killed and I had to take to sea all on my own. I've been going round in circles here for three years.

"I can't tell you the number of times I've tried to reach England, but I've always been turned back. It won't happen again as I've given up trying."

"You've made up your mind to stay in France, then?" Ivan said in astonishment. "Are you going to ask for political asylum?"

Ulysses made a face.

"I don't know yet."

Why did Ivan get the impression that Ulysses was hiding something from him? It became even more pronounced when they returned to the meeting room and Ulysses asked Henri Duvignaud to take him back to Paris.

"Paris?" Henri Duvignaud asked in amazement.

"Yes," Ulysses answered offhandedly. "Some friends have invited me to spend a few days with them on the boulevard Voltaire, but you can let me off anywhere you like and I'll manage on my own."

A few days later, despite his lack of enthusiasm, Ivan had to accept Mona's offer to work for the Marcellin Berthelot College. Instead of being posted to the canteen as previously discussed, he was made to join the most arduous of services, the cleaning department. He had to scrub the classroom floors, empty the trash bins, refill the chalk boxes, and coat the blackboards with a kind of varnish. The worst job was sweeping the ice-cold recreation yards that the frost had made slippery and dangerous. Since all this work had to be completed before the students arrived and before the gates opened at 8 a.m. it meant that Ivan had to get up at the crack of dawn, down a cup of Blue Mountain coffee, or perhaps not, and, shivering from the cold, walk across the windswept parking lots of the André Malraux housing estate and through the awakening streets to the college.

His life was beyond understanding. Once again he wondered why he had refused to become an apprentice to a chocolate maker only to end up in this wretched situation. When he lived in Guadeloupe his heart beat with happy anticipation. What had happened? Why did bad luck never loosen its grip? He had no friends: nobody he could count on and nobody in whom he could confide his distress. Ivana seemed to grow further and further away. The most she did was to give him a double-quick peck on his forehead in the morning and another one in the evening before locking herself up in her room. He could no longer put up with the constant reprimands from Hugo, and especially from Mona who, since she had found him a job, thought she could order him about.

On Fridays Ivan made his way piously to the Radogan Mosque, named after its imam. He didn't go just to pray since he was engaged in constant conversation with this God who had created him and now seemed to have forgotten him. Why did He tolerate the evil and wickedness of the living? He could never get this question out of his head. He liked to go to the mosque because he loved mixing with this humble crowd of men who prostrated themselves in the direction of Mecca. During these moments he felt his solitude melt away. He got the impression of joining a fellowship of brothers who were as destitute and vulnerable as he was and who were hoping that one day happiness would finally arrive.

One Friday a new imam made an appearance. Unlike Imam Radogan, a colorless individual who could hardly speak French, the new imam cut a fine figure. He looked a lot like Ulysses: brown skin, straight black hair, sparkling eyes, and a strong, powerful voice. Ivan was soon bombarded with information about him because you can't imagine the gossip that is rumored around in places of worship. In the mosque's refreshment room no subject was left unturned by the faithful while they sipped their mint tea. The new imam was called Amiri Kapoor. He came from Pakistan and had lived for a long time in Kano, the holy city in northern Nigeria.

Ivan had been deeply moved by his sermon.

"Take control of your life," the imam had declared in a vibrant voice. "Refuse to be treated with contempt, to be snubbed as if you were children, good-for-nothings. By every means possible, and I repeat by every means, we must destroy the world around us, and on the ruins build a more hospitable haven for mankind."

This wasn't the first time Ivan had heard this type of

discourse. But that day it had a particular resonance for him. He felt invested with renewed energy, prepared to brave everything. How he would have liked to talk to this imam. Unfortunately, when he pushed open the door to the waiting room a dozen devotees were already seated in line and he left disappointed.

It was that same evening he received a call from Ulysses inviting him to dinner. Ulysses had kept his word: he had left the camp at Cambrésis and found a job in Paris. Ivan was jealous. Finding a job in Paris, and well-paid into the bargain, was nothing short of miraculous. He would never have such luck. Although he had no inclination to continue his friendship with this lapsed Muslim who drank alcohol, he accepted the invitation, knowing full well how miserable his evenings were at the André Malraux housing estate. Ivana would lock herself up in her room with her typewritten notes and her class books. Hugo sooner or later would go and meet one of his Guyanese friends. All that was left was the company of Mona, who put on simpering airs and hummed little songs. Or else he would watch silly films on the television.

Contrary to expectations Ivan began to take a liking to Paris. He knew he would never conquer this city and there would never be a place for him. Yet its energy at all hours, day and night, was as stimulating as a drug. Every one of its boulevards whispered a catchy tune in his ear that made him want to dance. Everything was so different from gloomy Villeret-le-François. Passersby seemed more open-minded and happier. It was as if he was in love with a woman whose beauty and virtues made her inaccessible.

Ulysses lived in the very center of Paris in a handsome building on the boulevard Voltaire, which had the serious disadvantage of not having an elevator. Ivan had to hobble up the six steep flights of stairs covered with a threadbare carpet. When Ulysses came to open the door, Ivan had trouble recognizing him. Gone was the immigrant cramped into a shabby-looking parka and trousers he had met a few weeks earlier. Ulysses was wearing the latest fashion, dressed to the nines like Mansour used to be, in a salt-and-pepper suit with a large blue silk scarf tied around his neck. Where did this transformation come from? How could he account for it? Ivan refrained from asking and followed his host through a maze of well-furnished rooms to a charming bedroom in the middle of which was a bed covered with a richly embroidered Moroccan blanket.

"My goodness! You must have won the lottery!" Ivan said to Ulysses jokingly.

Ulysses shook his head seriously.

"I told you, I've found work."

He lit a cigarette, for not only did this lapsed Muslim drink alcohol, he also smoked.

"It's a special kind of job which I'll describe to you because I think for a boy like you, built like you are, it might very well suit you. You've no idea of the nightmare I endured for three long years at the Cambrésis camp. I can't describe the filthy showers and toilets that had to be shared between ten and twelve men. I'll spare you the revolting food served up in bars that went by the name of restaurants. No, I'm talking about the constant promiscuity, the daily rape of women, teenagers, and even children: in short, all those who were particularly vulnerable. I had the good fortune to meet a couple who helped me get out of there."

After a moment's silence he continued, slightly embarrassed.

"They offered me the job of escort."

"Escort?" Ivan repeated, somewhat puzzled. "What does that mean?"

Ulysses became even more embarrassed. He gestured vaguely.

"I think it's an English or Spanish word, I don't know exactly. Anyway, it doesn't matter. You know, women are very different from what they used to be. They're not what our countries tell us they are. Women have a will of their own, they have energy, they have desires, I mean desires of the flesh. They know what they want and they want men capable of satisfying them and helping them taste the pleasures of life. Every type of pleasure, you know what I'm saying?"

No, Ivan did not know what he was saying.

"What are you talking about?" Ivan asked again.

Ulysses decided to lay his cards on the table.

"What I'm saying is you can make thousands of euros a month if you know how to use the tools you were born with. How long is your penis?"

"What!" Ivan shouted, thinking he had misheard.

Ulysses waved a calming hand.

"I'm joking, I'm joking. Let's be serious. At the present time I'm escorting three women: one of them is the manager of an advertising company, another is an actress with a promising career, and the third is a cosmetic surgeon. None of them balk at giving me all the money I need."

Gradually the truth dawned on Ivan, for he was not entirely naive. Worse than anything he might have imagined, Ulysses surrendered his body to women in exchange for money. He was nothing better than a prostitute. A bitter taste of bile filled his mouth. He almost vomited, then he stood up and headed rapidly for the exit.

"Don't be ridiculous," Ulysses said, trying to hold him back.

Ivan was no longer listening. He dashed down the stairs, landed on the sidewalk, and in his haste almost knocked over a passing couple. Without knowing exactly what he was doing he crossed the boulevard and began running, the likes of which he hadn't done for years, and people stood in fright to let this tall black man run past, swifter than the legendary Thiam Papagallo. He pushed open the gate to a square which, during the day, was crowded with babies in their strollers and children pedaling their tricycles, but for now was deserted, and collapsed onto a bench whose cold surface penetrated his clothes. He couldn't stop feeling nauseated, disgusted, and soiled. He would have liked to become the small boy again when Simone soaped and lathered his body and poured calabash upon calabash of warm water over his head. While he remained petrified with disgust, a young man approached him and with an unmistakable smile, simpered, "Aren't you cold?"

Ivan's blood boiled over and he lost control of his hands which grabbed the seducer's throat. This is what the world had to offer: prostitutes, homosexuals, escorts, every type of depravity.

We have managed to reconstruct exactly the events of that fatal evening. We use the word "fatal" on purpose because, having attempted to follow and understand him all through our story, to our thinking it was at that very moment Ivan's radicalization came to completion. Up till then certain events, such as the deaths of his beloved Alix and Cristina, had not radically changed him. Suddenly all these incidents took on a striking new meaning: the death of Mansour and the depravity of Ulysses assumed a decisive character.

The screams of the man who Ivan had grabbed around the neck did not fail to attract the attention of passersby who were making their way to a concert at the Bataclan. By punching and kicking they managed to free the victim. But Ivan was so strong and tall he was able to escape, and jumped into a taxi cruising along the boulevard Voltaire. The taxi driver was a Guadeloupean, Florian Ernatus, who, seeing a man of his race in difficulty, and being pursued by a horde of white folk, naturally came to his aid. Such behavior is becoming increasingly rare and deserves to be mentioned. As for white folk, they have always killed each other: for example, the Nazis and the Jews. Black people, on the contrary, inspired by their theory of Negritude and racial solidarity, once believed they owed it to themselves to help each other. Nowadays such ideas have become obsolete.

"Where are you going?" Florian Ernatus asked Ivan, pushing hard on the accelerator.

"I don't know. Oh yes, take me to Villeret-le-François," Ivan stammered.

Lying flat out on the back seat while the lights of bars and buildings flew past as the taxi picked up speed, Ivan, who never talked about himself, began to tell the story of his life.

"It's the same for everyone," Florian told him, shrugging his shoulders. "You think things were different for me? First of all, I've never known my father. After pestering my mother, she ended up telling me his name was Bong, a Filipino who cleaned the cabins on board the cruise ship *Empress of the Seas* when the company used to make the Antilles their port of call. My mother was nanny to the baby of a rich family of mulattos who were traveling to celebrate their tenth wedding anniversary. Was she telling the truth? I've no idea. For years I walked barefoot or with sneakers because I didn't have the money to buy a solid pair of shoes. There was a time when I worked on the Filipacchi plantations. Unfortunately, one fine day a gust of wind blew down all the banana trees and I found myself out of work. Then I worked for the Salomon pig farm but the pigs caught swine fever and the facility had to close. It was in Paris I found work again. This taxi isn't mine, I'm just the driver."

What Florian didn't say was how he'd searched everywhere for his father. He had gone to Jamaica where the cruise company had its headquarters and was hired three times in the ships' kitchens. But among the hundreds of Filipinos who cleaned the cabins he never found trace of anyone called Bong.

We can only give thanks for the way Florian Ernatus treated Ivan. He drove him to Villeret-le-François and, despite the twists and turns he had to make, no thanks to his GPS, he didn't charge him a penny. Once they arrived at the André Malraux housing estate Florian helped Ivan climb the stairs in Tower A where Ivan hung out. He accompanied Ivan into Hugo's tiny apartment, opened the futon and put him to bed like a mother would have done. We can now certify that from that moment on a visible change came over Ivan. He became increasingly somber; never a smile, even less a burst of laughter, and always prepared to dissect the slightest incident in his daily routine.

Ivan spent the week huddled up on his futon, his forehead covered with compresses. Ivana missed two days of classes to look after him. Even though Mona insisted it was just a bad cold and there was no need to call the doctor, Ivana was worried. Finally Ivan opened his eyes, got dressed, and went to the mosque, determined to have a conversation with the imam Amiri Kapoor. He sensed that this man would change his life.

Amiri Kapoor received Ivan in his office whose luxuriousness amazed anyone who entered it. In this shabby-looking mosque, once a gymnasium, a gift from the municipality to its growing Muslim population, he had managed to create a space filled with beauty. Black and gilded calligraphies covered the walls as well as photos of the main places of worship in the world: Mecca rubbed shoulders with Golgotha, Notre-Dame in Paris, and Westminster Abbey. The imam's profile had a lot going for it. He was the son and grandson of two imams, moral rigorists who proclaimed loud and clear the name of God in the small village of Ragu located a few kilometers from Lahore. He was fifteen when his father forced him to write a letter of congratulations to Ayatollah Khomeini, who had just declared the fatwa against Salman Rushdie. "So must perish all bad Muslims," his father had thundered. The imam had then spent three years in Medina, that austere city where the call of the muezzins rang out from early morning on. When he had lived in Kano he had done wonders revamping and reorganizing the institutions of this holy city where all too often the call to prayer was little more than a monotonous recitative.

Amiri Kapoor cast a penetrating look at Ivan.

"First question: why did you convert to Islam? I know that Christianity reigns in the part of the world you come from. Why such a conversion?"

Ivan hesitated for a moment.

"I don't know really. I lived in Mali. In the compound where we lived my sister and I were the only Catholics and I always felt foreign, out of place. I believe, too, that I wanted to get closer to my father with whom I didn't get along."

The imam looked surprised.

"You have a sister, then?"

"A twin sister," Ivan replied, unconsciously infatuated every time he mentioned Ivana. "I came out of our mother's womb first. I'm a boy. These two reasons should have been enough to make me feel superior. But I feel nothing of the sort. She is so accomplished and I'm so inferior, I adore her."

"You should only adore God," the imam cut in sharply.

This brutal reprimand upset Ivan.

The imam continued more gently.

"Is your faith in God as sharp as a weapon? Are you capable of killing for it?"

Ivan once again hesitated. Although he had belonged to the death squad which had killed El Cobra, he had merely obeyed the diktat of the Army of Shadows out of fear or cowardice. It was not the result of a personal decision.

"Yes," he claimed, nevertheless. "I'm capable of doing it."

There then followed a long exchange of looks. Amiri Kapoor understood that this simple-minded boy, incapable of using his wits, was, however, made of exceptional stuff, the material for making first-class disciples. All it needed was to help him get rid of a few dregs, such as this excessive love for his sister.

He rummaged through the drawers of his desk and brought out a fat file, which he opened.

"Are you free on Tuesday and Thursday evenings?" he asked. "If so, I'll put you in charge of helping the students at the Koranic school. You'll reread their homework, grade them, and help them get closer to God. I feel you're capable of doing that."

After a moment's silence he continued.

"I must confess that in exchange for your services I can only offer a small payment. You know the financial situation of the mosques in France."

Ivan waved his hand.

"It's not a question of money between us. I'd do it for free if you asked me."

How surprising life turns out to be! In one week Ivan was offered two types of decent jobs. The principal of the Marcellin Berthelot College, who had never paid him any attention, summoned him to his office. To Ivan's great surprise he was offered the job of replacing a school supervisor who had been hospitalized for many months following an unfortunate car accident.

"You won't have much to do," he assured Ivan. "Simply supervise the students during their study period. Madame Mona Hincelin tells me you were an excellent pupil in Guadeloupe and I can easily get your file from the education authorities."

Ivan gave thanks to God, who for once seemed to be treating him well.

Henceforth he divided his time between the Marcellin Berthelot College and the mosque's Koranic school. He had a soft spot for the hours he spent at the mosque for, without really knowing why, he loved to be around young people. He who had never heard of the expression "second and third generation" immediately understood its meaning. These teenagers had never been to the country of their ancestors. It was unknown territory. Born in France, they believed themselves to be French, proud at having built the Eiffel Tower or having dug the Saint-Martin canal. Some of them were grandchildren of Harkis and knew full well that their grandparents had given France more than a helping hand when it was needed. They lived in blissful ignorance about themselves. Until the unexpected insult "filthy Arab" flew out because of a lost pencil sharpener or a torn text book. Of course, they had curly hair and a creamy pale complexion. But did that make them Arabs, they wondered? Moreover, what is an Arab? Those of them who investigated further discovered they were blamed mainly for their religion: Islam. They had trouble understanding that this mumbo jumbo on which they placed little value made them responsible for attacks committed in unknown lands as far away as Pakistan or Indonesia.

For the first time, Ivan was obliged to reflect on the meaning of Islam. A warlike religion, some people said. Aren't all religions warlike since they proselytize and take pride in the number of their converts? Misogynistic, others said. Isn't Christianity just as much? It wasn't that long ago when it questioned whether women were endowed with an immortal soul like men.

By contrast, Ivan disliked his new job at the Marcellin Berthelot College and considered his students pretentious, interested only in being admitted to the prestigious institutions of higher education. Most of his time was spent preventing the brutes in eighth grade from bullying the little pupils in sixth grade. He outfoxed rackets and set matters in order whereas before there was nothing but chaos; behind his back he quickly became known as Batman. When he learned of his nickname he asked Serge, a boy with whom he had become friends, "Batman? Why have you decided to call me Batman?"

Serge replied without hesitation. "Because you always fly to the rescue of the weakest."

Ivan was not satisfied with this answer. It was not what he wanted. He wanted to change the world. The only problem was that he still had no idea how to go about it.

He had hoped that the imam Amiri Kapoor could help him, but nothing had resulted from their meeting. Sometimes he got the impression that the imam was watching him and was taking time to think things over.

Needless to say Ivan and Ivana had less and less in common and lived more and more on different planets each day. Although Ivan suffered acutely from this situation, Ivana didn't seem to notice. She was happy and overjoyed at having all that she wished for. She had passed her exams and was admitted to the second year at the police training school. She had already been put in charge of minor duties and was proud of patrolling unsafe neighborhoods, standing guard outside schools, helping parents with children cross the road, and sometimes even volunteering for traffic duty. On Sundays she remained invisible. There was no longer any question of Ivan having lunch with her. She would go on visits to Notre-Dame, Montmartre, the Châteaux of the Loire, and especially to the Château of Chambord of which she was particularly fond. "Built at the heart of Europe's biggest enclosed wooded park, Chambord is the largest château in the Loire valley. It enjoys extensive gardens and hunting grounds listed as classical monuments." Ivana's close friend was Maylan, a blonde police student originally from Bulgaria and endowed with a pretty little voice. Already imagining herself as Sylvie Vartan she sang solo in concerts organized by charitable associations. Ivana and Maylan were inseparable. When they were not together, they were conversing endlessly over mobile phones glued to their ears. For all these reasons Ivan hated her.

Why did Ivan agree to go to Fontainebleau where Maylan was performing at her parents' farm? It was probably Spring that was lending him wings. His veins seemed to be injected with fresh blood. Instead of the blazing sun of Guadeloupe followed by long periods of rain, or the suffocating heat all year long in Mali, this change of seasons was beneficial. The same landscape was transformed month by month as if by enchantment, as if a magician had waved his magic wand over it.

Maylan's parents lived on a large farm not far from the forest of Fontainebleau. For their daughter's concert they had left nothing to chance. In the main courtyard they had set up huge white tents housing round tables and chairs. If it hadn't been for the disastrous smell of a nearby pig farm blown in sporadically by the wind, everything would have been perfect. Ivan took his seat next to his sister who very soon met up with her friends, whose company she seemed to enjoy. On the stage two men performed a duo: *Perrine était servante, Perrine était servante chez monsieur not' curé. Dingue Dengue Dongue.* It was an old traditional song from the region, Ivan was told. Apparently the guests loved it and it brought the house down. Ivan was not amused and after an hour he could no longer put up with the boredom and the insipid warbling of the guests. Leave, he had to leave.

He got up, whispering in the ear of his sister, who was somewhat surprised.

"I'll be right back. Don't worry."

He went out and found himself on the main road. Since the arrows of the sun's rays were becoming sharper and sharper, sweat began to roll down his face. He had no idea where the station at Fontainebleau was and decided therefore to hitchhike. He had to wait until a fifth car stopped, and a fair-haired boy at the wheel of a Volkswagen popped his head through the window.

"Where are you going, my friend?" he asked affably with a smile.

Coming from a complete stranger, Ivan was surprised by his familiarity.

"I'm going to the station at Fontainebleau."

The fair-haired guy burst out laughing.

"You're going in the right direction. If you walk straight for another twenty or so kilometers you'll get there."

Faced with Ivan's bewildered look, he continued.

"I'm joking. Get in. I'm going to the station myself so I'll drop you off."

He went on with the same familiarity.

"My name's Harry. What's yours? Where do you work?"

Ivan was incapable of answering such a question.

His companion insisted.

"At La Pallud's? At Dumontel's? What's the name of the stud farm?"

"I don't work on a stud farm," Ivan protested. "I was invited to a concert."

"A concert? I thought you worked at Dumontel's. They employ a lot of people like you."

Like you? What did that mean? Harry, therefore, had taken no notice of his elegant wild-silk suit, his fine stiff-collar shirt, and his expensive shoes, the elegant leftovers from his time with Mansour. All he had noticed was his color. All he had memorized was the black man, the nigger, as they used to say, and in his eyes Ivan could only ever be a subaltern. Before switching on the engine Harry rummaged among the cds in his car.

"Shall I put on Coluche? Would you like to listen to him? It's a repeat of his best sketches."

Ivan was caught unawares and could only stammer a reply.

"Coluche? I don't know him."

He had a vague memory of a fat man in overalls, his

hair in a fringe over his forehead. But he had never paid attention to his monologues.

"I can't believe it," Harry exclaimed, staring blue-eyed. "You've never heard of Coluche or his Restos du Coeur charity?"

Aujourd'hui on n'a plus le droit,
Ni d'avoir faim ni d'avoir froid.
Dépassé le chacun pour soi,
Quand je pense à toi je pense à moi.

(Today we have no right
To go hungry or be cold.
Gone is everyone for himself
When I think of you I think of me.)

What fault have I committed? Ivan wondered as the car drove off. Did Harry know the names of the famous drummers from Guadeloupe and Martinique? Fortunately they soon arrived at the station and Ivan mumbled his thanks.

When he arrived at Villeret-le-François, Mona was reading the cards in the living room.

"Back already?" she said, surprised. "Where's Ivana?"

Thereupon she continued without waiting for an answer.

"Today the cards are predicting nothing but misfortune. Black on black. Jack of spades on jack of spades."

Relations between Mona and Ivan had taken a turn for the better. In the early stages she had agreed with Hugo and considered Ivan a good-for-nothing. She constantly compared him to her son, a minor history teacher who was highly rated in his college in the provinces. Gradually she began to treat Ivan differently. We might think it was because of his attractive physique. His penis squeezed into his tight trousers always seemed on the point of popping out, and reminded Mona, partial to handsome males, of the time when she accumulated lover upon lover. Let's not get carried away, however. Let's say rather that Ivan's character and helpfulness brought out the best in him. He would accompany her to the market at Croix-Nivert, pushing her caddy loaded with provisions which he then hauled up the steep stairs of Tower A.

Ivan sat down in front of the television, determined to wait for an explanation from his sister. What pleasure did she take in the company she kept? Had she forgotten the plans she had made when they lived in Guadeloupe? Unfortunately, around 10 p.m. Ivana called Mona to say she was spending the night at Maylan's. Increasingly depressed, Ivan opened his futon and tried to get some sleep.

The next day Ivan once again went to meet Imam Amiri Kapoor to force him to confront his problems. Ivan found him immersed in his Koran while sipping a cup of coffee.

"What brings you here?" he asked warmly. "I only hear good things about you. The youngsters say you're an outstanding teacher."

Ivan curled up in his chair and answered glumly, "It's not the impression I get. In my opinion nothing seems to be going right."

Thereupon he began to describe in detail his latest misadventures and made no attempt even to hide his setbacks with Ulysses.

The imam listened to him attentively without interruption. When Ivan had finished, surprising even himself at having plunged into the waters of this malaise

which he carried deep down and had never really sus-
pected, the imam drew a typewritten sheet from a
drawer in his desk and handed it to Ivan.

"First of all you must read," he ordered. "Read. Only
knowledge can save you. There are answers to a lot of the
questions you ask."

Ivan cast a look at the list of books. He found the names
of authors and books that Ismaël had indicated when
Ivan was a member of the Army of Shadows, and even
further back when he was at school with Monsieur
Jérémie at Dos d'Âne: Frantz Fanon, Eric Williams, Wal-
ter Rodney, and Jean Suret-Canale. He had never taken
the trouble either to buy them or study them, something
which he now regretted.

"Wait a minute," Ivan said. "I haven't told you what is
torturing me. You know full well what my twin sister
means to me. I would even say she is everything for me.
But here, we are growing further and further apart. She
is absorbed by her studies and the life she leads in
France. I mean nothing to her anymore and that's what
is extremely painful for me."

The imam shrugged his shoulders.

"Women are narrow-minded," he let out. "I would say
frankly you love your sister too much. It's an unhealthy
feeling. If she is growing apart from you, let her go. It
will be good for both of you."

Nobody had spoken so brutally to Ivan. What a cage,
what a dungeon, what a prison his life would turn into if
Ivana no longer illuminated his existence. The imam
continued.

"Put your words into action, that's what you need to
do. I'm going to send you to a group of young men who
will help you become a man, a real man. I understand
what you mean. Western society, in which we find

ourselves immersed, will perish because it is too sure of itself and accumulates blunder upon blunder. What matters is that it doesn't drag us down with it."

The following weeks Ivan felt increasingly alone despite the promise the imam had made him. Ivana was away most of the time: language courses abroad, vacations in the sun. Together with Maylan she had traveled to Faro in Portugal, a small seaside resort. She even managed to go three whole days without calling her brother.

In the meantime Hugo and Mona, feeling cramped in their apartment, urged the two youngsters to find their own accommodation. Mona, who had more than one string to her bow, found some lodgings, though badly situated, it must be said, opposite the Croix-Nivert market. From morning to evening you could hear the market vendors shouting their sales pitch on such and such an item. All day long there was also the stench of fruit, vegetables, meat, and fish. Unfortunately the deal didn't go through as the twins' income was inadequate. This merely disheartened Ivan further. He knew all too well there was no place for him in this country which proclaimed so generously to be the home of human rights. If he disappeared who would even notice? Ivana perhaps. Then she would find consolation nestling her forehead against Maylan's breast.

It was on October 2nd that Ivan finally met Abdel Aziz Isar, whom the imam had recommended. Remember this fateful date of October 2nd, since we believe it marks the beginning of the end. Abdel Aziz Isar lived in Villeret-le-François in an apartment block in slightly better shape than Ivan's. Here, the elevators worked and the entrance halls were not overcrowded with drug dealers. Ivan got a cold reception since Abdel Aziz distrusted the lame ducks Amiri Kapoor insisted on sending him. Although a Muslim, he was born in Varanasi in India, on the left bank of the Ganges, the holy river where his father, Azouz, owned an elegant women's clothing shop. In 1948, during the bitter partition of India, Azouz had refused to leave the country of his birth, believing that every religion could live together in harmony. When his shop was burned down for the third time and he was left for dead on the sidewalk he made up his mind to move to Dhaka with his family. Abdel Aziz therefore had grown up with tales of violence and terror.

He asked Ivan curtly, "What do you expect from me? What do you want to do with your life? Do you want to stay in Europe or leave for one of our countries?"

"I would prefer to remain in Paris," Ivan replied, thinking of Ivana from whom he never wanted to be separated. "But whatever the case, I'll carry out any mission you want me to do and wherever you think fit."

Abdel Aziz inspected Ivan from head to toe.

"Do you know how to use a weapon? And explosives?"

"Yes, I do," Ivan claimed. "In Mali I was a member of the national militia where we learned those sorts of things."

Abdel Aziz looked him straight in the eye.

"Have you ever killed a man?" he suddenly asked.

Ivan hesitated then repeated his usual explanation.

"Yes, but I was part of a commando whose members had been delegated. I was obeying orders. It was not a personal decision."

Despite his surliness, Abdel Aziz, nevertheless, offered him mint tea served by a young woman with a ravaging smile and fawn-colored hair covered by an elegant black scarf.

"My wife, Anastasie," he said by way of introduction.

And with an unexpected lyricism, he added, "We met in Fallujah. Yes, the desolation of Fallujah was the setting for our love, a love so strong it has resisted many a pitfall. We have three children. Three sons."

Ivan was heading for the door, having finished his tea, when Abdel Aziz let fly an arrow.

"You don't have a beard."

Ivan stopped in his tracks, his hand on the doorknob.

"A beard?" he repeated, a little surprised.

Abdel Aziz's beard in fact was silky and well-combed and added a certain maturity to his still-juvenile face.

Ivan continued apologetically.

"It's a recommendation in the Koran, not a commandment."

From that day on, however, he grew a beard, which Ivana and Mona unanimously criticized. However much he rubbed his cheeks with essential oils, the beard remained skimpy and sparse and didn't suit him at all. After several weeks he resigned himself to shaving it off.

What Abdel Aziz didn't say was that during his numerous stays in Fallujah he was on intimate terms with the highest dignitaries of the regime. He worked on behalf of the committee that administered the city. He was in charge of implementing convictions pertaining to the law and was thus involved in all the public executions. He executed adulterous women by shooting them in the head. He cut off the hands of thieves. He branded deserving criminals with a hot iron. In short, he was nothing more than an assassin. What Abdel Aziz didn't say either was that his wife, Anastasie, was the daughter of one of Saddam Hussein's generals.

Ivan was not to see Abdel Aziz for another two or three weeks and even thought he had forgotten him. It was then he received a text message summoning him to a meeting where he encountered a dozen boys, some of them very young, still teenagers, no more than seventeen or eighteen. Most of them lived in Syria, Lebanon, Iran, or Iraq and had taken part in numerous punitive expeditions. They were in Paris prepared to obey orders from the supreme commanders to carry out attacks. What type of attack, nobody knew yet. Ivan was struck by the presence of two girls, two twins, Botul and Afsa. Originally from Turkey, they had lived in Brussels and had recently settled in France. In Brussels they had been part of an ensemble, The Amazones, hoping one day to become famous singers. Unless death mowed them down beforehand; an eventuality of which they were not afraid. Wasn't death the supreme consecration? Botul and Afsa were to have a considerable influence on the life of Ivan. He became their friend and visited them daily in their apartment on the outskirts of Villeret-le-François. They impressed on him a host of complex feelings. He admired their slender silhouettes, their sparkling eyes, and their thin upper lips which revealed two sets of dazzling white teeth. Above all, he admired their turn of mind. He would have liked his sister to be like them: rebellious and ridiculing, casting a critical eye on society and manifesting a permanent distrust of the West. Instead of which, Ivana became more submissive and conformist by the day. She accompanied Maylan to movies and concerts and enthused about films and books that were devoid of interest, but for her were remarkably successful.

"You're not interested in anything," she blamed her brother. "You don't like anything. You complain about everything."

She was right, Ivan told himself. He very likely deserved to be blamed. But how could you pretend to be someone else?

Since Botul and Afsa had given him tickets for a performance by a group with the surprising name of The Singing Berbers, he didn't hesitate to invite Ivana, who to his surprise categorically refused to accompany him.

"You don't want to go?" he asked.

She put on her poker-faced look.

"I assume that most of the spectators will be North Africans. Quite frankly, I don't like Arabs."

"You don't like Arabs!" Ivan exclaimed, stupefied. "How can you say such a thing? It's as if someone said they don't like Blacks. The Arabs are our friends. Or rather, our brothers," he corrected himself, remembering Monsieur Jérémie's lessons. "I even consider them to be role models, intellectual leaders. They were colonized like us. In Algeria they paid a terrible price fighting for their freedom."

Ivana remained unflustered.

"Perhaps you're telling the truth," she said. "What I do know is that Arab men cannot look at a woman without flirting with her and making crude advances. And the women with their ridiculous headscarves stand there watching them as if they were gods."

The twins, Botul and Afsa, soon confided in Ivan a hidden secret in their lives. Up to the age of twenty, stuck in a family obsessed with their problems of survival, their father a night watchman, their mother a cleaning woman, they had been lovers. No man or woman suited them. They slept in each other's arms and made passionate love. Only the contours of each other's body satisfied them. One night their sleep had been brutally interrupted. They had seen the archangel Gabriel seated in tears at the foot of their bed. Looking straight at them, his eyes brimming with tears, he told them how the nature of their relationship offended God. They were committing a crime which would close the gates of Paradise to them forever. This scene had had a devastating effect on them. They had become conscious of their fault and no longer sinned, putting an end to their relationship.

You can imagine the effect such a confession had on Ivan. Of course he had always known that, twin or not, the feelings and desire he felt for Ivana were unnatural. He had never thought, however, that they offended God. He reassured himself by saying he had never committed a reprehensible act. He had never brushed against his sister's body in an indecent manner. Had he voluntarily deluded himself and hidden the truth? Was Ivana in fact a cause for damnation?

Henceforth Ivan's malaise became acute. His fear of guilt constantly haunted him. Apart from that, he told himself, his life was beyond reproach. He prayed five times a day, he fasted during Ramadan, and on Fridays he never failed to go to the mosque. Moreover, despite his meager income, he gave alms whenever it was possible. He piously read and reread his Koran.

If there was someone who realized Ivan's radicalization, it was Henri Duvignaud, the lawyer, who learned about his quarrel with Ulysses. The reasons appeared obvious, but he decided to invite Ivan to dinner to be clear in his own mind. Henri Duvignaud was a fervent adept of the pleasures of the night. For him life began at sunset. Paris was a series of bars where alcohol overflowed, restaurants where you ate well, and places where you met open-minded and sophisticated individuals. He took Ivan to The Caravansérail, situated at the Porte Maillot, whose chef had lived for many years in Japan then China before settling down in Paris. Underneath his frivolous appearance and the perpetual celebrity smile on his lips, Henri was an excellent judge of men. He sensed that Ivan belonged to that species of humans who could be turned into the most dangerous of rebels.

As soon as they were served the starter, a delicate pastry stuffed with scallops, Henri interrogated Ivan.

"I hear you no longer see Ulysses?"

Ivan downed his glass of grenadine and nodded.

"What have you got against him?" Henri insisted. "He's a nice boy and very deserving as well."

"Very deserving?" Ivan exclaimed. "Do you know the job he's doing?"

Ivan burst into a fit of anger.

"He's a prostitute for women in exchange for money."

Henri looked Ivan straight in the eye.

"Would you have preferred he stayed in Cambrésis and continue to be raped because of his looks and insulted because of his color, or that he continue to do humiliating jobs for a few euros a time and in the end be beaten to death like Mansour? Is that what you would have wanted? Is that what you would have wanted? That he stays in hell? The world is a nasty business and, as the African proverb says, nobody gets out alive."

Ivan pushed away his plate and Henri Duvignaud continued in no uncertain terms, "Don't judge! Please don't judge! Turn your back on me too, since you can't bear to hear the truth."

Ivan leaned forward and his words hissed though his lips.

"So you give your blessing to every base act in the world? For me, you're just as despicable as Ulysses. And for you, the word of God doesn't count?"

"If God exists, which nobody knows for sure," Henri joked. "He is Love. You never think of that characteristic."

Ivan stood up and in an unintentionally theatrical

voice said, "I think we no longer have anything to say to each other."

Thereupon he strode out of the restaurant and disappeared into the night. He walked straight ahead not knowing exactly where he was going and found himself in an elegant and brilliantly lit neighborhood. Unwittingly he gave the passersby embittered stares as if they were guilty. Guilty of what? Of feeling happy with themselves whereas he felt so ill at ease? After a while he collapsed on a bench in anger. On seeing him, a couple of lovers who were necking stood up in fright and fled. Ivan remained seated for a long time. When he decided to continue on his way, he came across a metro entrance which led to the regional express. By talking to him of God's love, Henri had touched a sore point. He suddenly thought he had been unfair to Ulysses, who was a victim like himself and seeking to survive as best he could.

At this time of night the regional express was deserted. A group of women from Eastern Europe dressed in long flowery robes were singing so as to distract the passengers from the young pickpockets who were stealthily robbing them. Every time Ivan set foot in this smelly, drafty place he felt the same repulsion.

He finally arrived at Villeret-le-François. In the warmth of the night, Ivana was sitting on one of the benches set around the housing estate flanked by the inevitable Maylan. They had just seen a film, and chattered on loquaciously explaining that they couldn't remember the exact title: *French Fried Vacation* perhaps?

As they climbed up the filthy stairs Ivana seized him by the arm.

"I haven't yet told you the good news. I'm so glad," she declared. "Out of all the applications, the municipal police of Villeret-le-François have selected mine. Mine, can you imagine! That's where I'll do my internship next month."

"If you're happy then I am too," Ivan replied. "But what will it change?"

"I'll be just up the road," Ivana retorted. "I won't have to get up at dawn like I do now, quickly down my breakfast, and take that horrible express metro which is always overcrowded."

Once they arrived on the third floor, Ivan headed for his sister's bedroom as usual for a chat when she held him back.

"I'm dead beat. Good night and sweet dreams."

Stupefied, he watched her close the door behind her.

Ivan then spent the worst week of his life, watching for the slightest smile or the slightest gesture which could explain Ivana's behavior. What was she hiding from him?

One evening returning home from the Marcellin Berthelot College he bumped into a man waiting in the tiny living room: young with a dark complexion, like someone of mixed blood, and fairly handsome. The stranger jumped up and cried, "So you must be the brother! The twin! I'm very pleased to make your acquaintance. I'm Ariel Zeni, you sister's best friend, if I may say so."

Ivana came out of her room dressed to the nines and smelling of perfume. On seeing her, Ariel hummed jokingly the well-known song by Adamo for the benefit of Ivan.

"May I have your permission, monsieur, to escort your sister?"

The couple disappeared in a burst of laughter. Ariel Zeni, a foreign-sounding name, could he be a Jew? Ivan, who never watched the news broadcast over and over again on television, knew very little about the Israeli-Palestinian conflict. Sometimes he was moved by seeing houses in ruins or women in tears beside their wounded children, but that was all. Up till now he had felt neither sympathy nor antipathy for the Jews. He had never understood why the Nazis had hounded them relentlessly, seeking the Final Solution. He still didn't understand what people blamed them for. Is it a crime to form a close-knit, united community? Suddenly the fact of being a Jew took on the looks of a rival. Was Ariel a rival?

Ivana returned home shortly before midnight with the saucy look of someone who has had a good time.

"You're still up?" she exclaimed in surprise on seeing Ivan glued to the television.

"Who is this Ariel?" thundered Ivan. "He's a Jew, isn't he?"

Ivana rolled her eyes.

"Do you have something against Jews?"

Ivan grabbed her by the wrist.

"How long have you known him? What's going on between you two? Where did you go?"

"You have no right to ask questions," Ivana said curtly. "Besides, I won't answer you."

The next day, while he had practically forgotten Abdel Aziz Isar, given the agony he was going through, Ivan received a text message from Abdel Aziz asking him to come and see him. On that particular day Abdel Aziz was alone, and a little less cold and uptight than during the previous visit.

"The plans for the attack are taking shape," he declared. "It will probably take place on Christmas Eve so as to make an impression. The form it will take will be different from previous attacks as the directives have changed. Mass attacks leaving sixty or eighty dead are no longer on the agenda. The leaders prefer carrying out simultaneous skirmishes on the same day at different locations. They are therefore planning a hostage-taking at a police retirement home, another at a Jewish school, and another probably in a church."

Abdel Aziz handed Ivan a well-filled envelope and some typewritten sheets of paper. His mission was to go to Brussels and retrieve a load of firearms.

"You will go to this garage, the Keller Garage," he declared. "Ask for Séoud and rent a car for three days. It's quite enough for a round trip from Brussels. Don't give your real name of course. This is your ID card. In Brussels, go to number thirteen on the rue d'Ostende where my cousin Zyrfana lives. There you will take the batch of weapons he will have hidden in musical-instrument cases. You have nothing to fear. If the police stop you en route, your ID card says you're an instrument maker and your business is selling violins, cellos, and guitars. You will bring me the haul and I'll use it when needed."

In his current state of mind, Ivan perceived this mission to Belgium as a welcome break. Two days later he set out along the motorway with a feeling of liberation. He left behind him his worries and anxieties regarding his sister and had the impression of being a new man. The sun had risen and was sending him an inviting smile from high in the sky. His blood began to flow again briskly and warmly in his veins. He drove for hours and then stopped in a rest area to eat. Against a noisy background of jazz music, customers were eating French fries and downing mugs of beer called Mort Subite, a name that at first delighted him then made him think. *Mort Subite?* Sudden Death? Wasn't that what the jihadists wanted? To take their own lives in order to be admitted to the Garden of Allah and enjoy the delights of seventy-two virgins? Suddenly such ideas seemed to him absurd and childish. How could this be a satisfactory solution? Was that how you could change the world? By killing yourself? Isn't it better to stimulate our minds and brace our muscles to plan for a revolution? He no longer knew or understood what had guided him. He vaguely recollected Monsieur Jérémie's objections. Unfortunately he hadn't listened properly and didn't remember much about them. He drove the last few kilometers to Brussels plunged deep in thought.

Brussels cannot be compared to London, Paris, or New York. Smaller in size, it looks more like a country cousin in comparison with its more sophisticated relatives. Yet it exudes an old-fashioned charm. Ivan enjoyed driving along its boulevards, less jammed with traffic than in Paris and lined with well-pruned trees.

Unfortunately he got lost and it took him almost an hour to find the rue d'Ostende, a quiet alley in a neighborhood where the shops had nothing to offer except items from elsewhere: prayer mats, kettles, burnooses, hijabs, burkas, prayer beads, Korans, and multicolored straw sponges. Europe had suddenly vanished and been replaced by faraway cultures. Passersby, too, came from elsewhere, from North Africa, Turkey, India, and Pakistan.

Zyrfana was a colossus with a hooked nose, very convivial and jovial, unlike his cousin. He embraced Ivan like an old acquaintance.

"How was the journey?" he asked. "Not too many police on the road? Ever since the last attack, the place is teeming with them."

Ivan replied that much to his surprise he hadn't seen a single one. Zyrfana owned a nice apartment and led Ivan into a room tastefully furnished, its walls lined with photos of Muhammad Ali.

"I wept like a child the day he died. He's my hero," he explained to Ivan. "Not only because he converted to Islam. It's because he turned his body into a temple. We must do the same and each of us must make a masterpiece of his body. In fact, I was just about to go to the gym. Do you want to come with me?"

Ivan retorted that he hadn't the slightest sports outfit on him; not even a pair of swimming trunks.

"No problem," Zyrfana said, and dashed into his bedroom, returning with a pair of striped shorts.

The two men climbed down the stairs. Night had fallen and the air started to feel cool. More and more passersby filled the sidewalks. One by one the shop windows lit up and this cosmopolitan neighborhood exuded a kind of reassuring intimacy. Music could be heard wafting in from somewhere. Zyrfana and Ivan headed for the Equinox fitness center. For almost two hours, despite his fatigue from the journey, Ivan pedaled, skipped, lifted weights, and stretched left, right, and center. This state of physical exhaustion was oddly beneficial. Ivan became the little boy he had once been when he used to dive headfirst into the water at Dos d'Âne and swim out to sea. When finally he returned to the beach, exhausted, he would cuddle up against his sister.

Zyrfana turned out to be an excellent cook: a seafood pie and an apricot tart. When Ivan complimented him on his dinner, he said sadly, "If you had come here a month ago, you would have complimented my wife, Amal. She was a real chef."

Ivan sensed that Zyrfana would like for nothing better than to go on talking about her.

"Where is she, then?" he asked.

"She left me," Zyrfana explained gloomily. "When she learned that it was me who provided the arms for the last attack at the airport, she left in a shot. Even worse, she took our little Zoran with her. I've been all alone ever since."

"Left!" Ivan cried. "So she wasn't a real Muslim?"

"Better than you," Zyrfana fired back vehemently. "Her father was a much-respected imam in Lahore. She was fourteen when her father took her on her first pilgrimage to Mecca. She could quote the Koran by heart. But she said that we hadn't understood its message at all; that we were using the wrong method to change the world. We didn't comprehend the word of God, who ordered us to love each other and not kill each other."

How like Ivan's own interrogations these thoughts were. How similar they were to Ivan's own preoccupations!

Perhaps Amal was right? Who knows?

Zyrfana got up and rushed into his bedroom, returning loaded with photo albums showing a chubby baby, then a small boy standing firmly on his two legs: Zoran, on every page Zoran. There was no doubt about it, he was a very cute child.

"You're not yet a father!" Zyrfana pointed out. "You don't know what it's like to have a child, a son. He's the one who wants to make you change the shape of the world, with the help of Kalashnikovs, if need be. So that he won't be banished to the back of the class because of the color of his skin or for any other futile reason. So that he won't be mocked by his classmates or turned into a scapegoat. So that he won't have a jobless future, but one with marvelous prospects. Before I had Zoran I was a good-for-nothing. It was him who made me what I am: a warrior, a soldier of God."

Ivan remained silent, even though he understood perfectly what Zyrfana had gone through. Zyrfana was describing the story of Ivan's own life. He too had been ignored by his teachers. He too had been mocked by his classmates. He too had been jobless at the age of twenty.

Two days later he set off back to France. As on the outward journey, he didn't meet a single police officer. He handed over to Abdel Aziz three cellos, three violas, as well as countless guitars whose cases had false bottoms filled with firearms.

"With that, we'll make a nice little night music," Abdel Aziz joked.

Ivan obviously didn't get the allusion to Mozart, but he understood perfectly that Abdel Aziz was making a witty joke.

We know what you are thinking. Once again you're going to blame us for not paying enough attention to Ivana, for not describing her moods in as much detail as for Ivan. Forgive us, dear reader. We shall attempt to make amends.

Ivana had changed enormously over the past months. The curvaceous, smiling young girl had been transformed into a young woman of amazing beauty. Her eyes, tinged with a deep melancholy, went straight to the heart. Ivana was torn by remorse. She found herself like a driver in a car traveling at full speed along a rough road, knowing full well the outcome will be fatal. She too, like Ivan, was well aware that the feelings they both shared were not natural. But she had always done everything in her power to control them. She was now at the end of her tether and resorted to drastic measures. Of course she didn't love Ariel Zeni. Moreover, how had she met him? In the most banal way possible: he was a monitor at the police training school where she had attended classes. Having lived for many years in Israel he was a specialist in the fight against terrorism, for although

Tel Aviv had not become a safe city, at least it was not the place of living dangerously it once was. Its buses were no longer death traps.

The whiteness of Ariel's body disgusted her, reminding her of the cheap blancmange Simone was fond of. Accustomed to her brother's bulging member, she found Ariel's flat and lackluster under his police uniform. But she had made up her mind to marry him, to go and live with him in his modest apartment in Clamart and bear his children.

One day when she was especially distressed, she had let herself be kissed. Although his mouth had seemed insipid and tasteless, she had consented to marry him. She had even gone so far as to fix a date for the engagement ceremony where they would invite their friends and Ariel would slip a lapis lazuli ring, which he boasted had belonged to his mother, on Ivana's finger.

How could she tell Ivan of her wedding plans? How would he react? In despair she decided to ask Mona for advice. Whereas Hugo and Mona had always considered Ivan a good-for-nothing, even a bad sort, they had always adored Ivana. She was the daughter they had never been fortunate enough to have. They loved her gentleness and extreme helpfulness.

One evening when they were both alone, Ivana asked Mona, "Have you ever found fault with the way Ivan and I feel for each other?"

Mona set down her cup of jasmine-scented tea and shook her head.

"You're twins. In other words, a single person split in two and divided into two different bodies. You can't be considered like everyone else, like normal people. No, I've never found your attitude shocking."

"How can I tell him that I'm engaged to Ariel?" Ivana

continued. "How will he take it? Don't I risk being slapped on both cheeks or receiving a fatal blow?"

In order to gain time Mona downed her tea, then made up her mind and very slowly said, "It's obvious he won't be happy to hear it. But you must tell him the truth quickly. The longer you wait, the more difficult it will be for you."

But Ivana could never pluck up enough courage to reveal her plans to her brother. She rebuked herself. She blamed herself in the morning when she scaled the streets, which were starting to be fraught with an icy wind, setting off for the police center. She blamed herself in the evening when she returned to the André Malraux housing estate. It gnawed at her, it worried her sick and made her more desirable, and Ariel Zeni couldn't take his eyes off her.

In the meantime Mona plied her with questions.

"Have you told him the truth?" she asked every day.

Ivana would shake her head.

"No, not yet," she said. "You can see how moody he is."

In actual fact, Ivan could only think of the attack whose date was getting closer. Abdel Aziz had given all the instructions. But there remained a few points to clear up: would they attack at dawn or wait until nightfall? The plan was as follows: together with the help of three associates, Ivan would burst into the police retirement home. The four men would shoot down as many victims as possible, quickly go back to the car parked on the rue du Chasseloup-Laubat, and drive straight to Belgium. This time there was no question of contacting Zyrfana again, but instead they would take refuge with a certain Karim who lived in the small town of Molenbeek. Ivan was scared to death and by no means enthusiastic. Not at all enthusiastic, in fact. He had no inclination to murder a series of retired police officers afflicted with all the sufferings of old age, some of whom were frankly bedridden. How could such an act change the world?

The municipal police center was composed of two identical buildings linked by a gravel path alongside the sidewalk: on one side the retirement home, named René Colleret after an obscure secretary of state for housing, and on the other, the training center, named La Porte Étroite (The Narrow Gate) as a tribute to the novel by André Gide. Ivan wondered why they didn't attack the second building, filled with young and vigorous police cadets. Okay, they weren't armed, but their officer instructors were quite capable of defending themselves.

This feeling of uncertainty lasted for almost a week, until shortly before midnight on the evening preceding the attack Ivan smashed open the door of his sister's bedroom with a mighty kick. He was beside himself and seemed inebriated, although he never touched alcohol. He was streaming with sweat and his eyes were red and bulging.

"What do I hear?" he screamed. "You're the mistress of that bloody idiot?"

Ivana gently placed her hand over his mouth as she had done hundreds of times when they quarreled as children.

"Listen, I'll explain what happened."

Without waiting, Ivan sent her sprawling on the bed with a knee jerk, then, throwing himself onto her, he ripped off her clothes, stripping her attractive body naked. At the same time he stripped down to his blue Calvin Klein briefs, which he wrenched off in one go. His hands groped Ivana's throat and breasts and she began to moan.

"Take me, take me, if that's what you want!"

"I should have done it long ago," Ivan retorted savagely.

But just as he was about to penetrate her with his monstrous erection, he got up, looked at her apologetically, and ran out of the bedroom.

Ivana managed to sit on the edge of the bed, and called out in a whisper, "Come back, come back."

Her tears streamed down her cheeks making glistening streaks along her face. Why exactly was she crying? Because of this carnal act they had both so desired and seemed unable to accomplish? Ivana cried all night long. In the morning she sadly slipped on her police uniform and set off for the retirement home, which she reached at 6:30 a.m. Every morning before starting classes in The Narrow Gate building she spent one or two hours helping the nursing auxiliaries who adored her and nicknamed her "Little Mother Teresa."

But we know what's bugging you. You want to know what became of Ivan and his monstrous erection. Let's rewind. Adjusting his clothes as best he could, Ivan ran out of his sister's bedroom, shot across the living room, and landed outside the front door just as Stella Nomal, the neighbor, back from the movies, was opening the door of her small apartment. Stella Nomal was a young Guyanese girl come to Paris to study law. Unfortunately she had no success with her law studies and at twenty-two found herself without a job. Ivan knew Stella because for over a year they had both rubbed shoulders cleaning the classrooms and sweeping the dead leaves from the recreation yard at the Marcellin Berthelot College. There was once a time when Stella had been greatly attracted to Ivan, such a handsome stud, but, confronted with his total indifference, she had resigned herself to looking elsewhere. When she saw him on the landing half undressed, attempting to button up his fly, she exclaimed, stupefied, "What on earth is going on?"

Without listening, Ivan dragged her brutally inside her apartment. Without saying a word he threw her onto the sofa and violently penetrated her. Faultfinders will say it was a rape, for that's what any non-consensual sexual relation is called. We will not argue this point. Rape or not, Stella savored the pleasure which was long overdue. But suddenly Ivan burst into tears.

"What's the matter, my darling?" Stella sweetly murmured. "You seem to be so unhappy."

Ivan dried his eyes with his fists and for the first time in his life launched into a confession he had never shared with anyone.

"You're sexually attracted to your sister?" she cried, both shocked and excited. "Is that possible?"

He remained deaf to her questions and went on talking. Stella and Ivan spent the rest of the night cuddled up against each other, sleeping, dreaming, making love, and discussing intimate matters. Ivan cried a lot and Stella comforted him.

"If you desire her so much," Stella asked, "why didn't you make love to her when she asked you?"

"She is both the light of my life and my damnation," Ivan continued sadly.

When Stella awoke at six in the morning, she found herself alone in bed. She automatically got dressed and set off on her daily routine to the Marcellin Berthelot College.

The following day when Ivan's face was sprawled all over the front pages of the press together with unflattering comments such as "brute," "assassin," and "monster," Stella thought she had dreamed the previous night. Was this the same man who, bruised and vulnerable, had pressed himself up against her and sucked her breast like a child? Was this impenitent barbarian Ivan Némélé? In despair she went to find the psychological support unit which had been set up by the city hall of Villeret-le-François. The psychologist was a pretty woman with a scatterbrained look, not at all like a psychiatrist. She listened to Stella without saying a word, then asked, "Do you realize you came close to death? He could have killed you."

"Ivan!" Stella cried, shrugging her shoulders. "He wouldn't hurt a fly."

"And yet he murdered sixty people at the retirement home," the psychiatrist retorted.

Angel or demon? Ivan was definitively classified in the second category.

The details of the attack at Villeret-le-François are common knowledge since they made headlines the world over, even in the tabloids of Indonesia and Turkey. The attack was especially loathsome as it targeted retired police officers who had devoted their lives to defending their community and who were now victims bent by the weight of their years. However, there is one aspect which caught Henri Duvignaud's attention and which nobody would understand if he hadn't read *The Ballad of Reading Gaol* by the famous Irish author, Oscar Wilde. Below are a few lines from this ballad:

Yet each man kills the thing he loves
By each let this be heard
Some do it with a bitter look
Some with a flattering word
The coward does it with a kiss
The brave man with a sword.

We shall now describe the facts we have been able to piece together. When Ivan and his three associates got out of their car parked at the corner of the rue du Chasseloup-Laubat, given the early morning hour, the neighborhood was asleep, virtually deserted. Only some stray dogs were rummaging in the dustbins. Ivan and his co-assassins arrived at the René Colleret retirement home at 7 a.m. on the dot. One hour earlier a shrill alarm had sounded to wake up the residents and inform them their sleep was over and a new day was beginning. The nurses would soon be scrambling up the stairs, pouring onto each floor, and taking the pensioners who could no longer control themselves to the toilets. Taking advantage of the situation the nurses would reassure the pensioners, since old men are as terrified of the night as little children. They are scared to death by darkness. They imagine it filled with menacing or frightening creatures. In the dormitory on the second floor ex-sergeant Piperu, who had always been an amateur poet, was feverishly writing down his nightly dream in a spiral notebook as he did every morning. He had no idea that in a few minutes' time a bullet would pierce his chest, and his hands would let fall his bloodied notebook containing an unfinished text. In the basement kitchen the employees were busy preparing the breakfasts that would then be taken up to the rooms.

All Ivan and his companions had to do was to enter each room and fire at anything that moved. Ivan remained calm and determined for it wasn't the moment to harbor vain misgivings and wonder whether this was the way to change the world. He had to accomplish his task.

Yet we all know that one blip is enough to bring a perfectly well-oiled machine to a grinding halt. This time the blip was called Elodie Bouchez, the latest recruit in the contingent of health-care workers. Previously Elodie Bouchez had dreamed of becoming a nurse but had failed the profession's entrance exam. She had made do with a career as a health-care worker, at first with a pinch of contempt until gradually she had begun to like it and to carry out her work conscientiously. That very day, because of delays on the regional express metro, she arrived late for work. From the pavement she could hear the *rat-tat-tat* of the Kalashnikovs as well as the screams of the wounded and wondered what was going on. Could it be an attack? Not out of the question, given the times we were living in. She ran therefore to a bar close by named A Verse Toujours (Keep Pouring) to raise the alarm. The bar had only just opened and the server, a young curly-haired Arab, was half-heartedly mopping the tiled floor. Both of them dashed to the phone and called for reinforcements from city hall.

In the meantime Ivan and his associates had arrived on the third floor of the retirement home. That's where Ivan found Ivana leaning over the gendarme Rousselet, who was ashamed once again of having relieved himself in bed. Ivana and the gendarme Rousselet got along like a house on fire: Rousselet had been posted to Deshaies on the Leeward Coast of Guadeloupe for many years and he knew the island inside and out. Both of them remembered the golden sand of the beaches, the grandiose sea, the view that stretched as far as the island of Antigua, and the almond trees whose large varnished leaves turned sometimes green, sometimes red. They reminisced too about the wooden shacks radiant under the sun despite their poverty and the children of every color playing together.

Hearing the noise made by the assassins entering the

dormitory, Ivana looked up and collapsed on gendarme Rousselet's bed clutching the old man's bony shoulders. She looked Ivan straight in the eye. All the love and desire they felt for each other was revealed in this look. They relived their entire life like those who have come close to death might. Ivan and Ivana therefore relived every moment from when they emerged from Simone's womb on a warm, fragrant September night right up to this gray frosty autumn morning. Some memories lingered more than others. When they had begun to stand on their own two feet Simone would measure them against one of the house walls. For a long time they stayed the same height as each other. Then one year Ivan began to grow and within a few months had grown taller than his sister. At the time Ivana admired in bemusement his body that stretched out beside her. What a magnificent package of muscles. They had accompanied their mother many times to the choir and sang with the same childish voices that nobody noticed. One fine day a miracle occurred: unexpected, like every miracle.

At the church of Dos d'Âne, like everywhere else in Guadeloupe on August 15th, there is a ceremony for crowning the Virgin Mary. For the occasion the priests search for the most light-skinned children they can find as well as the prettiest kids of mixed blood. They deck them out with a pair of angel's wings and a loose sky-blue robe and have them climb up the altar to place a crown on the head of a plaster statue representing the Virgin Mary.

In the meantime a children's choir stands in a corner of the church churning out psalm upon psalm. Ivan and Ivana were members of this choir. One day Ivana's voice burst out of her throat supreme and filled the nave with its harmony. Ivan listened to her and wondered what marvels his sister's body contained. From that moment on Ivana was given a wide array of names such as "siren" and "nightingale" and was invited to perform solo in all the churches of Guadeloupe. Following a concert at the cathedral in Pointe-à-Pitre a writer who had just been awarded the Prix Carbet named her "The Magic Flute." Such terms proved that Ivana was outside the normal order of things.

The day of the attack Ivan didn't think twice. Without hesitating he aimed his gun at Ivana and fired. It was the only thing to do, the only act that had meaning to it. Ivana understood perfectly. Consequently she arched her breast in order to acknowledge the blessing from the bullets. Fatally wounded, she collapsed at the foot of the bed. After this, Ivan's intention was to turn his arm against himself and commit suicide. Alas, things turned out quite differently.

City hall had alerted the French gendarmerie intervention force who dispatched two squads of sharpshooters led by Sergeant Raymond Ruggiani. He urged his commando to take the jihadists alive, thereby getting them to talk and obtaining information on those who were giving the orders. Before Ivan had time to react as he intended, Raymond Ruggiani had fired at his legs. Ivan collapsed, knocking over his co-assassins as he fell. Covered in blood, they were thrown into an ambulance and rushed to the hospital at Villeret-le-François.

Several thousand kilometers away, given the time lag, Guadeloupe was still plunged in darkness. A night frequented by the usual suspects, Little Sapoti, the monstrous Bête à Man Hibè, and Masala Makalou; just another ordinary night. But not for Simone who always slept like a baby. She had gone to bed with a burning fever as if she were suffering from malaria, dengue fever, or the zika virus—in short, one of those many diseases common to countries where the mosquito reigns supreme. Three times she had got up to down a cup of water to prevent her teeth from chattering so as not to wake Father Michalou lying by her side. Simone was glad she had married him. He only had one fault: he liked to scribble their accounts on a slate and complain they didn't have any money. In any case, not enough to go and spend Christmas at Villeret-le-François, he declared categorically. Tired of hearing him repeat the same thing over and over again, Simone, who hadn't seen her children for some time, bypassed him and negotiated with Ivana, who had obtained a loan from her employer to have her mother and stepfather come for Christmas.

In her agitated sleep Simone saw her mother in tears and knew she was bringing her terrible news. But what? Feeling oppressed she woke up before dawn and cautiously climbed out of bed so as not to disturb Father Michalou, who always slept soundly after having sex. In the dining room she automatically switched on the radio to get the latest news. Another bomb attack in France! This time in a police retirement home, the speaker announced. She would normally have shrugged off the news since it was the third attack in two years, but an unexpected pain ripped through her breast. This time, she felt it, things were very different. They would concern her directly.

And she was not mistaken. She was about to drink her coffee when three men dressed in suits and ties burst in and stammered frantically, "Simone, your daughter's been killed in a bomb attack!"

"Killed!" exclaimed Father Michalou, who at that very moment emerged from the bedroom.

"You must not waste time. You must go straight to France," the three men sent by the town hall shouted.

"Where do you expect us to find money for that?" Father Michalou said.

"We'll pay," the three men replied in unison.

Don't be surprised if at that time there was only mention of Ivana. Ivan's identity, like that of the other terrorists, had not yet been clarified; that would take several days. On the other hand, it was easy to identify Ivana Némélé, a police cadet from Guadeloupe, a volunteer helping the team of care workers.

Consequently, by early afternoon, the entire island of Guadeloupe knew that once again it had produced a martyr. In fact, nobody was surprised. Although Bernadette Soubirous and other Mother Teresas were white of skin, the island was packed with unbeatified black women, husbandless, penniless, who nevertheless had raised their children out of respect for God's commandments and the church. A TV crew made a point of interviewing Simone. Unfortunately she cried so much she was of no help, repeating over and over again: "*Pitite an mwen! Pitite an mwen!* (My poor little darling!)"

To compensate they filmed Father Michalou, who had time to slip on his best suit and look his Sunday best. Everyone will be world-famous for fifteen minutes, Andy Warhol declared, and that's what happened to Father Michalou. He explained smugly in front of the cameras that although Ivana was not his biological daughter she was certainly his spiritual child. He had known her from the time she was born: the midwife had placed Ivana in his hands when she came out of her mother's womb. In order to back up what he said he went and fetched Simone's photo albums from the chest of drawers, showing Ivana at every stage: from the toddler making her first steps, to the young girl showing off her first front teeth, to the teenager exhibiting her first straightened hairdo.

As news of the bomb attack gradually spread around the island, people stormed onto the buses and charabancs and converged at the Pôle Caraïbes Airport from where they had learned Simone was to fly off at the end of the afternoon. Those who had the possibility went and prayed for a moment in church. It was by no means a carnival atmosphere. On the contrary, there were no masqueraders daubed in tar, no masqueraders with horns, and no *akiyo* band. Joy was not on the agenda. An air of distress hung in the air, mixed with pride because at last a girl from Guadeloupe was making headlines. In the Air Madinina plane, the overexcited crew offered Simone glass after glass of champagne, shrimp cocktails, caviar, and salmon canapés which she left untouched for Father Michalou. The eight hours flew by in minutes.

When Simone arrived at Orly Airport, the frenzy came to an abrupt end. Two self-important-looking men were standing in a corner brandishing a placard.

"Are you the mother of Ivana Némélé?" one of them asked coldly enough to make you shudder.

He and his colleague had been sent by the authorities at Villeret-le-François. The attitude of these two men, so different from the warmth Simone had left behind in Guadeloupe, made her blood run cold. Fortunately she could count on Father Michalou and nestled up closer to him.

Since the two emissaries did not have a car, they had to pile into a G7 taxi which set off for Villeret-le-François. Although it was barely nine in the morning a crowd was already forming in front of the imposing town hall:

bystanders had come for a look as well as a load of journalists from the press and TV stations. Cameras flashed and reporters had been sent from as far away as Marseille, Nice, and Strasbourg. In a dismal room on the first floor, the crush was unimaginable. The mayor, a tall, wishy-washy individual whose white face was lined with a colorless moustache, was attempting to deliver his homily over the noise.

"France has been smitten," he declared, "by this new tragedy, horrified by what has just happened, a monstrosity which adds to so many others. France is bathed in tears, afflicted, but remains strong, will always be stronger, I can assure you, than the fanatics who want to destroy it."

Nobody paid attention to Simone and Father Michalou. Nobody was of the same color and they felt lost and isolated. *Where is Ivan?* Simone wondered frenziedly, having expected to see him at the airport. She had called him but received only an unintelligible gurgling in response. Where could he possibly be when such a tragedy had struck his family? To say nothing of his special feelings for his sister, he had always been a loving and considerate son. He wouldn't leave his mother alone in such circumstances. The more time passed, the more Simone's heart grew increasingly anguished and filled with dark premonitions regarding her son. Hugo and Mona were of no help and were as surprised as she was by Ivan's absence. She could find nobody to answer the questions that were breaking her heart.

During this time of extreme distress, she was dealt two shattering blows. The first occurred when she had to go and identify her daughter's body the day after she arrived. The hospital at Villeret-le-François numbered a team of specialists whose reputation was firmly established and who were nicknamed "the embalmers of death." They weren't exactly embalmers since the art of embalming has long gone out of fashion in France. They were genuine experts who knew how to restore the velvety smooth texture to cadavers riddled with wounds, how to draw a smile again on twitching lips, in short, how to recreate an illusion of life. The team hadn't yet finished when Simone came face-to-face with the body of her daughter, whose sallow complexion and bandaged neck was squeezed into a white dressing gown at the bottom of one of the drawers in the morgue.

The second blow was dealt the day after, when she went to prostrate herself in the temporary morgue at the Cathedral of Saint Bernard du Tertre. She almost fainted at the sight of all those coffins and heady-perfumed flowers that were slowly wilting. She had to wait several days and several nights before hearing a vague explanation for Ivan's absence.

One morning while she was sadly downing her breakfast in Hugo's and Mona's modest apartment, Henri Duvignaud, the lawyer, marched in accompanied by the mayor, who had come in person to express his condolences. Henri Duvignaud grasped Simone's ice-cold hands.

"Be brave, Madame Némélé," he said. "What I'm about to tell you is terrible."

He told her that Ivan was seriously wounded, since he had been a member of the commando of jihadists, and was now at the hospital in Villeret-le-François.

"The ballistic tests have not been completed," Henri continued, "but from what I can deduce Ivan is also his sister's assassin."

Here we are obliged to wallow in pathos despite our dislike for it. On hearing these words, Simone fainted.

She might even have passed from this life to the next if Mona hadn't possessed a well-stocked pharmacy in the bathroom. Mona poured mint spirit between the clenched teeth of the unfortunate Simone. She rubbed her forehead and temples with tiger balm. She made her inhale essential oils. After an hour of agitation, tears, and sobs, Simone came to and murmured in a dying voice, staring at Henri Duvignaud with her reddened eyes: "You're totally mad! Ivan had nothing to do with these jihadists. As for killing his sister, he would have been incapable, he adored her!"

"That's exactly why," Henri Duvignaud retorted, launching into a long tirade, using all the skill of a lawyer used to verbal jousting.

When he stopped, Simone, whose fiery gaze had never flinched, cried out, "You haven't understood a thing. Not a thing! My children are not perverts and I repeat, Ivan would never have killed Ivana!"

In the icy silence that followed, the mayor hastened to declare that the Regional Council would take charge of the return tickets to Guadeloupe for the deceased Ivana, Simone, and Father Michalou, as well as a delegation from city hall led by an officer by the name of Ariel Zeni. Despite the separation of church and state, the Regional Council would also pay for the cost of the religious ceremony at Dos d'Âne. Did Simone know Ariel Zeni? Did she know he was her daughter's fiancé? He would come during the afternoon to pay his respects and present his condolences.

It would be a grave mistake to think that all French Antilleans, Guadeloupeans, and Martinicans alike suffer from the complex of "lactification" as denounced by Frantz Fanon in his famous work entitled *Black Skin White Masks*, and that they feel flattered by the slightest mark of admiration and esteem lavished on them by white folk. Often the opposite occurs. Ariel Zeni sensed it immediately when he came to pay his respects to Simone and her family. As soon as he entered the apartment, a flow of hatred struck him full in the face. His identity changed. Suddenly he was seen as a slave trafficker on the coast of Mozambique, advocate of hard labor on the Ivory Coast, and plantation owner of acres of sugarcane on an island in the Caribbean. He had just mutilated one of the slaves' shins and cut off a leg. Despite the fact that his grandparents had been victims of the pogroms in Poland, despite the fact his parents had barely escaped the concentration camp in Auschwitz, and despite the fact he considered himself to be one of the West's most pitiful victims. There is no need to recall here the Nazis' Final Solution, which everyone is familiar with.

But Ariel and Simone quickly got along very well together since they shared the same intense love for the deceased Ivana. Above all they shared the same blind tenacity, refusing to yield to what was slowly becoming the implacable truth. For them, Ivan was not a terrorist. They couldn't explain what he was doing in the retirement home at Villeret-le-François that morning. He hadn't killed his sister: such an idea was out of the question.

"I didn't know Ivan very well," Ariel repeated, "but he seemed a happy, open-minded, level-headed boy."

"He was a badmouther," Simone added. "But his heart was as good as gold. When he was little he refused to eat the hens we were raising in our farmyard or the rabbits from our hutches. 'They're our brothers,' he used to say. 'We're alike.'"

For Ariel and Simone it was all one big mistake which one day would be cleared up. Together they asked permission to go and visit Ivan, who apparently was at death's door, at Villeret-le-François's hospital. Ariel was convinced that his rank as police officer would open every door. Alas, they were met with a refusal. The three remaining jihadists, one of whom had died in the meantime, were not allowed visitors. A line of ferocious police officers guarded the entrance to the pavilion where they were located.

In her grief, Simone was not entirely alone. Henri Duvignaud came to see her every day, but they ended up quarreling again and Simone barred him from entering the apartment. She also received a visit from Ulysses. Poor Ulysses! He had given up his lucrative job as escort and had fallen in love with Celuta, a girl from his own country blown on the wind of misery to Paris where she house-cleaned. They were now squeezed together in a miserable maid's room. His activity as an escort, which for Ulysses was just another job, had since changed nature and he now believed it betrayed his heart and soul. Even worse, little did he know that Celuta prostituted herself for quick sessions with the bourgeois where she worked in order to make ends meet. Isn't life surprising? It has a sense of humor which doesn't make everyone laugh.

It was thus, arm in arm, that Ariel and Simone went off to the airport at Orly to fly back to Guadeloupe. Father Michalou walked behind looking furious since this tenderfoot white boy had stolen the show from him. The journalists now ran after Ariel, holding out the mike for him. Ariel, who was rather frail physically, swaggered contentedly, with an excited expression on his juvenile face.

"The words color and race should be banned," he clamored fervently. "They have caused too much harm to mankind. Whole sections of the world have been plunged into obscurantism and servitude because of this vocabulary. So many people have been assassinated because of it while others, so-called discoverers, conquerors, and the righteous, belonged to societies authorized to dominate. I have never thought Ivana's color to be different from mine. For me, only her soul counted."

We will not dwell on this stay in Guadeloupe more than necessary. We shall merely indicate certain facts. A considerable crowd was waiting for them on arrival at the Pôle Caraïbes Airport. A convoy of every type of vehicle headed for Dos d'Âne, which had never experienced such crowds in all its history. On several occasions we have underlined the ugliness of Dos d'Âne; it was as if a toad had been squashed by a car and thrown on the side of the road. Yet the day of Ivana's funeral it assumed a singular beauty. Invisible hands had packed the much too tiny church with arum lilies, tuberose flowers, and Canna lilies. Every commune in Guadeloupe, Martinique, and Guyana had sent delegations of schoolchildren dressed in white to wave tricolor flags. There were representatives of religious associations, priests, and even a contingent of cloistered nuns who had come down from the heights of Matouba where their convent was located. In his homily the mayor underlined how this day brought the overseas departments closer to France. Not only did they share the same family allowances and unemployment insurance benefits, they were united in the unspeakable suffering inflicted by an unparalleled event. After the mayor, Ariel Zeni stepped up to the pulpit and recited a poem of his own composition which brought tears to everyone's eyes:

"She was our ray of joy / she was the little rose we watered / she was the sweet-smelling breeze that cooled the sweat on our necks."

This poem figures on page 301 in *An Anthology of Poetry from Guadeloupe*, published by the well-known Haitian-Canadian publishers Mémoire d'Encrier. By common agreement the religious ceremony dedicated to Ivana Némélé, cut down in the prime of her youth, was unforgettable. Those who were lucky enough to attend were transformed. Gone were any self-centered and selfish ambitions; such a tragedy urged each and every person to give meaning to life and fight to improve the common lot. Ivana Némélé, who had dreamed of becoming a police officer so as to help and protect the destitute, had become a role model and an example for all. After the ceremony, once everyone had gone home heartbroken and reflecting on the day's events, Estelle Martin wiped the smile off her face and announced the incredible information on the evening news that Ivan Némélé, the twin brother of the saint who had just been buried, was one of the terrorists and had died at the hospital of Villeret-le-François. Hearing such news, the inhabitants of Basse-Terre and Grande-Terre came out on their doorsteps and began to weep. My God! Have pity on Guadeloupe! Whereas she had just appeared to the world as the birthplace of a martyr, her image was now downgraded to the birthplace of an assassin.

Shortly after midnight a comet shot across the sky spreading its unique tail and everyone realized that such a night was out of the ordinary. From that moment on, Simone Némélé occupied a special place in the national narrative of Guadeloupe. (But is there such a thing as a national narrative? Guadeloupe is an overseas department. Its only national narrative is that of France.) Simone, a humble woman in appearance, had given birth to both the best and the worst. She had borne in her womb an angel and a demon. Booklets began to be sold in the markets for a few centimes. They described the life of Simone and had a photo of her on the cover which was taken at the church in Dos d'Âne, her hands crossed over her heart and her eyes raised to heaven. These booklets were published by the Bénizat printers, already known for their best-selling *The Key to Your Dreams* and *Ten Ways to Success*, translated from the American.

Once she had recovered from her grief, Simone went along willingly with the game plan. She formed a prayer circle which grew so quickly it became the heart of a sect called The Shining Path. From that moment on she changed her appearance radically, adopting the attire befitting for someone who was half supernatural and filled with faith and love. She no longer combed her hair, which now resembled the tangled mop of a fetish child from certain countries in West Africa. She refused to wear any sort of color and dressed strictly in loose white albs tied at the waist with a cord, made free of charge by Madame Esdras, the dressmaker. She renounced wearing shoes to go barefoot and her nails grew gray and sharp like clam shells.

Every third Sunday, accompanied by her disciples, she climbed up to the altar and returned lost in prayer to the central nave. During this time Father Michalou sulked. He hadn't held in contempt all this religious nonsense throughout his life only to be forced into it in his old age. He often thought of taking off on his own, of leading a quiet life, in other words of leaving Simone. He couldn't make up his mind, however, since he loved his old woman who had suffered so much and was so good at making love. It was then that Simone committed the act that made him balk. One fine day she abandoned him just like that and went to live in a house given to her by one of her disciples. She no longer needed a man. God was enough.

Several points in our narrative remain wrapped in mystery. What happened to Ivan's body, which was not shipped back to Guadeloupe? It appears he was hastily buried with the other terrorists, thrown into a common grave in the cemetery at Villeret-le-François. His loyal friends walked behind the coffin: Hugo, Mona, Henri Duvignaud the lawyer, Ulysses, and Stella Nomal. Mona sobbed openly and shook her head, repeating tirelessly, "He didn't deserve to die like this! He didn't deserve to die like this!"

As for Stella Nomal, she didn't say a word and wondered what double-faced Janus she had made love to. The police arrested Abdel Aziz, but could hold nothing against him. Once he was released he returned home to his native land together with his wife, probably to continue his misdeeds. For a few weeks everything calmed down and life went on as usual as it always does.

Then in December an event occurred in Guadeloupe which was to have considerable consequences far beyond the borders of this little island, as far as Martinique, Guyana, and Suriname, and even as far as some English-speaking islands such as Trinidad and Tobago. The month of December in the Caribbean is calm and reverential. The season of Advent is focused on the coming miracle whose memory is celebrated faithfully on the 25th. The weeks leading up to it are strung with carols, some of which are local favorites: *Michaud veillait la nuit dans sa chaumière* or *Voisin d'où venait ce grand bruit qui m'a réveillé cette nuit*. The hurricane season is over. The great winds are sound asleep. The sea turns gentle, as good as gold, and the flying fish flashing along the surface deck it out with silver during the day. On the night of December 20th a group of strangers showed up at the gate of the Briscaille Cemetery in Dos d'Âne and asked where the tomb of Ivana Némélé was located. You must forgive their ignorance for they were a group of Haitians alerted by a mysterious star that had begun to shine above their homes in the village of Petit Goave. It hadn't left them for a second and had protected them during their crossing. No overzealous coastguard had confused them with the illegal immigrants seeking to infiltrate forbidden territory. They stood around Ivana's tomb intending to cover it with candles and flowers and to spend the night in prayer. That's when a television crew, alerted by the rumor, came to film them. Henceforth every year on the fatal date of December 20th people make the pilgrimage of "our little wounded sister" or "petite soeur de la blesse," as Ivana came to be known. So as to fully appreciate the fervor contained in this name you need to know that the Creole word *blesse* associated with Ivana means roughly "scar" or "wounded." It refers of course to the scars dealt by life which are never erased and always remain a wound in both body and soul.

MORE ABOUT THE UTERUS: THERE'S NO ESCAPING IT

We know that for you, reader, there remains a mystery. You believe it more important to clarify Henri Duvignaud's words when he introduced himself to Simone. On that day he didn't hesitate to use the word *crime*. In his words there was no doubt Ivan was his sister's murderer. Yet to our knowledge he hadn't seen Ivan, even though on several occasions he had taken advantage of his status as lawyer to request permission from the town authorities to visit Ivan on his hospital bed. Each time the response came back that Ivan was much too weak and had lost too much blood to see visitors. On what, therefore, did he base his argument? You are probably asking the question, *Why attach so much importance to Henri Duvignaud?* It's because our lawyer was gifted with a superior intelligence. Besides his brilliant law studies, he had passed the entrance exam to the prestigious School of Political Sciences in Paris and had studied three years at Harvard, the best university in America, which enabled him to speak English as good as his French. Back in Paris he had become a loyal follower of

André Glucksmann, quoting entire pages from his book *La cuisinière et le mangeur d'hommes* (The Cook and the Cannibal).

Henri Duvignaud had firm ideas on the subject of Ivan and Ivana. He would shrug his shoulders when he heard certain allegations. According to him the sad fate of Ivana was a striking illustration of this globalization which was blowing us an ill wind. Nowadays, it's a well-known fact, very few people spend their entire life from birth to death in their homeland; there are no longer borders which lock you in till kingdom come; in other words, no longer a pattern of life all mapped out. Ivana Némélé, born in Dos d'Âne in Guadeloupe, had been shipped kilometers from her native island to a suburb of Paris called Villeret-le-François, where she found herself mixed up in a drama and overtaken by events that destroyed her petty reality. Naturally, the story of Ivan and Ivana put an end, as if we needed another one, to the myth of Negritude. The notion of race no longer implies the question of solidarity. Worse still, it lost its meaning ages ago. What excited Henri Duvignaud was rather the individual interpretation of these uncommon destinies.

In order to back up his arguments he quoted Dr. Eisenfeld, a world-famous specialist in fetal medicine who was a friend of his. He had become a close friend because he had got his son off a heavy prison sentence for dealing drugs. In their mother's womb, Ivan and Ivana had first been a single egg. Then a mutation had occurred. The professor had assured Duvignaud that such an occurrence is not rare. Quite frequent in fact, although we don't know the exact cause. Perhaps a change of metabolism or hormones? As a rule, when such an event occurs the mother is afflicted with fever or bleeding. Such a mutation probably occurred shortly before she gave birth. Simone Némélé, therefore, already stressed by other factors, didn't notice a thing and the egg, split in two, emerged into the world. This explains why Ivan and Ivana had remained so close to each other. The time needed to adapt to two distinct lives had been too short. What complicated matters further was that the fetuses were not of the same sex. One was a little female, the other a little male. As a result they had elaborated a very intimate working arrangement: cuddling up together, kissing, and penetrating each other whenever they fancied.

Professor Eisenfeld had explained to Henri Duvignaud that these different occurrences were purely mechanical. They implied nothing sexual or pleasurable. It was perhaps merely a way of sharing their flow of vital energy. The moment of birth had not helped matters since it had caused a deep trauma by conferring distinct lives on Ivan and Ivana. They had kept the habits and nostalgia of a time when they lived in close communion. In fact they dreamed of nothing better than to return to this blissful period.

Are you more or less convinced now? But, you will object, if that's true, why did Ivan kill Ivana? On that point Henri Duvignaud became less categorical and more hesitant. His words became confused. He advanced into unknown territory, largely composed of suppositions. Ever since the world has existed, poets and philosophers of every nationality have repeated over and over again that love and death are one and the same and conjure up the same notion of the absolute. They are impermeable to the whims of time, public opinion, and the ups and downs of life. The Guadeloupeans in their wisdom have understood it full well since the two words *lanmou* (love) and *lanmò* (death) are separated by the flip of a single vowel. Ivan and Ivana, unable to lose themselves in each other in the flesh, believed that death could be the only way out. Ivan wanted to prove their eternal love by giving it, and Ivana by accepting it.

Are you fully convinced? Perhaps not. Some of you will consider that all they needed to do was make love together. Let's not go back over that: because they couldn't. Their education forbade them.

We have said over and over again that the attack at Villeret-le-François aroused sharp disapproval throughout the world, in India, Indonesia, Australia, and England, to name just a few countries, and was called The Second Massacre of the Innocents, alluding to an episode in the Bible. Even those who, deep down, detest the police and privately call them "pigs" or "murderers" were profoundly shocked by the fatal blow they had been dealt. The description of this infamous day made headlines in all the papers. That's how it landed in the hands of Aïssata Traoré, who you may recall was the cousin of Ivan's wife. On reading the Canadian daily *Devoir*, she dropped the cup of coffee she was drinking in amazement. Aïssata Traoré had resigned from an important job at McGill University in Montreal and gone to teach in a small college in Chicoutimi. Now that she was in a smaller town, she had plenty of time to devote to her favorite occupation: writing vicious political pamphlets. She had recently published two essays one after the other, both of which had caused a sensation: "The West and Us" and "Terrorism from the Victory at Bouvines in 1214 to the Present Day." She had dyed her hair red to prove that black women are free like the rest of us to choose the color of their hair, but that's another story.

Although she led an intense sexual life, the night she spent with Ivan remained unique for evermore in her memory. Seldom had such a partner seemed so gentle, so considerate, and so strangely child-like. She quickly grabbed her phone and called her cousin in Kidal. The latter was in tears, half in a daze. Somebody had painted scarlet graffiti over her house: *Wife of Assassin = Assassin*. As a result she no longer went out. The day before yesterday she had gone to the state store to buy two kilos of broken rice and had been physically and verbally abused by customers furious at seeing her come and go as she pleased. Her son's nurse no longer dared take little Fadel out for his walk since people formed a crowd behind her and tried to throw stones in his stroller.

"It can't go on like this. They'll end up killing you," Aïssata exclaimed, aghast. "You must leave Mali."

"Where do you want me to go?" the unfortunate Aminata moaned. "We haven't a single friend or relative under the sun."

"Let me think it over," Aïssata replied. "I'll call you back."

During the next several days Aïssata moved heaven and earth and did the rounds among her relations. All in vain. Nobody wanted to be mixed up with a jihadist who had finally got what he deserved. It was then she came across the name of Henri Duvignaud, who was often mentioned in the French press. He alone would dare take on the defense of Ivan, protected by his profession. It so happened that Aïssata and Henri Duvignaud had known each other long ago when they were students in Paris and both attended classes at the prestigious Political Science School on the rue Saint-Guillaume. They had even started to flirt once over a cup of tea.

Aïssata bombarded Henri Duvignaud with emails, text messages, and WhatsApps. He finally answered and, despite the distance, they both agreed they would endeavor to clear Ivan's name and explain how a little Guadeloupean had found himself mixed up in affairs which he perhaps didn't fully understand, without lapsing into hagiography or idealizing him. What form would their defense take? Perhaps they would co-write a book that would be edited by a major publisher. Henri Duvignaud boasted that he had connections with Gallimard, Grasset, and Le Seuil. After much discussion Henri Duvignaud left a simple word on Aïssata's cell phone: "Come!"

Aïssata and Aminata met up again in an Apart-Hotel on rue Léonard-de-Vinci in the aristocratic sixteenth neighborhood of Paris. Whereas Aïssata adored this city and dreamed of settling down here, Aminata, who was visiting for the first time, took an immediate dislike to it. She was not at all taken by its avenues filled with gleaming cars or its tall buildings, so tall they blocked the sky. Where was the sun, the moon, the stars? Vanished. All day long people and objects were bathed in the same yellowish, diffused light. One evening her footsteps took her to the banks of the Seine. She cried at seeing this river humiliated, obliged to flow between rigid embankments of stone and iron.

We shouldn't be surprised if Aïssata was able to lodge in these luxurious surroundings, for on the quiet she was rolling in money. A Canadian banker known for his extreme right-wing ideas had financed her handsomely for years. She kept this liaison secret for two reasons. Firstly, she didn't want to add her name to the sad list of black women who marry white men or make love to them. Secondly, her extreme left-wing ideas obliged her to dissimulate her behavior. Yet it was thanks to her lover's money that she had gone to India and written about the condition of women and the Untouchables. It was also thanks to his money that several of her books had attacked the dictatorships in certain Arab countries and in particular had denounced on many occasions her favorite topic of Europe's damaging politics.

Aminata and Aïssata flung themselves into each other's arms. They both recollected their connection to the handsome, muscular Ivan. On the other hand they forgot entirely about Ivana, who they perceived as a formidable rival and sensed was in full possession of her brother's heart. It had been some time since Aïssata had seen little Fadel, who was going on for two. He looked like his father with his almond-shaped eyes and full lips over an attractive mouth. But Fadel's looks and smile had turned mawkish and over-sentimental, unlike the gentleness which had characterized Ivan. It was obvious Fadel would never become an avenging warrior. Aïssata would have liked for Ivan's son not to be a loser like his father before him.

The day after they arrived, Henri Duvignaud came to pick up the two women for dinner. He had booked a table at the Astoria, a smart seafood restaurant situated close by. Before leaving, he clasped Aminata's hands.

"Don't you worry," he said softly. "Aïssata and I will do everything we possibly can to clear his memory and explain why Ivan became a terrorist."

Aminata wriggled herself free.

"My husband was not a terrorist," she cried. "Don't you ever speak of him in those terms."

Aïssata managed to calm her cousin and the dinner went off without further incident. The three guests even reached a sort of agreement. Eating his coconut ice cream, Henri Duvignaud murmured sadly, "We're all of the opinion that the world must change. Unfortunately we don't know how."

The very next morning Aïssata and Henri Duvignaud set to work. Before even having drawn up the first line of the book they were thinking of writing together, they had come up with the title: "The Reluctant Terrorist." Here was a provocative title capable of producing articles in the press and generating major sales, Henri Duvignaud claimed.

They set themselves a strict schedule. Every morning Aïssata took the bus to the office of Henri Duvignaud, who had reallocated his clients' appointments to the afternoon or evening. A secretary hired for the occasion dispatched hundreds of letters to those who had met Ivan in Guadeloupe and Mali. Unfortunately the answers were few and far between, since both places belonged to an oral tradition. The inhabitants were more interested in inventing ridiculous stories about their neighbors than answering questionnaires. Nevertheless, the book gradually took shape.

It was only natural that Henri Duvignaud drove Aminata and Aïssata to Hugo and Mona's place. The latter had never got over the drama that had occurred close to their modest three-room apartment located in a quiet suburb of Paris. Mona, especially, had never got over the death of Ivana. Ariel Zeni often came to visit as well. His story had made headlines around the world and he had been jokingly nicknamed "the bashful lover." He had elaborated an unlikely theory explaining roughly why Ivan was present among the terrorists. Everyone knew Ivan was jobless and penniless. As a result he had hired his services blindly to this death squad without knowing what was expected of him. His explanation had the sole merit of reviving and regretting the memory of the deceased, Ivan as well as Ivana. Consequently Ivan, too, was gradually draped in the colors of sainthood.

Remarkably, Mona had got closer to her neighbor, Stella Nomal, whom previously she had ignored. Now they were on first-name terms and voiced endless strings of "my darling," "sweetie pie," and "honey dear." Stella Nomal did the shopping for Mona at the market and supermarket. She took her washing to the laundry and bought her essential-oil balms from the pharmacy to soothe her osteoarthritis. The truth was that both women were hiding something secret which was raging in their breasts.

A major event had occurred, in fact, several weeks earlier. Ivan's death and the role he had played in the attack had been made public. The papers had a field day portraying him. They published a photo of him taken at a certain angle so as to make him look like an assassin. They never stopped repeating that, contrary to common belief, Ivan Némélé had been radicalized ages ago; in Mali, in fact, where he had helped murder an important head of the national militia. He had managed to escape because he had benefited from complicity at the highest level. Who? Nobody knew exactly but there was an ongoing inquiry. In short, Ivan Némélé was a very dangerous individual.

One evening Stella Nomal burst into the living room where Mona was knitting a baby's vest for her fourth grandchild who had just been born. She collapsed into an armchair and burst into tears.

"I cannot bear the way they're treating him. I can't live without him," she had moaned.

"Him? Who's him?" Mona asked.

Without further ado, as if she were throwing off a great weight, Stella described the extraordinary night she had spent with Ivan the day before the attack.

"He had never paid attention to me before he threw

himself onto me. There was nothing brutal about it and it couldn't be considered a rape. On the contrary. I let myself go without a word of protest. I was sizzling under his touch," she tried to explain, struggling to find her words. "It was as if I were consumed by fire. I felt he had lit a slow fire of glowing embers inside me. Sometimes he stopped and brought me back to earth. We caught our breath again before climbing back up into seventh heaven. I don't know how long it lasted."

Mona, in a state of excitement, couldn't hide her curiosity and asked piles of indiscreet questions until Stella Nomal stopped her, sobbing even louder.

"I can't tell you anything more. I have known many men but I can't compare those moments with any other. I'm telling you a secret. Please don't repeat it to anyone else."

Mona often had to take a grip on herself not to reveal anything to Hugo. Sometimes the truth was about to escape her lips and she had to restrain herself as best she could.

Shortly afterwards, on December 20th to be exact, another unexpected event occurred: yes, the same date of December 20th when a group of hallucinating Haitians had followed the miraculous star which had guided them to Ivana in the graveyard at Dos d'Âne. Like the Three Wise Kings from Galilee following the evening star, like Christopher Columbus and his three caravels stubbornly following the sun, as Sheila says in her song. There, any resemblance stops. Christmas in Villeret-le-François, in fact, is nothing like Christmas in Guadeloupe. No neighbors assembling in front of their homes on a balmy night for a concert of Christmas carols. No anxious pigs sensing the end is nigh and that they'll soon end up as blood sausage or in a casserole. At

Villeret-le-François there were few reminders of the anniversary of this sublime mystery which had impacted the whole of mankind. The town hall, for example, had strung up a few multicolored bulbs on the branches of the trees that lined the main avenues. On Saturdays, a fat man disguised as Father Christmas had his portrait taken with the children in a local supermarket. Christmas in Villeret-le-François was rather a sad time, especially for the homeless and those without a family, who were increasingly numerous and didn't know which way to turn.

So as not to succumb to this morose atmosphere, Aminata and Aïssata had not objected to Mona decorating a Christmas tree in honor of little Fadel. It's true Fadel was Muslim. But doesn't the Koran reserve a special place for Jesus? Consequently, is it blasphemy to grant Him an extraordinary birth symbolized by the Christmas tree? Oblivious to all this quibbling, the child, filled with wonder, stretched out his excited hands towards the Christmas-tree lights. It was then that Stella pushed open the door and came in without knocking as usual, since she had a duplicate of Mona's keys. From her expression it was obvious she had something important to say. Her face was stamped with an exceptional urgency, her eyes raised upwards, and the blue scarf she wore when it was raining, and of course it was raining, floated around her head. It was as if a mischievous artist had painted in his fashion *The Tidings Brought to a Black Woman*.

"Sit down," Mona said, busying herself around her. "Would you like a cup of tea?"

Stella Nomal didn't reply. Taking Mona's hands she opened her raincoat and gently ran her hands over her stomach, whose soft round contours nobody had yet noticed.

"I'm carrying his children," she declared piously.

"Whose children?" Aminata asked in a sharp tone of voice, for she disliked Stella Nomal, finding her indiscreet and intrusive. She couldn't bring herself, either, to confess that quite simply she was jealous of the pretty Guyanese girl.

Stella Nomal cast Aminata a look that went straight through her, and continued in the same solemn tone of voice.

"I'm talking about Ivan, of course. I've just come back from the doctor. He said I'm expecting twins. His twins!"

Mona managed to prevent Aminata from hurling herself on Stella and kept her seated, whereas she herself burst into tears. Meanwhile Aïssata feverishly looked for her cell phone so as to inform Henri Duvignaud of this unexpected turn of events. The lawyer was not available. He had gone to Calais that morning, where they were demolishing "the jungle." His association had a hundred or so minors on its hands, all of whom were determined at all costs to make it to England, and he was at a loss as to what to do with them. Despite her customary self-control, Aïssata, too, was on the point of bursting into tears. A violent disappointment had pierced her heart. The memory of that extraordinary night had been terribly screwed up. This Ivan, who she thought so different, who occupied a special place in her memory, was finally just a man, a womanizer, like all the others: capable of making love to three women and remorselessly procreating little bastards.

Therefore, out of the three women surrounding Stella Nomal, two were absorbed by selfish considerations. Only Mona was touched by the miraculous nature of this pregnancy. Ivan, shunned by everyone, expedited into a common grave in the cemetery, had come back to life and taken his revenge. It deserved a celebration: fireworks streaking their illuminations across the sky, a 21-gun salute, and firecrackers exploding around people's feet. Failing that, champagne glasses filled with the sparkling liquid. Mona had nothing of the sort to offer, except for a bottle of La Mauny rum. Aminata and Aïssata, however, were already on the point of leaving.

In the regional express metro taking them back to Paris, absorbed in grief, they were oblivious to the looks of the other travelers surprised by Aminata's gasping and mumbling. Once she had arrived at rue Léonard-de-Vinci, Aïssata revived a habit she had developed in Chicoutimi: she would go and sit alone at the back of a bar and pretend she was lost in her thoughts. Fans of exoticism would then flock around this black woman seated all alone. Sometimes she would follow them, and it was an effective way of healing her troubles. In Paris, apparently the lovers of exoticism are less bold than in Chicoutimi since nobody approached her and, forsaken, she sadly left the bar and went back in the rain to her Apart-Hotel.

The following morning she met up with Henri Duvignaud in his office and told him of the surprising denouement which had occurred in Villeret-le-François. The lawyer got all excited and exclaimed, "Twins, you say?"

"That's what she said," Aïssata replied halfheartedly.

"Can you imagine if she's telling the truth," Henri Duvignaud cried, more and more excited. "We'll call them Ivan and Ivana and they'll write the sequel to their story."

Aïssata shrugged her shoulders. "Perhaps they'll give a new version of their father's life, very different from the one we are planning to tell."

"Whatever," Henri Duvignaud said. "The truth doesn't exist. We lawyers see it every day. There's the truth spoken by the accused, the truth spoken by the plaintiff, and the truth spoken by the witnesses, and we have to navigate and find a compromise between all their statements."

Thereupon he took Aïssata by the arm and dragged her outside to a restaurant called The Glow Worm.

EPILOGUE

We have come to the end of the wondrous and tragic life of Ivan and Ivana, dizygotic twins. We have done the best we can and have verified the exactitude of the facts down to the slightest detail. However, if Henri Duvignaud is telling the truth, this is merely our interpretation and one version among many. We can already hear disagreeable remarks. On the subject of Ivan: "What a ridiculous idea to have imagined a Guadeloupean becoming radicalized and a terrorist! It doesn't make sense."

Our answer to this is that you are mistaken. Mrs. Pandajamy, a respectable researcher working in the Caribbean for the European Union, is adamant that in the ghettos on the various islands, young men are converting en masse to Islam and leaving to fight in the Middle East.

As for Ivana, you seem to think her character is hardly convincing. You think it odd that given her beauty and her charm she was not seduced by some impenitent womanizer while she was a teenager in Dos d'Âne, and that she kept deep in her heart an undying love for her brother.

But what shocks you the most is this platonic love between our two heroes. The problem is that you place too much importance on sex. Love is pureness of the heart which does not necessarily imply physical consummation. We have decided not to change a single word of our story. You can take it or leave it.

RICHARD PHILCOX is Maryse Condé's husband and translator. He has also published new translations of Frantz Fanon's *The Wretched of the Earth and Black Skin, White Masks*. He has taught translation on various American campuses and won grants from the National Endowment for the Humanities and the National Endowment for the Arts for the translation of Condé's works.

On the Design

As book design is an integral part of the reading experience, we would like to acknowledge the work of those who shaped the form in which the story is housed.

Tessa van der Waals (Netherlands) is responsible for the cover design, cover typography, and art direction of all World Editions books. She works in the internationally renowned tradition of Dutch Design. Her bright and powerful visual aesthetic maintains a harmony between image and typography and captures the unique atmosphere of each book. She works closely with internationally celebrated photographers, artists, and letter designers. Her work has frequently been awarded prizes for Best Dutch Book Design.

The two contra-curves on the cover are formed from an enlarged, trimmed, and tilted *S* taken from the Fabrikat Hairline font by Hannes van Döhren. Using the yin-yang symbol as a starting point, our designer Tessa van der Waals had in mind the image of two children spooning in a womb. The colors come from a detail within the novel: the sweaters knitted for the twins in Mali.

The cover has been edited by lithographer Bert van der Horst of BFC Graphics (Netherlands).

Suzan Beijer (Netherlands) is responsible for the typography and careful interior book design of all World Editions titles.

The text on the inside covers and the press quotes are set in Circular, designed by Laurenz Brunner (Switzerland) and published by Swiss type foundry Lineto.

All World Editions books are set in the typeface Dolly, specifically designed for book typography. Dolly creates a warm page image perfect for an enjoyable reading experience. This typeface is designed by Underware, a European collective formed by Bas Jacobs (Netherlands), Akiem Helmling (Germany), and Sami Kortemäki (Finland). Underware are also the creators of the World Editions logo, which meets the design requirement that "a strong shape can always be drawn with a toe in the sand."